Newt so Fast

Newt so Fast

A novel of mystery and magic

Emily McVie

The Vegan Witches of Redondo Beach

Book 4

A Wordploy Book

Newt so Fast
©2022 Wordploy Press
wordploypress.com

Cover by Elizabeth Mackey
www.elizabethmackeygraphics.com

Thanks to Pam Eaken, David Castle, and Ed Teja for your magical help in creating this book.

ISBN: 978-1-7360668-3-6

Dedicated to Mom

Chapter 1

What was out there? With my eye pressed to the peephole in the front door, I couldn't make out what was standing on the other side in the dark. It wasn't slouching like the undead, so it must be a person. And logically speaking, would a zombie have rung the doorbell? Yeah, good posture, definitely a live human being, a man, in fact.

He looked to the side. The light from next door revealed a mustache, a too-familiar face. What did he want? None of the best days of my life include a visit from Detective Nakamura. I let him in the house anyway.

"Detective Nakamura, how nice to see you," I said. "Are you looking for Emma? I think she might be out somewhere with Skylar."

His daughter Emma was in love with my friend and fellow witch Skylar.

"I'm here to see you," he said. "Thanks for letting me in without a warrant."

His mustache twitched at either end, unless I only imagined it. Detective Nakamura responded to the most surprising news with barely a raised eyebrow. If I watched carefully, I might see that black mustache go up and down a little when he spoke. It could be unnerving, especially if I was trying to keep something from him.

Why was he here? Why now? I wasn't currently trying to keep anything from him. I didn't know anything about the zombies and didn't want to know anything. The idea of dead people walking around gave me the willies.

Detective Nakamura headed for the kitchen. "What's with the commotion next door?"

"Our neighbor Georgina Clark-Whyte invited paranormal investigators to surveil our house. That's why I'm keeping the porch light turned off, for whatever difference it makes. They probably have infrared sniper video and whatnot. Georgina wants to catch us doing something weird."

"To justify shooting you?"

"Probably."

Georgina had shot a fire-breathing dragon that flew over her back yard. Detective Nakamura saw a video of that shooting, and when he found me wounded, he'd guessed the dragon must have been me — despite his unwillingness to believe that preposterous idea.

"Skylar made chocolate pecan scones yesterday," I told him. As we walked into the kitchen, he never turned his back on me. Far too cautious for that. If he didn't keep an eye on you, you might stab him or bonk him with a blunt object. I never got frustrated enough to want to hit him on the head, of course, hardly ever.

In the kitchen, he studied the ceiling so intently, I looked up too. I didn't see anything up there.

"That's a new flavor, isn't it?," he asked, still looking at the ceiling. "Chocolate pecan? We've had cranberry pecan, currant pecan, blueberry pecan, and something that was supposed to taste like bacon pecan but was actually more like smoke and seaweed pecan." He glanced at me. "Which was quite good, mind you. I'm only saying it wasn't bacon, really."

Detective Nakamura wouldn't say anything that might jeopardize his access to the scone supply. He adored Skylar's vegan scones, and who could blame him? She was a great chef, and the little touch of magic she baked into every item made them all irresistible.

As thoughtful as he was about praising the scones, he was equally unreserved about pursuing you to the ends of your patience if he wanted information about a case. He'd driven Skylar and me to distraction many times. And what went on in his head when he thought of magic? How could he think Georgina shot me yet not believe in the dragon she shot? He'd seen other clues about our magic. He tried to deny them. That was okay with me. I was wary of anybody knowing I was a witch. Fortunately, the detective didn't seem quite able to believe I'd actually turned into a fire-breathing dragon or become invisible. It was too strange. It didn't make sense.

If it made sense, Detective Nakamura, it wouldn't be magic.

With the coffee brewing, I told him, "Skylar is so far from her last real bacon, she has no idea what it tastes like anymore." I put the scone in the toaster oven and added wistfully, "I miss bacon."

He whispered, "I'll sneak you some real bacon if you'll do me a favor."

I looked around for someone who might overhear this little conspiracy before whispering back, "I can sneak myself out to get bacon if I really want it, and that would be a lot less effort than doing whatever favor you're looking for."

The detective reached inside his jacket, which gave me a glimpse of the semiautomatic pistol he wore in a shoulder holster. Then he placed a photograph on the kitchen table, the picture of a little girl. I recognized her. Angelina Martinelli, four years old. Her parents had reported her missing from their Redondo Beach home almost a week ago. No one had seen her since. The police had found no trace of her.

With my hand pressed flat against my chest, I stared at the picture for a few seconds. Then I looked at the detective. His expression was the same as it always was. That didn't look like good news to me. I prepared myself for bad news.

The toaster oven went beep-beep-beep-beep-beep. Why did it have to beep so many times? I slid the scone onto a plate and set it on the table. "Has she been found?"

"No. That's why I'm here. I'm hoping you can help find her."

I put a fork next to the plate. "Skylar and I already went around this part of the neighborhood, knocking on doors, looking under every shrub, moving everything on the ground that could have a hole under it. Everybody who lives in Redondo Beach has turned the place upside down."

"The police have done the same thing," he said. "Twice."

We looked at the photograph of Angelina. The scone sat untouched. The coffee maker finished and went quiet.

The detective cleared his throat. "The bad news is that she's been missing too long to be outdoors. The good news is that we've found no sign whatsoever that she was abducted. She's still in Redondo Beach somewhere, I just know it. We have to find her."

I put a mug down in front of him and poured coffee into it. "You given to magical knowings about people these days, Detective Nakamura?"

"I remember when Emma was four," he said. "She was the cutest thing."

"Still is," I said, "all these years later."

He pointed at the photo on the table. "We have to find this little girl."

I sat down across the table from him. "And you're asking me to find her? Even though I don't know where to look?"

"I was hoping you could…" He trailed off and took a sip of coffee. His eyes roamed the ceiling. What was he looking for this time? He put down the mug and cleared his throat. "I was hoping you could, you know, use your psychic power or something." He raised the mug to his lips and put it down again, waving his other hand. "To find her."

My face scrunched into a what-are-you-thinking look. "Detective, I'm not psychic."

"You can't hold the photo and get a vision of where the girl is? Magically?"

"Nope."

He sighed. We drank our coffee and looked at the table.

"Your scone," I said, pointing. "It's getting cold."

"There must be some way to find that girl," he insisted.

"Magically?"

He stabbed a bite of scone with his fork and put it in his mouth. He chewed for a long time and swallowed, took a sip of coffee. "I don't care how it's done," he said. "I've tried everything I can think of, everything that makes sense, and several things that don't. That little girl could not have vanished into thin air."

He stared at the battered remains of the scone and put down his useless fork. With his elbows on the table, he rubbed the sides of his face.

"I'll talk to a couple of people and see if anybody has ideas," I told him. "Maybe we can come up with something that works, even if it doesn't make sense."

"Thanks." He finished the last bite of scone, and I thought he was going to say how good it was. Instead he said, "I'm afraid I also bring bad news today."

"Like the missing girl isn't bad news?"

"I'm working hard to keep Angelina out of my bad news slot," he said, tapping his forehead. "The other bad news I'm bringing is definitely bad. Baldock Gunter escaped from Soledad prison several days ago."

I put down my coffee mug with a bang. "And you're just telling me about this now?"

"First heard it myself on the police alert system this morning. Then I called someone I know at the prison who told me they weren't even sure when the guy stopped being there. Guards realized at some point that he'd been gone for a while."

Baldock was a thoroughly evil sorcerer who'd tried to kill me and steal my magical power and very nearly succeeded. I'd only escaped by throwing myself off the Hermosa Beach Pier. Also, there was the little matter of the Minotaur that Baldock invoked. I could still feel its hot breath on my face and feel its claws in the flesh of my leg.

"Detective, you have no idea how dangerous Baldock is."

"Dangerous enough to turn you white as a sheet, I see." He stood up. "I know Baldock Gunter is a murderer. That's dangerous enough for me. We'll catch him. You just be careful until we do."

"Sure, sure. I'll stay indoors here at home and knit a sweater until you get cuffs on him." I got up and clattered my coffee mug into the sink. "I was hoping he could stay in the big house a little longer than this. What's it been, three months? And why was he sent to Soledad? They're the ones who let go of the first murderer you and I captured."

"Annoying, isn't it? I apologize on behalf of the California penal system for any inconvenience."

"Baldock will come for me. If you only understood what he's about, you wouldn't be joking."

"If it will make you feel any better, I'll put a watch on the house at night. They can sit in an unmarked car and keep an eye on the place. I'll tell them strictly no jokes."

What protection would mere police be against an evil sorcerer who can conjure the Minotaur?

"Don't bother," I told him. "Waste of the officers' time. I'll have to deal with it." I waved toward the front door.

Before we reached the door, another thought froze me in my tracks. "Say, you don't think Baldock took Angelina Martinelli, do you?"

"I do not. He was still in Soledad when Angelina was reported missing."

"You sure of that?"

"Why would he take Angelina? You know some connection here?" He held up the photo of the girl.

"Are you saying you need the idea to make sense?"

Detective Nakamura slipped the photograph into his pocket. "That would be my preference. Otherwise, I might start thinking the zombies got her."

"When I saw you at the door, I thought you'd come to accuse me of zombifying L.A. Thanks for not doing that," I said.

"My pleasure. Tell your neighbor to take her paranormal investigators up to the Angelus-Rosedale Cemetery, where they're sighting the zombies. Something is going on up there that has the police a little edgy."

I paused with my hand on the doorknob. "So the police are worried about the zombie apocalypse?"

"They're worried about people *pretending* to be zombies. Well, a few of the guys up there do think the zombies are loose." The detective shook his head. "I suppose there's some primal fear about dead people coming out of graves and walking around."

"Gives me the heebie-jeebies," I admitted.

"You don't believe in zombies, do you?"

"Of course not. On the other hand, some days I don't believe in police detectives either."

"After a long day, I feel the same way."

We both said "Good night" at the same time as I opened the door and squealed in fright at the two-legged creature looming out of the darkness. The horrible thing was ragged and bruised and cut up and staring at me with fire in its eyes. My heart thumped like a drum.

Detective Nakamura shoved me aside. He whipped out his pistol, cocked it, and crouched in the doorway in one swift move. He aimed at the awful thing swaying there.

"Oh, for heaven's sake," the thing said.

Nakamura gasped. He swung his arm aside and uncocked his pistol. Looking at the floor, he stepped back into the house and took a deep breath. He jammed the gun back in its holster. "Great," he said. "Now I have to file a report. 'Drew weapon to defend against zombie.' It will be years before I hear the end of this."

Peeking around the doorframe, I stared at the person standing outside in the dim light. "Emmeline?" I said.

The woman looked even more outraged than she had when the gun was pointed at her. She waved her hands in exasperation. To the detective, she said, "Can you believe this?"

He shook his head no.

Turning back to me, the woman said, "Emmeline was Skylar's other girlfriend. Do all pierced people look alike to you?"

Basically, yes, but I didn't say that out loud. I guessed again. "Candy?"

The woman brightened considerably. I think she smiled. "Right!"

"Detective Nakamura, this is Skylar's friend Candy."

"Pleased to meet you," he said with a level tone.

"Yeah," Candy said. "Look, what's going on with Sky and that lousy B-movie actress?"

"Melanie Gosford?" I asked. "What do you mean what's going on?"

"I saw pix on FB," Candy said. "Sky smashy-lips with Gosford the bitch-goddess. Are they shacking up like some Hollywood thing? Sky can do better than that."

Glancing at the detective, I wanted to mention that Skylar had indeed done better with his daughter Emma, but I let the opportunity pass. "You're one girlfriend behind at this point, and I'm sure Skylar would like to catch up on old times, but she's not home at the moment. I can tell her you came by if you like."

"If you'll excuse me, ladies," Detective Nakamura said, heading for his car.

Candy watched him go and then turned to me. "Kinda trigger happy, isn't he? I was worried he was gonna shoot off one of my nip rings." She laughed hoarsely, and all of her nose rings jiggled, along with the rings in various parts of her mouth, some of them connected by chains. Lower down I could hear the jingling of metal parts I couldn't see and hoped I never would.

"If he shot one off, at least you have spares," I said brightly. "I'm not sure when Skylar will be back. How about giving me your phone number, and I'll make sure she calls first chance she gets."

Since Skylar might be coming home with Emma, I wanted to make sure Candy was anywhere different. Emma had shown herself to be wildly jealous in the past, and Candy was a big girl who didn't seem to quite understand the "ex" part of being an ex-gf. The collision of these two might be explosive. And anyway, I wanted Candy to go away because she was not fun company.

She watched Detective Nakamura drive away and then scanned up and down the street. She squinted at the two people in Georgina's yard who were bent over some kind of equipment that was pointed in our direction. Maybe it was a paranormal ectoplasm detector or an astral light camera or who knows what.

"If my brother catches up with me, he'll probably kill me," she announced as she walked into the house. "I'll just hang around here until Sky gets back."

Chapter 2

Following Candy as she walked through my front door, I tried to think of some way to make her walk back out again. What if her brother showed up wanting to kill her? I wasn't eager to get in the middle of that situation. At the same time, I didn't feel like I could simply shove her outside to meet her sorry fate. I decided to let Skylar deal with her.

I texted Skylar, "Candy here."

While I waited for Skylar to get home, I needed something to keep Candy occupied. "How about a scone? Would you like a scone? I just made a pot of coffee."

"Say what? A scone? I hate scones. What kind of beer do you have?"

"No kind of beer in the house, I'm afraid. We have a bottle of merlot open. How about a glass?"

That idea made her nose scrunch up, which enhanced the overall zombie look. In the light of the kitchen, her clothes looked more raggedy than they had in the dark, and half her head was shaved with a mostly purple tattoo of a buffalo where the hair used to be. The hair that remained was short on the front and one side and streamed down her back in an orange tangle that looked like half a traffic cone.

"Bourbon," she said, her nose still scrunched. "Gimme a shot of bourbon, will you? I've had a hard day." She slumped into a seat at the kitchen table.

"Water? Ice?" I asked.

She shook her head.

"Shot of bourbon straight up." I got down the big bottle of Costco bourbon that we had for cooking and filled a cute shot glass I'd found at a garage sale. When I set the little glass down in front of her, Candy looked at me as if I'd lost my mind.

"One tiny shot glass?" she asked incredulously.

"Not a shot?"

"Not one shot *literally*. What part of 'had a hard day' did you not understand?"

She got up and eased me out of the way so she could get to the kitchen cabinets. When she located the drinking glasses, she pulled out a medium-sized tumbler and smacked it onto the table. Grabbing the bourbon from me, she sloshed in several shots worth and took a swig. "That's not bad stuff," she said, sitting back down and turning the bottle to look at the label.

I was still holding the shot glass and stepped over to pour its contents into Candy's tumbler. I don't care for bourbon, but this was starting to feel like an emergency. Knocking back the shot, I grimaced from the burnt-woody taste raging through my mouth and the fire burning down my throat. I plonked the shot glass down on the counter and regarded Candy, who was looking around the kitchen.

When her eyes landed on me, she raised her glass. "Here's to old times."

I nodded without bothering to pick up my empty shot glass, though I did consider getting a refill. One shot of bourbon is more than enough for me, but I don't usually have to contend with Candy.

The old times Candy was toasting weren't very old. I'd first seen her less than two years before, when she was protesting the sale of the café and plant nursery to Skylar and me. Or I should say, when the nursery was sold to my father. He did the deal. He could afford it. He wanted to give me something to do after I'd once again failed to come out of college with a degree. Now I ran the nursery and Skylar ran the café. We had a good time doing it when people weren't protesting or being murdered on the property.

With the glass in her hand, Candy tilted her chair so she was leaning back against the wall and crossed her feet on the corner of the table. Almost immediately, she righted her chair and pulled a crumpled pack of cigarettes from her pocket. "Mind if I smoke?" she asked.

"Yes."

She frowned at me for a moment as if she were trying to figure out if I was serious. Deciding (correctly) that I was, she tossed the cigarettes onto the table and leaned back against the wall. She started telling me about her brother.

My phone buzzed. Skylar had texted back, "Chocolate?"

I thumb-typed furiously, "Not candy candy. Your ex gf Candy. Where are you? Don't bring Emma."

After a minute, Skylar sent back a smiley face that was screaming rather than smiling along with the single word "Soon."

Candy was still talking about her brother. She said she did maintenance for a big apartment complex he owned in Redondo Beach. I wasn't sure exactly what she'd said, but now she was getting down to the important facts.

"He's a complete butt, my brother. You think detective what's-up-with-the-gun is annoying, you should meet my brother the butt. If he had a gun like that detective, I'd of been dead long ago. More likely I'd take the gun away from him and blow him away, blammo. He's such a wimp. That's the only reason he hasn't taken me out already. He's too afraid. And he should be. I'm not taking any crap off him anymore, you know?"

She didn't pause for me to say "Sure do" or "Atta girl" or "Excuse me while I go in the back yard and scream." Instead, she waved her glass of bourbon in the air and proposed a toast to her brother.

"Here's to brother Landon and the irksome whining wimps of the L.A. real estate biz. Without them we would have no place to live." She slugged back a gulp of the bourbon and started to cough. She had to swing her feet off the table and tilt her chair down to keep from choking. "That bastard," she said finally, wiping her eyes.

I handed her a napkin. She blew her nose into it and handed it back.

"If you saw all I do for that louse, week in and week out, you would cry. You would wonder why I haven't taken him out. You would want to know why I haven't had him arrested for total buttlessness." Candy cackled. "He's the world's most buttless brother butt bastard."

Tilting her chair back too quickly, she banged against the wall and the chair legs slipped out from under her. Somehow, she managed to straddle the chair and squat without falling to the floor. Blitzed people are capable of amazing acrobatic feats.

Righting her chair and sitting in it with all four legs on the floor, she picked up the cigarettes, looked at me, and put them back down again. She clutched at her glass, put it back down. "I'm good at fixing things. I'm really good at it. I can fix your car. I can fix that stove over there. I can fix anything that goes wrong in an apartment complex. Does my brother appreciate that? Does he say, 'Nice job, Candy. Thanks for being a team player'? No! He does not. Ever. You want to know what he told me?"

She paused and stared at me as if she actually wanted an answer. I fake-smiled and raised my shoulders to say, I dunno, what?

"He told me." She stopped and drank the last of the bourbon. "He told me the only reason he hired me to fix his apartments is that I scare the tenants so much, they don't call for repairs unless they're desperate. Can you imagine your own brother saying that? That is low," she concluded, thumping her glass on the table. "Don't you think that's low?"

I had to admit, that was low. Also clever.

With a little more bourbon in her glass, poured by bartender me to keep her from spilling it all over the kitchen, Candy ranted on about working for her brother at the apartments. When she was drunk enough, she finally told me the real reason she'd come to see Skylar. It had nothing to do with Melanie Gosford.

"You should have heard him shout," Candy said, trying to laugh and not quite succeeding. "Mrs. Fletcher in 32C told him about the water going everywhere, and I mean everywhere. You should have seen it. I took out the guts of her shower faucet with the water to the building still on. I'd always wanted to do that. The water shot out of the fixture like a fire hose and splashed against the wall of the shower and out everywhere."

Candy waved her arms to indicate what everywhere meant. She only sloshed a little bourbon across the room. I wiped it up while she carried on with her story.

"I told Mrs. Fletcher I'd be right back, I needed a part to fix the shower, and of course, the whole reason she'd called in the first place was because her shower drain was stopped up. Too much hair. It's always the hair." Candy shook her head sadly at the hair issue, causing her own orange mane to flop languidly back and forth.

"32C is on the third floor, right? Pretty soon the Steinbergs in 22C are blowing up my phone, both of them calling. Eventually, I answer the phone and tell them I'll be there as quick as I can. Half an hour later I'm at Subway having lunch, and the Steinbergs are calling every two minutes. They're shouting at the phone. Water is dripping out of the light fixture! Water is coming down the walls! Mr. Ngonamo in 12C is calling now. I'm eating my meatball sub and seeing all this water in my mind's eye, but mostly I'm imagining the look on my brother's face when he finds out, which he did."

Candy slumped in her chair. She pulled at the frayed collar of her sweatshirt. "That's why I can't go back to the apartments or he'll kill me."

"He won't literally kill you," said Skylar, who was now standing in the arched doorway to the living room.

How long had she been there?

I straightened up from where I was propped against the counter and waved to Skylar. "Over to you," I said and left the room.

Half an hour later Skylar came to my bedroom. She told me she'd put Candy in the guest room. "Just for tonight," she assured me when she saw the look on my face. "She's really gone downhill, hasn't she?"

"Well, not meaning to cast aspersions on your choice of girlfriend, but Candy was never much above sea level." I slapped shut the book I was reading about repotting orchids. "Sorry. That wasn't nice."

Skylar slumped onto the end of my bed. "It's all right. Candy was always a mistake. I mean, I should have taken a clue from how we first met her."

I nodded.

"Protesting!" Skylar said. "Always protesting! That girl would try to ban happy hour."

"Hmm," I said. "She might object to mom and apple pie, but I think happy hour is safe."

With a half-shrug of agreement, Skylar said, "I thought she was only a crank rabble-rouser until she cold-cocked her fellow protester who was stealing plants from the nursery."

"That's what endeared her to you, was it?"

Skylar pulled a wry face. "It did make me take a second look at her. I realized she really cared about doing the right thing. She's an ethical person, even if she is a bit violent. And she wasn't quite so outrageous looking back then."

"Well, she's outrageous looking now, and she didn't do the right thing by her brother."

"It's worse than you know," Skylar said. "Besides that little plumbing prank, she's organized protests of several real estate developments he's worked on for years. She got some of them torpedoed — multimillion-dollar deals."

"She needs to get out of the protest biz," I said. "She needs a new line of work."

"And a new place to live. I told her I'd go with her tomorrow to get stuff from her apartment. It's in her brother's complex."

"Before you do that, I wonder if you can help with a project for Detective Nakamura."

"Not likely."

"Sorry, I shouldn't say it's a project for him. He's only the messenger. He asked if I could use my psychic power to find that little girl who's missing."

"Psychic power?" Skylar stood up and waved her fingers like thought rays shooting out of her head. "He's a complete dip. His own wife is probably a witch, and he's clueless about magic."

"Most days, I have a hard time making sense of magic myself, and somebody taught me that if it made sense, it wouldn't be magic. Let's see," I said tapping my chin thoughtfully, "who told me that?"

"All right," Skylar said, "It's just that Detective Nakamura is so annoying. You should hear Emma tell how he hounded her all through her childhood. It was always, 'Do your homework. Do your chores. Don't hang out with that popular group of girls.'"

Tapping my chin again, I said, "Let's see, how much of that sounds bad?"

"You are in a mood tonight, aren't you?" Skylar complained.

"Drinking with Candy will do that to a girl."

Skylar looked startled. "You weren't trying to keep up with her, were you?"

"Wasn't quite that desperate, no. I did have a shot of bourbon that didn't fit into Candy's plans."

"I've never seen a shot of bourbon that wouldn't fit into that woman's plans, but never mind. What exactly do you want me to do about that little girl? What's her name?"

"Angelina. I want you to find a way to find her. Can we get psychic powers somehow?"

"I already asked mother if she could think of a way to find the girl. She couldn't. And there's no such thing as psychic powers."

"That's what you told me about possession," I pointed out.

Skylar flopped back onto my bed. "Proving me wrong one time does not mean everything I say is wrong."

"It does suggest you're not infallible."

"All right," she said, slapping her arms on the bed. "You're right. I could be wrong. What do we get from establishing that?"

"It gets you vexed. Vexation is the mother of invention."

"That doesn't sound right, but speaking of vexed, a woman wearing a navy blazer was in the café this morning complaining about the advice you gave her on repotting her orchids. I believe the term she used was 'orchid apocalypse.'"

"Zombie apocalypse, now orchid apocalypse. Thanks so much for reminding me of my failure." I picked up the orchid book and threw it onto the bed next to Skylar. "That woman was only the beginning of my lovely day. In the middle was a plant order that was messed up because I entered the right numbers in the wrong column. To finish off my day, along comes Detective Nakamura chased by Candy and bourbon."

Skylar flipped open the book. Pretending to look through it, she said casually, "Meanwhile, Emma and I really had fun at the mall."

Leaping out of my chair, I growled like a dog. I snatched the biggest pillow off my bed and pummeled Skylar with it.

"Ow, ow, ow," she cried, as my blows rained down on her mercilessly. She batted at the pillow with the orchid book. "Hey wait," she yelled between pillow whacks. "I'm vexed enough. I have an idea."

I paused my pummeling. "A good idea?"

"You won't like it."

With one hand on my hip I said, "Of course I won't like it! Did you come up with a little decorative edge to sew on my rotten day?"

She held up a teddy bear from the side of the bed I didn't sleep on. She was right about not liking her idea. My ex-boyfriend had given me that teddy bear.

"You could ask Killin," she said.

"I am *not* speaking to him."

"I said you wouldn't like it."

Killin Bardis had been my boyfriend for a while, on and off, until I caught one of Skylar's café employees — a pretty young thing named Dawn — straddling him with sexual intent. Well, it had gone way past intent to fully involved whamming and bamming. When I caught them, she didn't even have the decency to stop working at it, if that doesn't stretch the concept of decency too far.

Tall and dark, Killin was originally from Ireland, though you had to listen close to hear any Irish accent. He moved like a ballet dancer, and the flash in his dark eyes was echoed by the glint of a ruby stud he wore in one ear. He'd made my heart go banga-banga-banga from the first moment I saw him, but he'd cheated on me. Also, he might be an evil sorcerer. Definitely, he was a sorcerer. Okay, definitely he was an evil cheater. It was the extent of the evil I was unsure of. How bad was he, really?

After half-heartedly whacking Skylar with the pillow, I plopped it at the head of the bed and flopped myself back down in my desk chair. "*If* I were talking to Killin, what are you thinking I'd ask him?"

"Whether he knows how to find a lost little girl. He might, you know."

"I will not ask Killin for anything."

Skylar said, "Odd that you still have this teddy bear on your bed."

"I will not," I said. "I will not. I will not."

Chapter 3

Killin answered after the first ring.

I'd agonized all night about calling him. I knew I had to do it, but I wavered. I struggled. I couldn't bring myself to do it. I'd pick up my phone. My finger approached the call button and hovered there. My better nature said *You have to*. My finger said *I won't*.

After picking up my phone and putting it down again for the umpteenth time, unable to sleep, I went out to the backyard at first light. For Redondo Beach, it was a typical overcast morning in late June. Sitting on an old concrete bench next to the back fence, my phone lying next to me, I watched little birds peck around under the dogwood tree. Killin and I had sat on that bench any number of times. He'd first told me he loved me while I was sitting on that bench. It felt cold under me now, gritty with dirt. I stood up and brushed off the grit, sat back down.

Where had it all gone wrong?

Killin was always coming and going, disappearing for weeks at a time on missions that he wouldn't tell me about "for my own safety." On one trip to Prague, he'd been ambushed by a group of witches who conjured a magical tiger. In the fight that followed, the tiger's claws gave Killin a terrible festering wound that nearly killed him. My tears had healed the outer wound, but the evil magic lingered inside, still poisoning him, keeping us apart. And then I'd caught him with Dawn.

My blood boiled when I thought of that scene, the two of them joined on the floor of my garden shed. The image burned in my memory. My whole body hurt when I thought of it. Mostly, it was my heart that ached.

He was probably somewhere at the far end of the earth. The farther from me I imagined him, the closer my finger came to touching his mobile number on my phone, but my finger still said *I won't.*

I gave my finger a stern lecture: Put aside your own feelings and think of the greater good. Do it for Angelina, for her parents. I made a deal with my finger: Touch the call button, get Killin's help, and then never touch his call button again, ever. I'd give the teddy bear to Angelina.

The little birds scratched and twittered next to me. In the distance, a garbage truck roared, backed up, crashed a container around. I willed my finger to touch the call button and held the phone to my ear. The tinny sound of the ringing started, and then I heard his voice: "I knew you wouldn't be able to live without me."

My finger shot to the red disconnect button, hitting it hard, mashing into the glass. I yelled at the dead phone, "Arrogant cheater!"

The little birds flew away. Thrusting the phone in my pocket to keep from throwing it across the yard, I stood up and walked toward the house, moving fast, kicking any little object that got in my way — a couple of pine cones, a stray soccer ball, a pair of gardening gloves.

The phone vibrated in my pocket. I was not going to answer.

I walked away from the house, around the yard, and kicked the soccer ball against the back fence a couple times. Then I kicked it over the fence. I kicked the gardening gloves over the fence.

Back toward the house now, looking for a new target, I saw the garden hose lying sprawled in stray loops on the grass. Grabbing the end with the little spray gun on it, I whipped the hose into a neat circular pile next to the raised vegetable bed. I straightened up and kicked the coil of hose. My foot bounced off.

Yanking my phone out, I looked for Killin's voice mail so I could delete it. But I had no message from Killin. Detective Nakamura had texted a picture of Angelina. In the photo, she was crouched on the beach holding a tiny shovel of sand, squinting in sunlight, her head tilted sideways with a shy grin, long dark hair falling around her little face.

I sat down hard on the concrete bench and put my head in my hands. I had to focus on Angelina. I called Killin again.

"Are you driving?" he asked.

"No. Why do you ask if I'm driving?"

"We got cut off. I thought maybe you were —"

"Shut up," I said. "I need your help to find a lost little girl."

"How little?"

"Much younger than Dawn. Don't get your hopes up."

"Look, you don't understand what was —"

"I saw you, Killin!"

"But you don't know why! You don't know why I was doing it! You're so impatient. You always jump to conclusions."

Of all the stupid claims ever made by man, this had to be stupidest, most baffling load of rubbish ever dumped. I sat with my mouth hanging open for several seconds before I realized he'd hung up on me. I flung several curses at the phone, none of them magical, regrettably, and leapt up for another tour of the yard. Several objects I would have kicked were now on the other side of the fence. I kicked the fence. Not my best idea.

How dim did this man think I was? He supposed I didn't know why he hooked up with that impossibly cute little Dawn witch? Not that she was an actual witch. Not magical. Incredibly attractive, sexy vixen witch. Does he think I don't know how sex works? That I don't know why people have sex? Men!

Women, too, actually. I understood all too well why people had sex, since I hadn't had any for months. I kicked a couple of pine cones over the fence. Except I had that one fling with the guy in Germany. Under the influence of magic. And a bottle of wine. He was fantastic. I'd been meaning to find out what happened to him.

My phone buzzed. Ah, Killin this time. I touched the button and said, "Okay, tell me why you screwed that girl. I'm sure this will be illuminating, since clearly I don't know why a man would have sex with a girl whose clothes hardly want to stay on her skinny little body."

"Just hold on one second. I know what it looked like, all right?"

"Really? You know what it looks like when one naked person is riding another naked person? You can imagine that from my point of view?"

"Sorry. I should have told you before I did it, but I didn't think you'd understand."

"You get to be right!"

"Just — Would you be willing to let me tell you one thing?"

"Sure." I was running out of things to kick. It was time to finish this stupid conversation and find out if he could find the little girl. Move on, be done with it, done, done, done.

"It healed me," he said.

I tilted my head sideways, held the phone at arm's length, and squinted at it. I looked up at the gray sky. Did "It healed me" make sense up there? No, it didn't. How about over by the house? No, it didn't make sense over there.

"What are you saying?" I asked Killin. "What's "It" in that sentence? Healed you how?"

"Interacting with Dawn healed me of the evil magic," he said.

"'Interacting'? That's what you call it?"

"All right, having sex. It healed me of the magical poison from the tiger."

My mouth was hanging open again. After barking a quick laugh, I said, "Good one, Killin. You think I'm going to believe that? You really do think I was born yesterday. Why couldn't you just have sex with me?"

"Because you're magical. The poison inside me would have infected you. You knew that. It had to be a non-magical person. And it worked. I'm a new man."

"That makes no sense."

"Hayley, if it made sense, it wouldn't be magic."

"I'll call you back." I hit the red button on my phone and headed for the house.

Skylar was still half asleep. I woke her up the rest of the way.

"What's going on in the backyard?" she asked. "I heard shouting."

"Listen," I said. "can a man cure himself of evil magic by having sex with a non-magical person?"

She blinked sleepily a few times and stretched her shoulders. "We're talking about a man who's a sorcerer?

"That's the one."

"Hard to believe he'd trot out an excuse that ridiculous."

"Exactly my feeling."

"Still," Skylar said, reaching for her phone, "it wouldn't do to ridicule the excuse until you're sure. You might end up feeling like a fool."

"Wouldn't want that to happen," I said.

She flipped through her contacts and touched the number for her mother. I didn't mention that I'd already ridiculed the excuse, and I had that here-we-go feeling that comes a few minutes before you end up feeling like a fool.

Skylar reminded her mother about Killin bonking Dawn in the garden shed, which outraged her mother on my behalf. Then Skylar reminded her mother about the magical tiger attack and asked whether the Dawn bonk might have been part of a spell to cure Killin of the last vestiges of tiger poison. Skylar said "Uh huh" a couple of times followed by "Thanks. Love you." She hung up.

"Possibly," she told me. "Quite possibly."

I went to the window and parted the curtains so I could stare into the backyard for a minute. I thought about a few things I could take out there to kick over the fence. Behind me I heard Skylar get out of bed and pull on some clothes. She came to the window and drew back the curtains. We stood there looking out for a minute.

"What now?" she asked.

"Well, I'm *not* going to forgive him just because it saved his life."

"Reasonable."

We looked at the backyard for another minute. The little birds were back under the dogwood tree. A mockingbird perched on the fence sang a different tune every two seconds.

"Did he know any way to find Angelina?" Skylar asked.

"We kind of got sidetracked from that," I said. "Let me ask him again."

I hit Killin's mobile number on my phone, and he answered with, "So you forgive me?"

"Could we put that discussion on hold for the time being and focus on finding the little girl?"

"Why would I do you a favor if you won't even forgive me?"

"Because you're pretending to be a decent human being?"

He huffed. "You're not making it easy to be decent, but okay. Tell me what you need."

Skylar and I rolled our eyes at each other. I texted the photo of Angelina to Killin.

"I'm sending you a picture of the girl," I said. "She disappeared from home several days ago, and no one has found a trace of her. I'm wondering if you know some magical way to track a person's path into the past."

"She's a cutie," Killin said. "I do know a way to track a person, but you won't like it."

"Don't worry," I assured him. "I'm used to that. What do we have to do?"

"First, get about 20 gallons of blood. Any kind of blood will do."

"Oh, Killin, give me a break. That's gross." I looked at Skylar, and we both stuck out our tongues. "What kind of spell is this?"

"It's the spectral bloodhound spell. If you think that's gross, you should hear what goes into the seeing-eye-monkey spell."

"Never mind," I said tartly. "As you may recall, we're vegan witches, so blood is out of the question."

"I do recall that you're vegan," he said equally tartly, "and that's why I said you wouldn't like it. I get to be right again. I'm on a roll."

"So keep rolling," I said. "What's our second choice?"

"Hmm, I can't think of a second choice. It's the bloodhounds or nothing."

"Thanks." I hit the red button and looked out the window. "Back to square one."

A voice from behind me made me jump. "Why is everybody staring at the backyard?"

Shooting a glance over my shoulder, I saw Candy wearing sunglasses. A second glance told me that was all she was wearing — aside from numerous metal rings and studs, surrounded by countless tattoos, mostly of animals chasing one another across her body.

She put one hand on her head and the other on my shoulder to steady herself. "Did somebody take a shot at me last night? I have this strange memory that my brother sent a Chinese guy to take me out. Why is it so bright?"

"Just a bad dream," I said, pivoting slowly so she could maintain her balance while I walked out from under her hand. It didn't work. She swayed in the opposite direction and then overcorrected toward me so I had to catch her to keep her from falling.

"Easy, easy," she said, swaying. "Don't run around like a maniac. My head is throbbing."

I passed her to Skylar and went to the kitchen to make tea. Putting tea leaves into the strainer basket, I wondered if any plant on earth could substitute for blood in a magic spell. I was always thinking about substitutions like that. Skylar and I wouldn't use the eye of newt and toe of frog required by traditional spells. We'd found a lot of good substitutions, but changing the recipe usually changed the outcome of the spell, sometimes dramatically. So far, no one had been hurt. Not too badly, anyway. I mean, our neighbor Georgina had shot me while I was a dragon, but you could hardly blame the spell for that. Fortunately, Detective Nakamura had taken Georgina's gun away.

In my bedroom, I sat down with the tea at my desk and picked up Etshigal. This stone disk was an elongated oval about a quarter of an inch thick. It snugged perfectly into my palm. A couple of glyphs carved into its green and black surface spoke from a language lost to time. I had no idea what the glyphs meant, but within the stone you could find a world of knowledge about plants — if you could talk to stone.

I can talk to stone.

With Etshigal, I'd learned to start slowly. Otherwise, I'd be lost in it for hours. Cradling it in my hand, I released a greeting into the cool stone. A pulse of awakening came in return, followed by bursts of rapidly quickening streams, random currents of knowing. The language of stones has no counterpart in the human senses, but I think of it as talking. I posed a question about blood. My request rolled through the fabric of the stone like a wave and returned with nothing, only an empty wave.

I waited for more, but nothing came. That was unusual. I put down the stone and sipped my tea. I'd lost this stone when I jumped off the Hermosa Beach Pier to escape from Baldock Gunter, the evil sorcerer who'd now escaped from prison. On the pier, he was trying to steal my magic. A little blonde girl — one of a set of magical triplets — had retrieved the stone from the water and returned it to me. Now I was searching for another little girl and feeling a wave from the stone.

Coincidences? Connections? Insight?

I picked up the stone and asked the wave to carry me to a deeper answer. The stone had no idea what that meant. I felt waves wash forward and back, storming through the stone. It seemed as big as the sea. Swells crossed the wide expanse, north and south, lapping at lost islands, crashing on beaches in unseen coves, returning with nothing but the waves themselves. My imagination wandered in the waves. Under the water, green fronds swayed as colorful fish hovered and darted, dodging shafts of sunlight.

I clunked the stone down on my desk. Seaweed. What about seaweed?

Running to find Skylar, I found the house empty and a note on the kitchen table: "Taking Candy to get her stuff."

Then the doorbell rang.

The man at the door wore an unstructured sport coat over a pink button-down shirt and maroon tie whose geometric design somehow matched the sport coat. He was handsome in a classy way. His shoes were freshly shined. His eyes were an amazing shade of green.

I, on the other hand, looked like I'd just rolled out of bed and put on the T-shirt and shorts I'd gone running in the evening before.

I was about to tell him I already had solar on the roof and didn't want to answer a survey or sign a petition, but he wasn't carrying anything, and he was not smiling. He didn't look like the guys who want me to buy solar or answer a survey. Those guys don't generally wear thousand-dollar sport coats.

He could be a new neighbor. Please be a new neighbor. Why was he frowning?

"Something wrong?" I asked.

"My sister," he said. "I'm wondering if she's here. Candy Longstaff?"

"Ah," I said. "No."

His green eyes bored into mine for two seconds. Then his shoulders relaxed, and he gave a slight nod. He took out his phone. "When will she be back?"

"Never?"

He looked up from his phone and smiled. "I know what you mean," he said. "Look, sorry to bother you. I'm Landon."

A chill went through me. This was the guy who was out to kill Candy? Mr. Charming in a pink button-down? He put out his hand. I shook it. His grip was firm but not aggressive. I found myself a little reluctant to let go.

"Candy and I had a disagreement over the maintenance she was doing at one of my apartment complexes. I'm afraid she misunderstood my intentions."

"She didn't understand that you intended the water to stay inside the plumbing?"

Those green eyes regarded me for half a second before he barked a laugh. "Yes, you might expect that keeping the water in the pipes would be the simplest approach, but our Candy is creative. In any case, we need to sort it out. Do you happen to know where she's gone?"

Did I trust this man? Those green eyes were making me feel like I could tell this man anything.

Chapter 4

Should I tell Candy's brother where she was? His green eyes said yes. A little voice inside my cranium said no and suggested that I didn't know where her apartment was, so I could plausibly say I didn't know where she was. The little voice told me to just go for the half-lie. This little voice obviously wasn't my conscience.

"I don't know where she is," I said.

The wide-open pupils of the green eyes narrowed. Those eyes said they knew I'd veered from the truth. That might be the end of my little moment with Landon Longstaff.

"Hey," I said with new misgivings, "how did you know Candy was here?"

Landon gestured toward Georgina's house. "I saw it on the GhostOps feed. They got video of the encounter between Candy and a guy who pulled a gun on her. I enjoyed that, I have to confess."

"So you just happened to be watching this GhostOps feed and saw Candy?"

"She's the one who hooked me up with GhostOps in the first place."

His impeccable posture tilted slightly, and the faintest blush left his cheeks pink. "Actually, I think she got interested in GhostOps because of Skylar. And you." He cleared his throat. "Candy thought mysterious things were happening, which is typical of her. She sees conspiracies everywhere. Even in me. I'm just trying to run a business, and she thinks I'm part of some shadowy real estate cabal that's taking over L.A."

"Are you?"

"Oooo," he said, waving his hands on either side of his head. "Didn't you detect the secret handshake a few minutes ago?"

"Missed that."

"It's mysteriously easy to miss things that were never there," he told me with a wry smile. "The GhostOps people, on the other hand — they do catch some interesting phenomena. When it pops up on Instagram, I take a look."

He touched the screen of his phone. I was expecting him to show me the GhostOps feed. Instead, he studied the phone in a way that told me he was about to leave.

"As long as you're here, would you like a scone and a cup of coffee?" I asked him abruptly.

"Ah, I'd love to, but I'm on my way to a meeting." He looked at his phone. "And I'm going to be late."

He extracted a monogrammed silver case from a jacket pocket and held out a business card. "If you see Candy and want to help her out, give me a call. Without the job I give her, she'd have nothing, and I don't see how she can get by." Slipping the silver case back in his pocket, he waved his hand dismissively. "Protesting certainly doesn't pay."

I watched him walk to the BMW he'd parked at the curb. Candy had got him wrong. Even with his sport coat in the way, I could see there was nothing buttless about this guy. He spent time at the gym.

# # #

A few hours later, I caught up with Skylar at the café. She was combining several types of flour in a bowl. I asked if she knew about using seaweed in spells, and she said she'd never heard of such a thing. When she got the flours mixed, she dusted off her hands and called her mother, who had no seaweed spells either.

I went to my little office behind the front desk of the nursery and called Killin. He'd heard of two spells that used seaweed.

"One is for patching a leaky boat," he said. "I'm not convinced it's actually magic because your boat will still sink. Maybe not as fast. The other spell is to make a fish sing. I may have got that wrong. I'd drunk a lot of Guinness the night I heard about that one. Why are you asking about seaweed?"

"I'm wondering about substituting it for blood in your bloodhound spell."

After a few seconds, he said, "That makes no sense, so it could be magic. Other than that, I don't get it."

"Several years ago at Fresno State I had to take a biochemistry course, which I didn't quite pass, but I remember something about hemoglobin. It's the main part of red blood cells, and it binds oxygen using iron. If I remember right, seaweed has a similar molecule, only it uses magnesium instead of iron."

"That's it? That's your reason for substituting seaweed for blood? You're definitely nailing the doesn't-make-sense thing. Bear in mind that the spectral bloodhound spell is powerful magic. I don't think it's a good idea to mess with it that way."

"Why can't we just try it? It might work."

"Did I ever show you the YouTube video of the guy jumping off a barn with wings on his arms?"

"Three times," I reminded him.

"Did I not explain the significance of the analogy? Stepping off the barn is like casting a spell. As soon as you step off, you're heading for the ground. You have to land, only you don't know how that will happen. See?"

"Killin, where are you?"

"San Pedro."

"You're practically next door. Did you stick around in case you needed Dawn to give you a booster shot? Although, I guess technically it's you giving the —"

"Stop it!" he said. "I'm sorry, all right? I'm not seeing her. If you want to try the spell with seaweed, I'll help. Will that make you happy?"

# # #

Casting the spectral bloodhound spell in the backyard would have been handy, but with the GhostOps people surveilling us from next door, we decided to do it on the beach. That worked with the seaweed theme. We needed a lot of seaweed, so we got it from a commercial outfit, and Skylar liquefied it in her industrial-strength food processors at the café.

Out on the beach in the dark, we lined up buckets of seaweed glop that Skylar had liquefied down to the molecular level. Using stray pieces of lumber, we built a fire that we weren't supposed to have on the beach. Over the fire we hung an iron pot containing pinto beans and water. ("How charming," Skylar said. "At last we have a witch's cauldron.") We also had a grasshopper that Killin had caught. He assured us that no harm would come to the grasshopper.

I was clutching a little shirt that Angelina Martinelli had worn. Detective Nakamura got it from the girl's mother. The detective had asked if he could be there for whatever we were doing. When I said no, he guessed that we didn't want strangers around when we danced naked in the moonlight. I told him that was correct. Why not let his imagination run wild? I asked him to be ready in case something happened.

Fully clothed, with everything in place on the beach, Skylar and I squatted next to the buckets of seaweed. Killin began the story that powered the spell:

> Dad blast it, that was a time we had chasin' Pa Downey. Why, I don't reckon we ever seen the like of that there endeavor.

"Very funny," I said. "You are joking?"

"This is the spectral bloodhound story," he said. "You want it or not?"

Skylar and I stood with our hands on our hips, glaring at Killin. I asked Skylar if she'd ever heard a cowboy spell before.

"Not in all my born days," she said.

"Killin, where did you get this spell?" I asked.

"Turkmenistan."

"That makes no sense," I pointed out.

"There you go," he said.

Skylar and I waited. I tapped my foot in the sand.

Killin explained, "I think some guys from Texas were hired by the Turkmenistannis, or whatever they are, to consult on managing their cattle. American westerns are very popular there, I think. Somebody in the group lost a rifle, I think, and wanted it back. Somebody was a sorcerer, or maybe a witch got into the mix. I'm not sure."

"That's the haziest story I've ever heard," I said.

"You have to understand that there was a great deal of Zip 5 beer involved in my acquisition of this spell. People don't just give up their spells for fun, you know. You have to get friendly, get to know them."

"Get them drunk," Skylar said.

"Doesn't hurt," Killin said.

"And you still think you got the story straight?" I asked.

"My memory for spells has stood the test of better beer than Zip 5. If there's a problem here, it's your bleedin' seaweed."

Skylar and I looked at each other in the flickering light from the fire and shrugged.

"Should have worn cowboy hats," she said.

We squatted by the seaweed buckets. Killin started again.

Dad blast it, that was a time we had chasin' Pa Downey. Why, I don't reckon we ever seen the like of that endeavor.

Summer it was, blazin' hot, and the dogs was lyin' in the shade of the porch. They would not bestir theyselves for a bone or no other thing. After what they'd heard, who could blame them?

Flies buzzed and went still. Weeds that were green the day before crackled dry and lifeless underfoot. By the time the sun labored down to the crest of the Arden hills, Pa Downey had not returned from his dalliance with the woman named Doreen. We let him be. He could take care of hisself.

That night, heat lightening flashed above the hills. It showed up dim flickers in the house's south-facing windows. Sleep was a stranger that came to the door, called out invites to meet in deep mines that promised rich veins of rest, and gave up no more than hollow rumblin's.

In the morning, we put a pot of beans on the fire and stood back as quick as we could. Truth be told, we didn't need much fire to cook beans on this scorching day.

By midmorning we knew we would not keep up with this day even if we ran alongside it for all we were worth. No, we would fall in the dusty road. The cows drank from the trough before dawn and would not pause. They drank till they gave out and fell where they stood.

We told the dogs that Pa Downey had not meant what he said, but they would not come out to the trough. Those sorry hounds will not hunt again in this world.

Where was Pa Downey? The blood pulsed behind our eyeballs as we looked off to the south. The heat haze wavered across the valley, doubling the hills. It seemed the blood in our hammering veins would soon leave us to make its own way in the world.

That was our cue. Skylar and I tipped over the buckets of seaweed. The green glop slithered away from our feet, down the sandy beach. In the firelight the glop was dark as blood, but greenish, like bug blood. Fear prickled my skin. Were we about to invoke giant hunter insects? What was Killin going to do with the grasshopper? He pressed on with the story:

Looking out there, we saw him, Pa Downey, walking toward us afar off, little puffs of dust rising around his feet. We turned our heads and squinted against the glare, wiping sweat from our eyes. We saw several Pa Downeys, each walking his dusty way against the distant hills, wandering, straggling sideways, standing in one place with dust still lapping at his feet.

Dust devils. We were only seeing blasted dust devils. They staggered like drunkards out there. After a while, they were closer. We felt the air move.

A breeze brushed my face. Just wind off the water?

"Did you feel that?" Skylar whispered.

"Yes," I whispered back.

Over the sound of the waves coming onto the beach, a hissing noise came up, little splashings.

Them dust devils knew what was out there. Traipsing across the breathless land, they breathed in every dang thing that was there, everything that had been there. They whirled it all up inside and carried it along, carried it toward us. We could feel it, smell it.

Then they was on us.

The wind hit then, blowing my hair around my face. The empty plastic buckets clattered together and rolled across the sand. We grabbed at them, but they moved from under our hands as the wind swirled past carrying bits of stray trash. The fire blew hot, the flames churning around in a circle as a whirlwind came over and around us and passed up the beach, throwing sand against our legs. Another whirlwind was close behind, a stronger one. The wind shifted and jerked. My hair whipped straight up from my head and then to one side. The fire roared, the burning lumber turned yellow with heat, burning my eyes, and smoke blasted out in gyrating jets. Killin lifted up the jar holding the grasshopper. He was shouting now:

When them dust devils got on us, we watched weeds and trash blowin' all over hell and gone, up in the air and over the house. A grasshopper flew over the dogs, over the pot of beans, and disappeared up inside the wind.

The spirits of the dogs rose up then, all solid as whirlwinds. They barked and circled and multiplied until they were a pack of six. We tossed a raggedy shirt

of Pa Downey's in the air. They sniffed. They whined.
They circled, impatient to be off to find...

"Angelina Martinelli," we all shouted together. The whirlwinds
wailed around us and rattled the plastic buckets up and down the
beach. I threw Angelina's shirt into the air.

Black shrouds rose up from the seaweed spread across the sand.

Two slithering shapes gathered, each twisting in the air with a
moan that rose in pitch as the forms grew. They blotted out the
lights onshore in their passing. What were these things? They
didn't look like dogs. They weren't spectral hounds. What had we
made?

"Killin?" I shouted, but my shout was lost in the moaning of
the black shapes, the howling of the whirlwinds.

The fire had gone out. The sky was black. Over my shoulder,
flickers of lightning sparked over the sea. A stink of rotting fish
came and went as the wind shifted.

Crouching again, I closed my eyes against the flying sand and
reached to the place where Skylar had stood. My hand touched
bare sand and blowing trash. I called her name again and again,
barely able to hear my own voice.

The two dark shapes moved between me and the onshore
lights, going slower now, turning in place, undulating back and
forth as they went around, keening like lost children. These were
not dogs of any description. The hairs on the back of my neck
stood on end. Everything about this was wrong.

I wanted to run, but I couldn't leave Skylar. Had she run away
already? Again, I felt around where she should be. Close to the
ground, everything was moving. I kept my eyes screwed shut. My
hands snatched at plastic wrappers, hot embers, gooey chunks
coated with sand. It all felt alive. None of it was Skylar. I got to my
feet and backed up a few yards, holding my hands around my eyes.
I couldn't see Skylar or Killin. They were gone or lying on the
ground.

The lightning struck closer over the water behind me, followed
by rumbling thunder. Inland, lights twinkled faintly through dark
airborne shapes. Darkness bled out of the rotating forms. A little
at a time, they became transparent, only visible as shimmering

outlines against the onshore lights. The keening stopped. The shapes shivered in the air. They made sounds like giants straining to lift impossibly heavy burdens. With a blinding flash and a rending shudder, they tore themselves apart.

The shockwave knocked me down. I got up, backed away toward the water. Lightening struck with a crash. The water lit up, flickered, and went dark. The sequence began again — dark shapes turning with a keening noise, four of them this time. The air went perfectly still.

The stink of rotting fish rose around me. My stomach turned over, and I bent double, hands on hips, and clenched my jaws. I looked up. The forms in front of me were growing into things I was liking less and less, whatever they were.

Lightning flashed, boomed, flashed again and again. The ocean pulsed with green light. I squinted up and down the beach. Trash and plastic buckets littered the sand. I looked back and forth, behind me at the water, now dark as night. Everything was still except the swirling shapes in front of me. Skylar and Killin had abandoned me. I backed away from the shapes, toward the water. As I splashed along the edge of the surf, a flicker of lightning lit the ocean far out and my feet tingled with electricity.

I stepped away from the water. Lightning sparked again far out, here and there, with light that didn't blind me. Outlined against the flickering light, something else moved in the knee-high surf. Something was coming up from the water. An overpowering smell of spoiled meat enveloped me.

A person was walking out of the waves.

"Killin?" I called. "Skylar?" I stepped into the water.

The person didn't reply.

Behind me, the floating shapes ripped apart with a yellow flash. The sudden light revealed the figure walking out of the water. This wasn't Killin or Skylar. This wasn't a late-night swimmer. This person's face was half missing, and his reddish shirt was hanging in tatters as he walked straight-legged in the low surf.

Revulsion twisted through me, and I turned away. What had we unleashed with this spell?

I angled south down the beach, with the zombie on my right and six uncertain shapes turning slowly in the air to my left. The shapes were becoming transparent as ghosts and yet taking on more definite forms.

The zombie was easy to outpace, but the shapes were angling south too. They were clear yet somehow blotting out the lights. They were growing into huge blobs of darkness enveloping Redondo Beach.

I stopped running. I couldn't outflank something that was covering whole blocks of buildings. But as the shapes moved south, they came closer. A little at a time, each of them was collapsing into itself with squeaking jerks that got louder and came in rapid bursts, faster and faster now, like countless smoke detectors shrieking with lurching waves of noise. I stood alone in the dark with my hands over my ears. When would this end? How would it end?

Then the noise stopped. In the quiet that followed, waves splashed onto the beach behind me. Car horns blared on the Pacific Coast Highway. "Purple Rain" blasted from a club on the pier. The world had returned to normal except for the six shapes writhing in the air in front of me. Each form had collapsed to the size of a 55-gallon drum, only longer.

They were turning faintly white, glowing. They seemed to be swimming in the air, undulating like giant fish, swishing their tails. Maybe this was okay. Maybe the seaweed had invoked spectral fish instead of dogs. Maybe this would turn out all right.

Swimming in a pack through the air, the fish swooped up and back down, away from me. What if they were going to find Angelina? I ran after them. I couldn't let them get away. They'd find the girl without me. We still wouldn't know where she was.

The spectral fish swam toward the San Simeon condos — four- and five-story buildings that fronted the beach near a jetty. I ran after them, across the bike path and onto the steps that led up the sandy slope to the condos. The steps seemed to go on forever. This rise was like trudging up three flights of stairs.

By the time I reached the top, breathing hard, the fish were swimming through the spaces between the condo buildings. Could Angelina be in there? This was a couple of miles from her house.

I hurried up a walkway between the buildings and came out on Esplanade, facing Topaz Street, and couldn't see the fish. I'd lost them already. Turning back down the walkway, I looked up as the fish flashed overhead and swerved north. The walkways were deserted. Could non-magical people see these fish?

As I reached Esplanade again, the fish came back around the buildings. With a jerk, they all turned and stopped. Their tails barely moved in the air as their eyes focused on a single target. I didn't like the way they were looking at me.

The pale fish swam closer, their eyes fixed on me. What was it about their shape that seemed familiar, alarming? I backed against the building. They swished their tails, arrayed themselves in a half circle, cutting off all chance of escape.

These giant translucent fish, dark on top, white underneath, hovered in the air around me, and I knew what they were. These were the bloodhounds of the sea, able to sniff out prey across vast distances. The biggest one darted down a few feet from my face and opened its jaws, showing gleaming rows of jagged teeth — the face of a great white shark coming straight at me.

Chapter 5

The enormous mouthful of great white teeth opened around my head, smelling like the ocean, only deeper, wrong and appalling. I put my hands out to push it away and had one last thought: Did this beast eat Skylar and Killin? I had my answer a moment later, when the ghostly great white thing licked my face like a dog. I had just about peed my pants by that point, and the lick pushed me over the edge. All things considered, it was better than having my head bitten off.

The great white whimpered like a puppy, all of them did, wagging their tails. The one in my face licked me again.

Fish do have tongues, I think, but they're not like dog tongues, so the spell must have crossed bloodhounds with sharks, thanks to the seaweed. That was my logical assessment.

At the moment, logic wasn't uppermost in my mind. I was sweaty with fear and faint with relief that I wasn't shark bait. Also, I was worried about Skylar and Killin. I'd have to figure out what happened to them later, because these sharks were ready to hunt.

"Can you find Angelina?" I asked them.

They writhed around in the air and whimpered some more. Just guessing here, but these shark-dogs probably didn't understand English.

I jumped forward and held my arms out enthusiastically. "Okay, you guys, let's go find the little girl!" I pointed away from the building, and we all surged forward. They surged a lot faster than I did, and once again I lost them. They flew away making a noise that started with a squelch and ended with a bark — "Skark! Skark! Skark!"

They came back like good dogs, and the big one swooped around behind me and nudged between my legs. He (I decided he was a he) wanted me to ride him. I clambered aboard, straddling the creature behind its dorsal fin, thinking I'd jump off right away if it seemed too hard to stay on.

Careening up into the sky with a "Skark," the creature put an end to my plan to jump off. I held onto the fin for dear life, hanging off one side as we banked into a wide turn. We "swam" high enough to see the lights of L.A. stretching into the far distance. It would have been an awe-inspiring sight if I hadn't been riding on the back of a ghostly shark-dog whose intentions weren't entirely clear.

The shark-dogs were having quite a romp, veering off this way and that, but we were heading roughly in the direction of Angelina's neighborhood, so that was good. We passed several people who were out walking. None of them seemed to notice us flying past overhead, even though the shark-dogs were skarking now and then.

It took only a few minutes of wild flying to reach a two-story house a few doors from Angelina's home. We circled the house, with the shark-dogs skarking hysterically the whole time. I could see children through the second-floor windows. None of them looked like Angelina, but we were moving too fast to be sure.

Then the shark-dogs eased up against the house, wriggled, and passed through the wall. That scraped me off the back of my ride, and I barely had time to grab for one of those chains people use on their houses instead of downspouts.

Unfortunately, I missed the chain.

Fortunately, it wasn't too far to the ground, and the big bush I landed on hadn't been pruned into sharp points. Well, only super-sharp in a couple of places.

After clambering out of the shrubbery, I walked across the front yard, trying to find a window I could peek into. That wasn't going to look good if anybody saw me. Somehow, I hadn't made a plan for what I'd do if the dogs found Angelina, or might have found her. And what if the people in this house had kidnapped her?

It was time to call Detective Nakamura. He answered right away, and I gave him the address.

While I waited, the shark-dogs wriggled out of the house and zoomed around me like maniacs. They kept skarking at me and trying to push me into the house, so I let them batter me against the stucco until they figured out I couldn't go through in one piece. They all had hang-dog looks after that.

The big one got the idea to knock down the front door, which I was expecting, so I positioned myself in the way, just in case these ghostly fish were able to do it. Another shark-dog tried to move me aside, so I was struggling with them when Detective Nakamura arrived.

"You okay?" he called out as he walked toward the front door.

"Fine." The shark-dog stopped shoving me, so I was able to look normal. The detective obviously couldn't see the shark-dogs or he'd have his gun out. With any luck, he hadn't seen me struggling with them, but probably he had.

"Practicing your dance moves while you wait?"

"Yeah." It wasn't the first time I'd looked like an idiot to Detective Nakamura. I was used to it.

Peering at my forehead, he put his phone in flashlight mode and held it up. "You need to get that looked at."

I touched my head and found blood on my hand.

"Just a little shrubbery encounter."

One of the shark-dogs had sidled up to the detective and was rubbing against him. He didn't notice a thing.

"So you think Angelina is in this house?" he asked

"Not sure, but yes, I think so. You might say I tracked her energy to this house. What if they kidnapped her? Do you need backup?"

"It would be nice to have uniforms covering the back of the house, but 'I tracked her energy' won't look good in the paperwork I have to file. Let's just have a friendly chat with these people. Stand behind me, please. I looked these guys up. They're the Verratti family."

He rang the doorbell. After half a minute, the porch light came on and a man opened it.

"Back again?" he said. "I still don't know anything about the girl, and I've told your officers that three times."

"Sorry to bother you yet again, Mr. Verratti," Detective Nakamura said. "Do you mind if we come in for one minute?"

"We're putting the kids to bed," he complained. When the detective continued to look at him with an unchanged expression, he said reluctantly, "Oh, suit yourself," and opened the door wider.

The man eyed my forehead as I walked past him at the door. Detective Nakamura said, "This is Hayley West. She's our horticultural evidence consultant."

"Evidence?" Mr. Verratti said. "Looks like she's been in a fight."

"You know how it is with horticultural investigations," the detective said. "We need to finish up here and get her to the ER." He peeked around the arched doorway off the living room into the dining room, where an enormous table filled the space.

My shark-dogs were swimming gleefully around the house, skarking as they went. Nobody else noticed.

A little boy wearing Spiderman underwear ran out of the dining room, through the living room, and down the hallway with a girl in close pursuit who looked to be about 14. A slightly older girl yelled "Gotcha!" at the end of the hallway. Two little girls in pajamas were sneaking down a stairway in the foyer as the 14-year-old and the older girl came back, both looking at their phones as they herded the little boy and the two little girls back up the stairs.

"You have several children, Mr. Verratti?" Detective Nakamura asked.

"Twelve. A dozen kids. You want to arrest them? I can tell you plenty of misdemeanors they've committed."

"I wonder if we might meet them."

"Now?" He stared at the detective as if he were crazy. "I'm trying to get them to bed."

Clearly, it was the older children who were getting the younger children to bed, but the detective's expression didn't change. "Just a quick hello," he said, holding out his hand as though welcoming Mr. Verratti up the stairs of his own house.

Mr. Verratti went up the stairs with the detective and I following. At the top, Detective Nakamura spotted the oldest girl and asked if we could meet the younger children. The girl looked up from her phone only briefly, and pointed to three rooms off the hallway.

In the doorway of the second room, I eased the detective aside and walked over to two little girls who were sitting on the bottom bunk of bunk beds that had a slide leading down from the top. I knelt in front of one of the girls. She was adjusting the pajamas on a Barbie doll.

"Angelina?" I asked.

"Uh huh," she said without looking up.

"You having a good time visiting your friends here?"

She nodded enthusiastically, looking up at me. Seeing the blood on my forehead, she frowned. "You have a booboo."

"Hurt myself just a little. I'd better get cleaned up. Would you like to go home for a while?"

"I guess so." She handed the Barbie to the other little girl. "Ready for bed, Mary Catherine," she said.

The other little girl handed Angelina a baby doll. "Baby Jackie is ready too."

I said to Angelina, "Let's take her to bed at your house, okay?"

"Okay." She hopped down from the bunkbed. "Goodnight, Mary Catherine. Sleep tight."

"Don't let the bedbugs bite," said Mary Catherine.

Angelina walked out holding my hand, telling me all the things that Baby Jackie liked to do before bed. Detective Nakamura was on the phone to her parents.

In the hallway, Mr. Verratti squinted at Angelina. "That's not my child." He bent down to get a closer look. "Is it?"

"Nope," I said.

A couple of little boys in a room off the hall got into a noisy squabble about something, and from the other end of the house came a woman's hoarse voice, "You kids go to sleep this instant."

We went down the stairs with the shark-dogs swimming around us deliriously trying to lick Angelina. She screwed up her face as though she felt them. I patted their heads and waved them away. That was the last I saw of them.

Angelina's parents met us in their front yard and cried over their lost little girl, who didn't understand what all the fuss was about.

Detective Nakamura and I slipped away while they were blubbering.

I called Skylar's number and went to voice mail. What had happened to her and Killin?

Detective Nakamura gave me a ride home. "You're a hero, Hayley West," he said in the car.

"Oh well, any day now one of the Verrattis would have realized they had a ringer."

"For Angelina's parents, every minute must have been an eternity. And from the look of you, I can see that finding her was more involved than visualizing where she was with psychic powers."

"Well…" He didn't know the half of it and didn't really want to know. Certainly, I didn't want to tell him.

"I'll get you a commendation from the city for finding the girl," he said.

"Don't you dare."

He pulled into the driveway, which was already just about full of cars. I was relieved to see Skylar's car. Behind that was Emma's car. Detective Nakamura noticed the Hello Kitty in the back window of his daughter's Honda and said that he wanted to talk to her.

Before he turned off the engine, he asked, "Sure you don't want to go to the ER?"

"I'm fine, really. I'm wondering if Skylar's okay. I lost her out on the beach."

When we opened the car doors, we heard angry voices coming from the house. The front door was standing open. Two women were yelling at each other. I recognized Emma's high-pitched voice. By the time I was out of the car, I realized the other voice belonged to Candy. Skylar was pleading with them to calm down.

Grappling with one another, Emma and Candy burst out the front door before Detective Nakamura and I got halfway up the walk. Candy was a big girl, and I worried what she might do to Emma, but her father didn't seem the least bit concerned. He walked calmly toward them as if he were going to join an afternoon social.

When Emma pushed Candy away, Candy took a swing at the smaller woman. Before I could cringe, Emma had moved gracefully under the swing, and Candy was on her back looking up at the stars.

Next to me, Detective Nakamura murmured, "I taught her that."

Not bright enough to know she was outclassed, Candy scrambled up and tried again with a massive haymaker. Emma leaned out of the way, rotated in place, and kicked Candy's ass, literally, which sent the bigger girl sprawling on her face in the grass.

Emma stood over Candy and shouted at her, "You leave my girlfriend alone, you hear? So help me, I'll take you out if I hear you've been here again. I'll do worse than throw you on the ground. Do you understand me?"

Detective Nakamura stepped in then and put his hands on Emma's shoulders. She spun away and was about to take him down when she saw it was her father. Contorted with rage, her pretty face flushed crimson and her mouth sagged open. Her father had seen everything.

"What did I tell you about threatening somebody?" he whispered calmly but urgently.

She looked away. "I was angry."

"Exactly." He took her arm. "You can come home now. We'll get your car tomorrow."

"What about her?" Emma said, pointing at Candy, who was getting to her feet.

"Oh, I think Candy is going somewhere else," I said. Never to return, I hoped.

Glancing at Georgina's house next door, I saw the paranormal investigators in the front yard. GhostOps had captured the whole bash-up between Candy and Emma on video — the shouts, the tussling, the punches thrown, the take-downs. And Emma's threats. GhostOps recorded all of them with 8K high-resolution video and Dolby 5-channel digital audio.

Because the dust-up involved two women who were not celebrities, this recording would normally have raised only a brief flutter of interest on social media. But in exactly 20 hours and 14 minutes, the video would be propelled into the world's news by a horrifying assault.

Chapter 6

Blissfully ignorant of the future, Skylar and I celebrated our survival. Mostly I celebrated. Skylar was upset about the Emma vs. Candy bout, which was piled on top of worrying about what had happened to me during the spectral bloodhound spell.

"I thought those things ate you," she said, as she cleaned up the gash in my forehead. When she was satisfied that it didn't need stitches, Skylar cast a healing spell on it and put her arms around me. I felt tears wet my neck. "I thought I'd never see you again."

"Nah," I said. "I hardly ever get eaten by shark-dogs."

Skylar pulled away. "You kinda stink. Did you fall in a toilet?"

I ticked off the list of stink contributors on my fingers. "Peed myself about the shark-dog coming to bite my head off and then licking me instead of eating me. Sweated buckets, same reason. Rode on the back of a shark-dog. You probably noticed they smelled like week-old fish. Fell into a shrub with stinky berries on it. Oh, and before all that, zombie stink might have gotten on me. I'll take a shower." I stood up from the kitchen table.

"First," she said, "tell me what happened. I've been worried sick."

"Okay, I just told you the high points of the story." I sat back down. "Or maybe those were the low points. What happened to you and Killin? I was worried sick that the shark-dogs had eaten *you*."

"Didn't you hear Killin yell to run away?"

"Nope."

"I guess I only heard it because he grabbed my hand and yelled in my ear. He knew the spell wasn't going right. We ran up the beach. Then he realized he'd grabbed the wrong girl."

"Typical," I said, rolling my eyes. "Good thing he didn't grab me, though. Otherwise, I wouldn't have found Angelina."

Skylar jumped out of her chair. "You found her, really? That's fantastic!"

I stood up and we high-fived. Then we did a victory dance and sat down again.

"Wow," she said, "you really do stink. But you're a hero — a super-hero!"

"Superstink Girl," I said, striking a body-builder pose. "What happened to Killin?"

"He's okay. He was looking for you. We both were. After a while, I came home to see if you'd somehow made it back here and was about to go out again when Emma showed up. Candy was already here. You saw the collision."

"So Killin is still out looking for me?"

"As soon as I saw you, I texted him that you were home. He replied that he was dealing with zombies. You thought you saw a zombie too?"

"During the spell, yeah. Someone was walking out of the surf. In a flash of light, I saw that half his face was gone." I cringed, remembering the sight. "The rest of his face was not long for this world if that applies to a dead person. Also, he stank worse than I do now."

Skylar puffed out her cheeks in distress. "Probably it was some poor guy who got injured by our spell."

"I don't think a guy could be walking around alive with that much of his head missing."

"But you think he could walk around *dead* with his head missing?"

"Obviously," I said, waving my arms, "if he was a zombie."

"Except there's no such thing!" Skylar said.

"That's what you said about possession."

Now it was her turn to roll her eyes. "It makes no sense that people could walk around dead."

"And that makes me think magic is involved."

# # #

Time goes past so wickedly fast sometimes, you find yourself fleeing from one moment to the next like a woman bolting from a zombie that looms unexpectedly out of the dark. On other days, you're the zombie.

The day after the shark-dog adventure, I felt closer to being dead than undead. I'd been so excited about finding Angelina the evening before, I felt like a super-hero. Dang, I was a super-hero — casting a spell that called up shark-dogs, riding one of them through the sky, crashing into the shrubbery at the Verratti's house without breaking my neck, rescuing the lost girl from the sleep-overs she'd been enjoying.

Now I was sore all over, and I'd barely slept after being so hyped-up the night before. Every single one of my muscles hurt. My head felt like one big spasming muscle. My rear end was chapped from riding the shark-dog. When I looked at the jeans I'd been wearing, the seat was almost worn through. Sharkskin is rough stuff. I threw the jeans in the trash and considered climbing in with them.

Instead, I had a cup of coffee with Skylar in front of the morning news on TV. Number one story: The little lost girl Angelina Martinelli was found in Redondo Beach, to everyone's immense relief. The police reported that they found her thanks to an anonymous tip. That was followed by a brief statement from the girl's mother about how happy they were to have Angelina home again. Then, Ms. Martinelli looked straight into the camera with tears in her eyes and said thank-you from the bottom of her heart to the person who called in the tip that led to Angelina's discovery.

Skylar and I leaned against each other on the sofa. My eyes got a little misty, so I had trouble reading the texts from my two best nursery employees saying they wouldn't make it in to work that day. They didn't feel good. Well, guess what, your boss lady hurts all over, but somebody has to mind the store.

Actually, Ms. Martinelli's thank-you made me feel a little better. I guess that's what super-heroes live for.

While I was reading the texts, I almost missed a story on the news about a strange mess that had fouled a Redondo Beach beach overnight. That's how the news anchors said it, "Redondo Beach beach." They thought it was funny. The video of the beach showed a big green seaweed slick with two humped-up patches of white next to a wood fire that had an iron pot on it.

"Uh oh," Skylar said.

I looked up from my phone.

"The pot is full of beans," a live-on-scene reporter said. "But they're not ordinary beans. Each one has the face of a dog on it." The image zoomed in to show the little faces on the beans.

The reporter added that the white patches in the seaweed bore an uncanny resemblance to fish, and residents had reported a freak lightning storm followed by strange noises. He walked over to a man with crazy-wild white hair who stared directly into the camera. The man was wearing a Hawaiian shirt, and his purple-framed sunglasses were perched on top of his head. He gestured at the white patches. "They're great white sharks, that's what they are," he said into the microphone held by the reporter.

The man grabbed the microphone out of the reporter's hand and carried it over to one of the white patches. The cameraman scrambled to keep up. The wild-haired man pointed the microphone at the white patch. "See? Great white. Here's another one." He pointed the microphone at it. "You can tell these things were trying to be born here, trying to rise out of the primordial ooze like the first creatures to crawl out of the La Brea Tar Pits. Redondo Beach is the epicenter for alien life forms who want to repopulate the earth and join the shark people in Washington and Berlin. They —"

The program switched back to the news anchors in the studio. "Redondo Beach always entertains," one said to the other.

"And that wasn't a *pot* of beans," said the other. "That was a cauldron. Strange goings-on in the South Bay. In Compton last night…"

Skylar muted the TV. "I didn't think about leaving a mess on the beach," she said. "Our fingerprints are all over that cooking pot."

The doorbell rang.

"That would be Detective Nakamura," I predicted.

When I opened the front door, there he was, like magic.

"I've come to arrest you for littering," he said.

"How about a scone before you haul us off?"

"Please."

He wiped his feet on the mat and followed me into the kitchen. Along the way, I called to Skylar, "Detective Nakamura is here to arrest us for littering."

She came into the kitchen from the living room. "Are we entitled to a phone call?" she asked.

"No," I told her. "Just a scone."

"I'm late for the café already, and we only have two scones left. You hold him while I hit him over the head with something."

The detective lifted a cast iron skillet off the counter and handed it to her. "This ought to do it."

"Ha," she said. "You're trying to bait me into falling for a judo move." She put the skillet back on the counter. "I hope Emma doesn't think I have any interest in rekindling a Candy relationship that was never a good idea the first time around."

"That's something you'll have to take up with her, and I don't won't to hold you up if you need to leave. I do want to ask if you were involved in finding Angelina Martinelli last night?"

"Yes," she said. "Sorry about the mess on the beach. We'll clean it up."

"Not to worry," he said, holding up his hands. "I hired a crew to take care of it. Thank you for finding Angelina. If you girls ever run that sort of, ah, *procedure* again, I'll be happy to take care of logistics for you, especially the parts that might carry fingerprints."

"You want to be there when we cast a spell?" I blurted out. The idea horrified me. Detective Nakamura obviously knew that we were doing some kind of magic — not that he fully believed it — but having him watch us do it was unthinkable. Thinking about it triggered a deep fear in my gut that people would discover I was a witch and burn me at the stake.

I looked at Skylar, who was looking back with eyes big as saucers. Was she horrified too? Or upset with me for talking about magic? I blushed with embarrassment and shook my head NO at Detective Nakamura.

He cleared his throat. "Are you reluctant because we'd all have to be nude? Dancing in the moonlight? Like that?"

I stared helplessly at Skylar, who was now giving the detective a furrowed-brow what-are-you-on-about look. Suddenly that look flew off her face. "Yes!" she shouted. "That's it!" She shrieked with laughter.

Taking her arm, I nudged her toward the door and handed her the tote bag she used as a purse. "You can go to work while Detective Nakamura has a scone."

"Sure you don't want to give him hot cross buns?" she called over her shoulder on the way out.

"Sorry," I said to the detective, wishing he was the one leaving.

What was I going to do with him? I didn't want to talk about magic with a non-magical person — certainly not when that person was Detective Nakamura.

"Scone!" I said, opening the refrigerator. "Would you like blueberry or zucchini walnut?"

He was standing by the kitchen table looking the way he always looked, looking at me with a level gaze that always bothered me. I'm pretty sure it was intended to. "Could I have a blueberry to go, please?"

"Blueberry to go!" I said with relief, taking a scone out of the refrigerator and dropping it in a little paper bag. "Sure is getting warm these days, isn't it? Looks like a hot summer coming on."

I handed him the paper bag. He didn't say anything. He looked at the paper bag. I was about to mention that I also needed to go to work when he took a step toward me. That put him a couple of feet away. We're about the same height, so he's looking right into my eyes now, just about in my face. I feel like he's *in* my face. Blinking a couple of times, I start to edge out of the kitchen, but he steps forward to cut me off.

I look toward the door. "I have to go to work."

He's right in my face now. I glance at him and look away.

"You said you cast a spell. Did you sacrifice sharks on the beach?"

What a relief. A question I could answer. "We're vegans, detective. We only put out seaweed."

He put his hand on my arm. "Then why do those white humps that look like sharks have something in them that came from sharks? My forensics people tell me they do. Why do they have shark in them when you claim you didn't put it there? Did a shark magically jump into the seaweed? What did you do out there?"

I shook off his hand and glared into his dark eyes from a few inches away. "I went out, detective, and I found a lost little girl. I found a little girl that you asked me to find. You're welcome. I have to go to work."

I pushed past him and went down the hall to the bathroom. When I came out a few minutes later, he was no longer in the kitchen. The paper bag containing the scone was resting on the counter. I put it in the refrigerator. He could be all proud if he wanted to. I wasn't going to let a scone go to waste.

When I came out the front door, he was standing by the driveway. I locked the door and walked over the grass to go around him.

"I do appreciate your finding Angelina," he said. "You did a wonderful good deed. It's just that you do something that makes me trust you, appreciate you. Then you don't trust me. You think I don't know what it's like to be different, but look at me."

I opened my car door and did not look at him.

"I'm of Japanese descent," he called out. "My parents were locked up in a camp during the war. I understand about being different. You have these gifts, whatever they are. But when you act like they're top secret, some kind of national-security-level private knowledge, like you're a mysterious magical cult leader or some such, that's arrogant. That's suspicious. You see how that works?"

"Yes," I said, looking at him. "I see. You think you have a right to know my personal business, and when I won't tell you, you think that's suspicious. Well, you don't have a right to know anything about me. I haven't committed any crime." I got in my car.

"You littered the beach!" he shouted. "I paid to clean it up!"

"Thanks!" I shouted back, and slammed my car door. I got an oldies station on the radio and turned the volume way up. The loud part of "Stairway to Heaven" blasted out of the speakers. I didn't look at Detective Nakamura as I backed out past him. I'd risked my life to find that girl. Then he felt like a hero for cleaning up the mess. There was no way he would ever understand me. I wouldn't trust him if my life depended on it.

#

When I got out of my car at the nursery, three customers came up to me wanting advice about what plants to put under the trees in their backyard or in pots on their patio. I helped a gray-haired woman decide which ground cover to plant under her trees. The woman's neighbor, a handsome man in his 40s, bought annuals for his patio pots.

The third customer wanted more extensive help and looked like she could afford it. She was beautiful in a manufactured sort of way. She had a Hollywood haircut, by which I mean the cut and color had cost her *many* hundreds of dollars. The square-cut emerald hanging in her cleavage cost many thousands, as did the men's Rolex on her slim wrist. She waved around a big landscaping plan for her new house and said she wanted to pick out the plants herself.

Normally, I'd be thrilled with a customer like this, but I really wasn't in the mood to trail through the nursery after a woman who's directing me to add this plant or that one to the flatbed hand truck I'm hauling along behind me while all my muscles hurt and my head throbbed. She didn't ask for advice about anything. I was only a mule pulling a wagon.

When we'd filled one flatbed, I dragged it back to the front desk and got another one. A few minutes after I'd joined the woman again, Killin showed up. My prince! Well, he would do in a pinch.

"There you are," he said. "Could I have a word?"

"What's up?" I asked him after gladly taking a couple of steps away from the customer.

Killin pulled me a couple of yards further away next to the bougainvillea. "Zombies are up. I saw two last night, and I'm trying to figure out if we created them with our spell or somebody else just happened to do it on the same night."

"Skylar says there's no such thing as zombies."

"She told me the same thing right after I ran into a guy whose face was past its sell-by date."

"Sounds like the zombie I saw — left side of his face gone? Right side kind of oozing sideways? Shirt that was red once upon a time, a long time ago?"

"That's the guy. Around ten o'clock I came across a female zombie who was walking out of the surf near the pier. You didn't see her?"

"No, by then I was at the house where Angelina Martinelli was hanging out."

A woman laughed close behind us. Killin whipped around. The customer I'd been helping was now a couple of feet away with the leaf of a bougainvillea plant between her fingers.

"I couldn't help overhearing you mention that little girl," she said. "Funny that the authorities went to so much trouble to find her when she was just playing with her friends next door. What a waste of taxpayer money. I'd like these three plants." She pointed three times. "And I want to consider the hibiscus next."

"Of course," I said like a dutiful mule, if a mule could talk.

Killin stepped gracefully in front of me and swung the 10-gallon bougainvillea pots onto the flatbed as though they were props in a ballet. The ruby stud in his ear flashed in the early morning sun. The woman narrowed her eyes and watched him.

"Thank you, young man," she said, still looking at him. She leaned forward slightly, and the big emerald in her cleavage bounced back and forth.

A prickle of jealousy warmed my cheeks. Yeah, I guess I did still care about him.

"*No hay problema,*" Killin said, touching his fingertips to an imaginary sombrero without looking at the woman. To me he said, "*Hasta luego, señorita.*" He sauntered off.

After that, the woman looked at the hibiscus, and some purple fountain grass, and rosemary, and nine different types of bamboo. While she was deciding which bamboo would be best with no help from me, she mentioned that she'd bought several bamboo plants already, but someone had vandalized them.

"Who would vandalize plants?" I said. "I've never heard of such a thing."

"Oh, there are haters in this world," she said.

I was hating that I had to follow this woman around like a mule. I wondered if she was picking up my thoughts. After the woman paid and left all her plants on my flatbeds for her landscaping guy to pick up, I hated fixing the plant order I'd messed up on a previous day. After that, I hated the whole rest of the head-throbbing day, except for the half hour when a woman brought her two little boys to shop for bamboo (big day for bamboo), and the boys were absolutely fascinated with what I told them about the plants, beginning with the fact that bamboo is a type of grass.

After they left, I hated imagining a future with no husband to have little boys and girls with. Should I just go for it on my own? Who needs a man? After thinking like that for a few minutes, I knew it was time to go home, but I still had an hour until closing time and only one other person to help run the nursery.

Finally, closing time came. The landscaper of the woman who'd filled the flatbeds also came. I helped him load the plants into his pickup truck. And then I was going home — or so I thought. As I grabbed the keys to lock up, the plant order I'd straightened out arrived. They never brought a plant order at this time of day (or night, as it was getting to be). The delivery guy reminded me that I'd put "Deliver immediately!!!!!" in the comments section of the order form — four more exclamation points than I usually put. The company considered anything over three exclamation points an emergency.

I called Skylar and told her to go ahead and eat without me.

By the time I got away from work, it was dark outside. I was ravenously hungry and still hurting everywhere from my feet up to and including the top of my cranium. When I got home, I wanted to fall into bed and be done with the day. I could hardly tell the gnawing hunger of my empty stomach from the rest of my aches.

Skylar insisted that I eat something, partly because she had all the ingredients for a vegan stir fry laid out. I ate on the sofa in front of the TV news with the sound off as we usually do, only this time it was the 11 o'clock news instead of the 6 o'clock. I paid no attention to it as I shoveled the food into my mouth. A few shovelfuls in, I did remember to tell Skylar that it tasted good.

I also remembered to tell her about Detective Nakamura acting like I had to reveal my magic or I was a bad person. "He says he understands about being different. He says I should trust him. Yeah, right. Then he gets all mad and thinks he's SpongeBob SquarePants because he cleaned a little seaweed off the beach."

"Men!" Skylar said. That was her general assessment of any problem involving a male of the species.

As long as I was in complaining mode, I pressed on. "Did you really have to poke at him about dancing in the moonlight?"

"Yeah, sorry. See, the image of my girlfriend's father dancing naked was a problem that I had to deal with somehow. I could bang on my head until the pain distracted me or laugh at the whole idea. The correct choice seemed obvious."

Then she got into the spirit of complaining mode. "What were you up to, shouting about casting spells? I thought you didn't want to tell anybody you're a witch. I thought you were afraid of anybody knowing. If the wrong guy finds out, you might pay with your life. And Detective Nakamura might be the wrong guy."

"That's Candy," I said in surprise.

"Candy is the wrong guy?" She followed my gaze to the TV.

Several people were holding signs, waving their arms. Skylar grabbed the remote to rewind the DVR and turn on the sound.

The news report showed a demonstration at the Angelus-Rosedale Cemetery. For several days, on and off, several people had been protesting the demolition of a cinder-block retaining wall on the border of the cemetery and Normandie Avenue. The city wanted to replace the painted cinder blocks with a fake-stone wall that would be less appealing to local tag artists. Every few days, a crew had to come out and paint the wall to cover the graffiti. The protestors insisted on keeping the old wall as a "community resource."

We'd heard all this before but hadn't realized that Candy was one of the protestors. This report showed several close-ups of her.

"That girl will protest anything," Skylar said.

Then we learned that they were reshowing this old video of the protest and focusing on Candy for a reason. A reporter was on the scene, surrounded by the flashing lights of emergency vehicles and yellow police tape.

"What we know so far," he said, "is that the woman was savagely attacked by someone — or some*thing* — as she left the protest this evening. The woman has been identified as Candice Longstaff. Police have not found her body, so they have some hope that she is still alive. A search of the cemetery is underway as I speak, though the search is hampered by fog." His brow furrowed into a puzzled look. "Which is unusual for this time of year."

The reporter glanced off camera. "We now have an eyewitness who saw the attack." He walked over to a young bearded man who looked dazed. "This is Norman Agostino. Could you tell us, Norman, what happened here earlier?"

Norman nodded. His retro plastic-framed glasses had slipped down his nose. He licked his lips uncertainly and cleared his throat. "We were protesting here along Normandie." He pointed vaguely to his right. "Lots of people were honking their support as they drove by. It was great."

He cleared his throat again and pushed his glasses up on his nose. "Awhile after it got dark, we decided to call it quits for today. Candy said her car was on the other side of the cemetery, who wants to walk through the cemetery with me? We all said we weren't walking through the cemetery in the dark, not with this weird mist that was rolling along the ground. It was like a graveyard in a movie, you know? Candy said she wasn't afraid."

Norman stopped and took a deep breath. "She walked up the hill there." He pointed behind him. "The mist was thicker up there. In the distance you could see a faint purple glow. It was weird, man. It didn't feel right. Candy walked on up there. We called to her, told her to come with us, walk around on the sidewalk. She waved her hand and kept going. The next thing we knew…"

He blinked back tears. The reporter put his hand on Norman's shoulder. "The next thing we knew, a zombie came out from behind a tree and stalked up behind her and hit her over the head, like really hit her hard, you know? Really hard. It was awful. The zombie turned toward us with its arms flailing around and its head shaking back and forth. You know the way zombies do? Then, it lurched a step toward us like it would come for us next, so we turned and ran. Over my shoulder I saw the zombie drag her into the mist."

Chapter 7

We kept the TV on for a while after that first report, but nothing new came up about the assault at the cemetery. CNN aired a segment based on the info we'd already seen in the local news reports.

By 1:30 in the morning, I had to give it up, exhausted after my long day. When I went to bed, Skylar was still wide awake in front of the TV, beside herself with grief and anger and guilt. She kept saying that if only we'd let Candy stay with us, maybe she would have gotten drunk in our kitchen instead of going to the protest.

I remembered what Skylar's mother always said: If only "if only" were magic, we could do anything. I didn't say it out loud.

#

Light was seeping through my window blinds the next morning as someone shook me.

"Wake up," a woman's voice said. "It's getting weirder."

That's not a valid reason to wake a person up. I was sure of that, possibly the only thing I was sure of as I tried to focus on Skylar from my tangled sheets. The light was too dim to see her face, but I thought I recognized her voice, and I'd always suspected she was the kind of person who would wake somebody up just because things were getting weirder.

I rolled sideways and looked at the clock: 5:53. "It's weird that you're waking me up four hours after I went to bed." I pulled the sheet over my head, which didn't work out because the sheet was twisted all over the place. I must have wrestled with it for the whole four hours.

"Sorry," Skylar said. "I've been watching the national news, and they have new information."

I pulled down the part of the sheet that was over one ear. "Okay, tell me."

"Are you sure you're awake?"

"No." I rubbed my hand across my face. "If I hurt all over, that means I'm awake?"

Skylar turned on the lamp next to my bed. She brushed the hair away from my forehead.

"Your cut healed up already," she said. "Didn't I cast the healing spell on your whole bod?"

"If you did, it failed miserably."

"Hold on."

She left and came back with a handful of herbs. Waving her hands and chanting a string of nonsense words (nonsense to me, anyway), she cast the spell. It was very relaxing. I fell back asleep. My phone buzzing on the bedside table woke me up. Probably someone with new information about things getting weirder. I ignored it. Why had I left the stupid thing on?

"It's Sander," Skylar said.

Grabbing the phone, I saw the Caller ID — Sander Nilsen — and touched the answer button, unsure whether I'd answered in time. "Sander? Sander?"

"Hayley, hi," he said in his high reedy voice. "Sorry to bother you so early. I remember you're an early riser?"

"Yes," I assured him. "I was already awake." I shrugged at Skylar.

"You're welcome," she mouthed at me.

"What's wrong?" I asked. "Are the girls all right?"

Sander was the father of blonde triplets. They were about five-and-a-half years old, and they were the cutest trio of witches you were ever likely to meet. I'd met them in the Angelus-Rosedale Cemetery, where a magical pattern called the Waterway had its main portal. The triplets had the ability to "walk" the Waterway.

Sander had become a friend in recent months. He had the potential to be more than just a friend, but he was one of the shyest men I'd ever met. How he'd ever gotten married and fathered children was a mystery. Sander was one of the few men on the planet who Skylar liked, and she kept pushing me to pursue him. I was afraid I'd drive him away if I seemed too aggressive.

"The girls are fine," he said. "No problem, really. I don't understand why they want me to talk to you, so I apologize for bothering you. I tried to call last night, but I guess you were busy."

"Just moving plants around," I said. "And you aren't bothering me at all, Sander. What's going on?"

I heard a little girl's voice in the background say, "Tell her about the Wiza." Two other little voices chimed in with the same message.

Sander said to them, "I'll tell her, just hang on."

To me, he said, "We visited the cemetery yesterday afternoon."

"Not your usual day," I said.

"Her birthday," he explained.

Sander's wife had died a year or so before in an accident on a movie set. She was buried in the Angelus-Rosedale Cemetery. He and the girls visited her grave once a week. I'd often thought his loss was too recent. He was still grieving. That's why he didn't see the potential in our relationship that I did. Or maybe he just didn't like me that way.

"After we arranged the flowers, we visited the pool."

In the background, I heard a little voice say, "We put out a cupcake, too. Tell her about the cupcake with the candle for Mommy's birthday."

"Yes," Sander said, "a chocolate cupcake. That was the girls' idea."

"With a candle," a little voice said.

He took a deep breath. "So we went to the pool. The girls love the place, but it still makes me nervous. They insist on going into it, and all I can think of is Anna being lost in there for weeks. Thank you again for rescuing her."

"I was glad to help." He thanked me almost every time we talked. Anna had been stuck in the Waterway because her magical energy had gotten low. The girls called that energy Wiza, after the

Wizard of Oz. Using my ability to walk the ancient Stoneway, I charged Anna up again and brought her out. In the process, I'd become the living bridge between the Waterway and the Stoneway, whatever that meant. I still had no idea.

"The girls were about to go into the pool, but as soon as they touched the water, they pulled back. They said something was wrong. They were very upset about it but couldn't explain why. When a cloud passed across the sun, I could see a purplish glow in the water if I didn't look directly at it. You know how you can see faint light out of the corner of your eye? The girls kept saying it was wrong, something wrong with the Wiza. They said you would know how to fix it."

"Me?"

It's nice when children have faith in you. It's terrible when that faith is misplaced.

"Sander," I said quietly, so my voice wouldn't carry to the girls at his end, "I don't know what's wrong. I don't know how to fix it."

"They say if you visit the pool, you can tell what's wrong."

I looked at Skylar, who pulled a wry look and shrugged.

"Getting to the pool is difficult at the moment. You've seen the news?"

"Uh, I don't follow the news much. What do you mean?"

"Last night a woman was attacked at the cemetery. A friend of ours. She was hit on the head."

"Oh no. Is she all right?"

"We don't know. She's still missing, and the cemetery is one big crime scene. We won't be able to visit the pool for some time."

"I see. The girls will just have to be patient."

A little voice in the background said, "I don't want to be patient."

A second little voice asked, "What's patient?"

A third little voice said matter-of-factly, "That's when you have to wait for UPS."

The second little voice said, "I don't want to wait. What are we getting?"

The discussion continued in the background as I told Sander that something else was wrong at the cemetery. "You've heard about the zombies?"

"You're kidding." He sucked in a sudden breath. "You're not kidding. The open graves."

"What?"

"When the girls and I walked through the cemetery yesterday, several graves had piles of dirt and stones next to them. At first, I thought it was some kind of maintenance. Then, I started to notice that the graves looked like they'd heaved up their contents from the inside." He stopped for a moment. "The girls were right. Something is wrong."

"I'll go with you to the cemetery as soon as it's open again. The police won't be able to find the pool, so that's safe."

The pool was protected by a spell that kept people from finding their way to it unless they could follow the magic. In fact, I originally found the pool by "talking" to headstones in the cemetery. That's my main magical ability, talking to rocks. It might not seem exciting, but you can learn a lot from rocks. If you lie around for millions of years, *something* interesting is bound to happen to you, even if you're a rock.

Here in the present, too much was happening to me, and it wasn't quite 6:30 in the morning. I signed off with Sander, promising to stay in touch and get together soon. I put the phone down and untangled the sheet from my legs.

"Those girls are so cute," Skylar said.

"They are cute all over the place 24/7. I don't know how Sander keeps up with all that cuteness."

"They need a mommy," Skylar said, not for the first time.

I found a pair of shorts in my dresser and pulled them on. "Should I go up there with my mommy hat on and take over?"

"Looking at it from Sander's point of view, he probably feels overwhelmed all the time. So he might think the mommy job is so challenging, you wouldn't be willing to step into it. You could invite the girls on outings to make it clear you're happy to deal with the challenge."

I was about to take off the T-shirt I slept in and stopped. "Skylar, that's a great idea. Why didn't I think of that?"

"So you forgive me for waking you up?"

I pulled the T-shirt over my head and threw it at her. "That depends on whatever weirdness you woke me up for. Something weirder than a zombie attacking Candy?"

"You should see for yourself. I recorded a CNN report on the DVR."

Pawing through my underwear drawer, I found bra choices that included only uncomfortable, tattered, and super-fancy. I went with tattered. "I need to do laundry."

"Our regular laundry day turned into spectral bloodhound day."

As I finished dressing, I looked at Skylar slumped against the doorframe. She didn't look so good.

"Did you get any sleep at all?" I asked.

"Maybe a couple of hours. I was too wound up to sleep. Worried. I wasn't convinced about the zombie, but Candy was always riling people up with her protesting. Now I don't know what to think. You want some tea?"

"Sure," I said, following her into the kitchen. "You think someone pretended to be a zombie to attack Candy?"

"That's what I thought at first. As I say, I'm not sure what to think now. You'll see in a minute."

When the tea was brewed and we were sitting in front of the TV, Skylar started the recording she'd made. "This first piece is about zombie sightings at the cemetery. A guy captured this on his phone. The soundtrack is mostly the guy repeating the F word to his girlfriend over and over as they figure out they're watching a zombie."

I watched as a figure in the distance lurched out from behind a pyramid in dim light. The Angelus-Rosedale Cemetery has several of these small pyramid-shaped mausoleums. Must be Rosicrucians or something. The guy taking the video moved toward the zombie. As he got closer, I could see that the zombie's once fancy suit had turned to rags, though it was still wearing a bright blue necktie. Its right arm was missing. A lot of its face was missing. It was seriously gross.

"Is that the thing you saw on the beach?" Skylar asked.

"No. The zombie I saw was missing the left side of his face. He had both arms but was going tieless."

The guy taking the video had gotten within 20 yards of the zombie, so I got a better look at it than I really wanted. It was walking dead all right. Then the zombie seemed to notice the guy taking the video, which was odd because its eyeballs were in bad shape. The zombie quivered in place for a moment, jerked back and forth a couple of times, and wheeled around toward the guy with the camera. At that point, a lot of dimly lighted scenery streaked by.

"The guy and his girlfriend screamed and ran away," Skylar explained.

"This was the same zombie that attacked Candy?"

"Candy's friends say the zombie they saw was different. Theirs wasn't wearing a tie and wasn't so obviously male."

"But this video was taken the same day? Yesterday? I can't believe the attack happened only yesterday."

"Only last night, in fact. But no, the zombie video was taken several days ago. It's been circulating on social media, apparently. Since the attack on Candy, the big news organizations are taking it a little more seriously."

"This video confirms the zombie stories we've been hearing from the area around the cemetery," I pointed out.

"As if somebody couldn't dress in a zombie outfit as a joke," Skylar objected. "Or as a disguise."

"If you saw one in the flesh, you wouldn't think it's a joke," I said. "And obviously, the zombies were around before we cast the spectral bloodhound spell, so we didn't create the zombies Killin and I saw on the beach, unless we also cast them back into the past by creating time travel."

"There's no such thing," Skylar assured me.

"You keep saying that."

"Sometimes it's true."

"You think it's true about zombies? You think they're either a joke or a disguise?"

"I'm keeping an open mind," she said as loftily as possible for a person who'd been up most of the night.

"That's weird, all right," I said.

She took a long sip of her tea. "That wasn't the main thing I wanted you to see."

She picked up the remote and fast-forwarded an hour. This time, she turned on the sound. The TV showed a CNN studio with a female news anchor I didn't recognize. A big banner across the screen said "Breaking News."

The anchor said, "CNN has gained exclusive access to new developments in the case of a California woman assaulted last night in a Los Angeles cemetery. The woman has been identified as Candice Longstaff, known to her friends as Candy. Eyewitnesses to the assault said Candy was struck on the head at the edge of the cemetery by an individual they described as a zombie. These witnesses said that the zombie then dragged Candy further into the cemetery, which was enveloped in an unusual ground fog."

The anchor looked slightly embarrassed about delivering this news and struggled to hide her discomfort. "Just moments ago, an FBI agent and another man reported to be an expert tracker entered the cemetery where the assault took place. To minimize disturbances to the crime scene, only two individuals went in this morning at first light. The FBI agent carried a high-resolution video camera. We can now bring you the unedited feed captured from that camera approximately 16 minutes ago. The first voice you hear is the expert tracker."

The TV now showed a weedy patch of grass with scuff marks across it.

"This here's the spot where the girl was hit. That squarish chunk of rock over there was undoubtedly used to hit the girl on the head. You can see the blood there and on the ground where she fell."

A hand entered the picture, pointing first at a flattened patch of weeds and then a pair of scuff marks.

"She fell here and was dragged by her armpits that way. Her shoes tore up this vegetation. Right here on this dirt patch we can see a clear print of the assailant. It's a small shoe, probably a woman's. We can measure that."

The two pairs of boots in the video were careful to skirt the path across the grass as the tracker and the FBI agent followed the scuff marks. The marks ended in a grassy area between a palm tree and a couple of pines.

"The girl was laid right here."

A boot traced an outline on the grass. At one end of the outline was a dark patch.

"The girl lay here for a while, bleeding. Since she's not here still, we can figure that either somebody picked her up and carried her off or she walked away. That's an awful lot of blood there, but head wounds sometimes bleed like a stuck pig, you know?"

The FBI agent said, "Yeah."

The tracker edged around the other side of the dark spot on the grass. He took two steps past that spot and pointed. The agent focused the camera on a patch of bare dirt, where a footprint was clearly visible.

"That's the assailant's print, and that person is not carrying anybody else. The assailant walked off thataway by her own self."

The tracker edged around the other side of the little clearing. "And the victim, sure enough, got up on her own two feet. You can see the grass pressed in here and here. And…"

The tracker trailed off as he followed alongside the tracks Candy had left.

"She's still alive!" I whispered.

"Well, this is the part where it gets weird," Skylar said.

"These tracks ain't right," the tracker said, crouched on the grass. "Look here."

The camera focused where the man was pointing to a series of footprints in the bare dirt. They just looked like regular footprints to me.

"What's wrong with them?" the FBI agent asked.

"Look at the heel, and look at the toe," the tracker said, pointing. "You see a deeper impression at either end?"

"Uh, I'm not sure I do."

"You don't — trust me — because it ain't there. This person was walking flat-footed, not like a normal gait. Do you remember this girl walking that way before she was hit?"

"I didn't notice that," the agent said, trying not to sound ignorant.

"This girl did not walk flat-footed before she was hit. She left perfectly normal prints back there on the hillside — same kind of normal prints as the person who hit her and dragged her off. The attacker's normal prints go off thataway."

The tracker walked a little further along the path. "These prints of the victim are different. It would be very hard for a normal person to walk like this. All the muscles in your legs would have to be held rigid. A normal person would use some of those muscles without thinking about it, without being aware of it. You couldn't help it."

"Are you saying that this girl turned into a zombie?" the agent asked.

"Well, sir, I ain't saying nothing like that. I've tracked a goodly number of men, women, and children, and all manner of animals. I have never tracked a zombie. And I've never tracked a person who walked like this." He pointed at Candy's footprints on the bare earth.

"What I believe we could say," said the FBI agent, clearly trying to sound knowledgeable now, "is that the attacker who's *supposed* to be a zombie is walking like a normal person through this whole incident. On the other hand, the victim who's taken a blow to the head is now walking like a zombie."

"You the FBI's point man on zombies?" the tracker asked.

The agent cleared his throat and said, "Well, I, you know…"

"You can say whatever you want about zombies later, son. Let's see where this girl went to."

Chapter 8

As I watched dumbfounded, the image on the TV broke up and went to black. Skylar muted the TV, while I continued to look at the news anchor moving her lips soundlessly. After a minute, I realized Skylar was looking at the side of my head.

"Well?" she asked. "What do you make of that?"

"If you woke me up so that I could explain what's going on, you're going to be disappointed."

"Weird, isn't it?"

"Yeah, one thing that's weird is the way it ended. What about the rest of the video? Where did the tracks lead?"

"Did you notice how embarrassed the news anchor looked after the video ended? I wonder if they hacked the FBI's video feed and then lost the connection."

"The news anchor looked embarrassed from the get-go."

"Whatever happened, that's all the video they've shown. I don't know where the tracks lead. Wasn't it weird what the guy said about the tracks?"

I drank a big sip of tea and then another big sip. "In a way, it makes perfect sense, although I might only think that because I'm not quite awake."

Getting up from the sofa, I went to the window that looks out on the front yard and opened the curtains. I think better when I'm looking at the outdoors. After another big sip of tea, I said, "Of course, the way it makes sense doesn't make any sense, so overall…"

I waved my tea mug to complete my thought, which wasn't anywhere near complete, so I walked to the coffee table, sat down, and banged my empty mug down on a coaster to act as punctuation at the end of my thought. Sometimes you just need sound effects when you can't think straight.

"I thought it was weird," Skylar summarized.

I slapped my thighs. "We're in agreement then. Weird."

Standing up again, I realized I had no destination in mind. Where was I going? Back to bed? Theoretically, that sounded good, but I wasn't sleepy anymore.

Skylar noticed that I'd stalled out. "Breakfast?" she asked.

In the kitchen, I made another pot of tea while she stir-fried leftovers to eat on toast.

"Let's think about this logically," I proposed.

Skylar laughed.

"I'm not joking."

"That's why it's so funny!"

"Come on," I said, pouring boiling water into the teapot. "How far would Sherlock Holmes have gotten with that attitude?"

"How far would Sherlock have gotten in a world of magic?" Skylar countered. "Where the facts don't necessarily make sense? Where the improbable is the norm?"

"We have to start somewhere," I said. "Even magic ends up making a certain kind of odd sense, once you know how it works."

"I'll grant you that," Skylar said, pulling two whole-wheat slices out of the toaster. "Everything makes sense once you know how it works."

She slopped half the contents of her skillet on a slice of toast and put it on the table in front of me. "*Bon appétit logique.*" Sitting down, she added, "Pardon my French."

I poured tea. The leftovers on toast were good. Skylar's added magic meant we always ate the best vegan food on the planet, even when it looked like slop on toast.

"So after Candy was hit on the head, she walked like a zombie," I ventured logically.

"Do we have to talk about zombies while we eat?" Skylar complained.

"What else is there to talk about?"

"The weather is nice."

I looked out the window. "Typical overcast June morning in Redondo Beach."

"Supposed to burn off and get into the 80s," Skylar said. "Light offshore breeze."

"Same as it ever was. That's it for the weather." I tapped my fork on my plate a couple of times. "So Candy apparently turned into a zombie, which is logical if you've been killed by a zombie, except the person who killed her was not walking like a zombie, so it doesn't make sense. Which means…" I looked at Skylar expectantly.

"It could be magic," she said dutifully.

"And could it be the same magic that's gone wrong at the Waterway pool?"

"Logically speaking, any two problems that don't make sense could have the same cause."

Putting down my fork, I made a face at Skylar. "You have a way of making logic sound stupid."

"Sometimes logic only moves the pieces around without making anything clear, you know?"

"Sure, but we have to start somewhere. What else can we do?"

Skylar held up her phone with a gleam of extreme cleverness in her eye. "Call Mother."

"That's your alternative to logic, call Mother?"

"I would have called her earlier, but I didn't want to wake her up."

When we had Skylar's mother, Lenora Bemis, on the line, we filled her in on what had happened at the cemetery. She didn't say anything until Skylar concluded, "So the zombie who attacked Candy *wasn't* walking like a zombie, but after the attack, Candy *was* walking like a zombie. What do you make of that?"

"All this zombie talk is certainly confusing," Ms. Bemis said. "I mean, many people have investigated claims that the dead can rise up and become zombies but nobody has found credible evidence. There's no such thing."

Skylar stuck out her tongue and gave me a smirk.

"That being said," Ms. Bemis continued, "if it looks like a zombie and walks like a zombie, it might be a zombie."

"Also smells like a zombie," I added, and told her about the zombie I'd seen on the beach and the other smelly one Killin had found.

"There you go," Ms. Bemis said. "I think you have to look at the facts logically."

I stuck out my tongue and gave Skylar a sweet told-you-so smile, which really made me feel like an intelligent adult.

Skylar threw up her hands in frustration. "How can we be logical about something that can't exist?"

"*Can't* might be too strong a word. We don't know of any zombies in the past, but someone could raise dead people out of their graves with the right magic. It would take a powerful spell, so one logical question is, why would someone do that? Why go to the effort of waking up dead people? Another question is, why did zombies show up in that particular cemetery and in Redondo Beach?"

"And why kill Candy?" Skylar murmured to herself.

"What was that?" her mother asked.

"I'm wondering why someone would kill Candy."

"She aggravated plenty of people, including her brother," I pointed out. "Did one of them kill her while pretending to be a zombie?"

"Or was she killed by a zombie pretending to walk like a regular person?" Ms. Bemis said.

"Hadn't thought of that possibility," Skylar said. "Are zombies crafty enough to walk like regular people?"

"Most of what we know about zombies comes from Hollywood," I said, "which might be stupider than actual zombies."

"If actual zombies exist at all," Skylar said, pounding her fists on her head. "Good thing we're looking at this logically."

Ms. Bemis agreed to ask other witches if they'd heard of any new developments on the zombie front. We didn't hold out much hope for that kind of news. Magical people were tight with their knowledge. Even well-meaning witches withheld info about magic for fear it could be used against them.

As for sorcerers, they were "completely untrustworthy, mostly," according to Skylar, who felt that way about males in general — despite the fact that her sorcerer father was one of the kindest, gentlest men I'd ever met.

On the topic of sorcerers, Ms. Bemis asked about Killin. The Bemis family saw the Killin relationship as my personal soap opera with consequences for everyone. I thought they were secretly hoping I'd forgive him for cheating on me so the soap opera would continue, though I was less sure they welcomed the consequences. Killin was so secretive about his activities. We were all unsure about his true intentions.

I told Skylar and her mother about my short conversation with Killin at the nursery that was interrupted by the eavesdropping customer with the big emerald hanging in her cleavage.

"Big emerald with little diamonds above it?" Skylar asked. Before I could answer, she added, "Compact frame except for these." She cupped her hands under her breasts. "About five-two, professionally blonded, very well put together?"

"You know her?"

"You don't know her?" Skylar answered in surprise. "That's Barb Vanderberry."

"I get the impression you think she's famous."

"She is famous!" Skylar said. "Celebrity chef? Chain of big-deal restaurants? Wildly popular YouTube channel? Millions of followers?"

"Sorry, I don't keep up with people like that. Is she a friend of yours?"

Skylar shook her head rapidly. Her eyelids fluttered, and her left arm jerked sideways. Finally, she managed to say, "No!"

She got up from the sofa and explained, while pulling on her hair with both hands, "She eats in the café, and after she's had a few bites, she comes into the kitchen and tells me what I did wrong in each dish. Several times she's insisted that I remake an entree the way she thought it should be done, while she looks over my shoulder instructing me through each piddly-assed step. 'Don't stir that so vigorously, dear. Not so much thyme, just a pinch. Where do you get your walnuts? They're not *fleshy* enough.'"

At least, I think Skylar said "fleshy." It came out as a low animal noise.

She stood there with her fists held in front of her like tight little wads of anger. "I hope you weren't nice to her in the nursery. She's a nuisance."

"Now, Skylar," her mother said from the phone, "you know how you've always been impatient. If you could simply deal with Barb Vanderberry calmly, I'm sure you'd learn something from her. She's a wonderful chef. I just watched her show about cooking with tonka beans. Have you seen that one? You could make some terrific dishes for the café with those."

"Especially if I want to get arrested. Did she mention that tonka beans are illegal?"

"She did say something like that towards the end, but she said not to worry about it. You have to eat a lot of them to have a problem. Did you know that?"

"I do know, yes. It's the feds who don't know, and they say it's against the law to serve them. Do you want me to get arrested?"

"If you get arrested, Hayley can get you out," Ms. Bemis said and laughed.

I'd used a magic spell to turn invisible and sneak into the Redondo Beach police station several times. Ms. Bemis found this hilarious. Skylar did not find this conversation funny in any way.

We signed off with Ms. Bemis and decided to go to work a little early. Just as we were walking out the door, Emma Nakamura walked in with a pout on her pretty face. She wasn't done up with the immaculate makeup she usually wore, and she didn't look happy to see us.

For that matter, Skylar didn't look happy to see Emma, but Skylar wasn't happy with anybody at the moment. They traded peeved expressions and half-hearted greetings. It looked like one of those general-upsetness situations that neither of them should take personally and that both of them would.

"My father is impossible," Emma said.

Skylar nodded impatiently. "We know that."

This wasn't the level of sympathy Emma had come for. She tried again. "You would not believe how he's been badgering me all morning. Honestly, I don't know how I maintain my sanity."

"Hard to say how you do that," Skylar told her. "We're going to work." She dug into her tote bag for her car keys.

"We're a little upset about the attack on Candy last night," I told Emma, trying to provide an excuse for Skylar's lack of sympathy.

Emma decided that she could up the ante on lacking sympathy. "What did Candy think she was doing walking alone through the cemetery? That was stupid. She was asking for trouble."

Skylar glared at Emma. "Candy was my friend, and someone killed her."

"Daddy says she's probably lying injured in the cemetery. They'll find her any minute, and she'll be okay. In any case, I do not understand how you could be friends with that woman."

I didn't understand how Skylar could be friends with Candy either, but I wasn't going to say it out loud. Skylar was simmering with anger already.

"How are you suddenly the judge of my friends?" Skylar said.

"I'm not judging. I'm just saying I don't understand it."

"You are judging her, and you're not honest enough to say so."

"So I'm a liar?" Emma demanded. "Now who's judging?"

"Why are you here?" Skylar asked.

"I told you, Daddy is impossible. I was wondering if I could hang out at your house for a while."

"Why aren't you going to work?"

"I called in sick."

Emma worked at a fabulous handbag shop at 2 Rodeo Drive. She didn't make a lot, but she got a discount on the shoes and little purses she craved.

Skylar peered at Emma's face. "You're sick?"

Emma elevated her nose a couple of inches and declared, "I don't feel well. I need a day off. Is that okay with you? I might take a nap."

"Sure. That okay with you, Hayley?"

"Of course," I said. "Make yourself at home. I might come back and take a nap myself this afternoon if I can get away."

"That would be nice," Emma said. "I hate to be alone. I wish you guys had a dog or a cat or something."

"We'll get you a gerbil," Skylar said.

The doorbell rang, and Emma looked alarmed. "That's probably Daddy. He said he wanted to talk to both of you today. I thought he'd find you at work. Don't tell him I'm here, okay?"

"Your secret is safe with us," Skylar said as Emma fled down the hallway. To me Skylar said, "Like he's not going to notice her car parked outside."

I headed toward the kitchen. "I don't want to talk to him either. Tell him I went to work already."

"Like he's not going to notice your car in the driveway," Skylar said behind me.

I kept going. Detective Nakamura could notice anything he wanted. I wasn't going to talk to him.

After Skylar opened the front door, I heard a voice I didn't recognize and reversed course to find out who it was. The young man standing in the open doorway was wearing a short-sleeved shirt with light-blue checks, open at the neck, and a Stetson hat.

"This is Detective Harris Duke," Skylar told me.

The man held up his ID. "Good morning, ma'am," he said with the slightest southern accent.

After casting the countrified spectral bloodhound spell, now we had a detective wearing a cowboy hat. His southern accent wasn't from the South of the country, though. Probably Bakersfield, California, I decided, birthplace of Merle Haggard and an honorary outpost of the true South.

"Where's Detective Nakamura?" I asked.

"I was about to ask the same rude question," Skylar said.

"Well, now, no need to be rude, is there?" the man said. His wispy blond mustache crinkled above an amused smile. "I'm here about a matter from the Pico-Union area. Nakamura's your local guy here?"

We nodded yes.

"Friend of yours? Or you just run afoul of the law pretty often?"

Our faces must have displayed several different flavors of bafflement. How did we answer questions like that? The detective's smile broadened.

"That's all right," he said. "No need to incriminate yourselves through past associations. May I come in?"

"We're on our way to work," Skylar objected. I think she'd figured out what was about to happen.

"I'll hardly hold you up for one teensy, tiny moment," he said. "I'd like a little help about a brutal assault that occurred in the Pico-

Union district of the city yesterday evening, in our big cemetery to be precise. You're aware of this crime?"

When we nodded, he stepped through the doorway, closed the door behind him, and took off his Stetson. A mass of blond curls came into view. The sight of all that blond hair springing out was almost comical, but we weren't in the mood to enjoy it. He motioned us toward the living room. We went. We sat.

"Now you," the detective said, looking at Skylar as he perched on the front edge of an easy chair, "are Skylar Bemis. Is that correct?"

Skylar nodded. I started to hope we could get through this interview with a few nods.

"The woman who was assaulted has been identified as Candice Longstaff. I believe she was a friend of yours?"

"Yes," Skylar said. "We were friends years ago."

"Had yourselves a little relationship going back a ways, I believe? And recently reacquainted?"

"Yes," Skylar said reluctantly.

"When was the last time you saw Ms. Longstaff?"

"That would be Wednesday."

Detective Duke looked at me. "You are Hayley West?"

I nodded.

"And when was the last time you saw Ms. Longstaff?"

"Same day. Wednesday."

"So, day before yesterday. That was the day Ms. Longstaff had an altercation here at your house with Ms. Emma Nakamura?"

We nodded.

"Could I speak with Ms. Nakamura, please?"

"Ah," Skylar said, squirming on the sofa next to me, "that would be up to her."

"Would you be kind enough to ask her for me?"

"Ah, yes," Skylar said. She took out her phone and touched Emma's mobile number. If she was hoping to fool the detective into thinking Emma was not in the house, this plan failed when we all heard a tune by a German electronica band playing down the hall and behind a door. It was Emma's ringtone, and it was unmistakably in the house.

Skylar pressed on anyway, saying into her phone, "You want to talk to a detective?"

I heard a single syllable from the phone. Skylar put her phone on the coffee table and told the detective, "No."

The detective smiled and shouted down the hall, "You're a suspect in the possible homicide of Candice Longstaff. You're going to have to face the music."

Chapter 9

While Emma pondered whether to come out for an interview with Detective Duke, we peppered him with questions about why on earth he suspected her of killing Candy — if Candy had indeed been killed. Skylar did most of the peppering, because I remembered a good reason for suspecting Emma: She'd threatened Candy the night before the attack in the cemetery. But how did the detective know about that threat?

With Skylar still insisting that Detective Duke was being ridiculous, I pulled up GhostOps on my phone. Their most recent post was video of a wolf emerging from a garden shed in Pennsylvania, where wild wolves haven't been seen since 1892. Obviously, this was a werewolf, according to the post.

Or a dog, I'd guess.

Here I was, a witch, being totally skeptical of werewolves. Who did I think I was? I made a mental note to ask Skylar about werewolves. She'd say there's no such thing, and then I'd have to argue with her. Seriously, werewolves?

Why was I winding myself up about werewolves? Oh yeah, I'd been woken up after four hours of sleep by someone telling me things were getting weirder. I looked up from my phone. Skylar was still arguing with Detective Duke. Emma was standing halfway down the hallway, still undecided about coming out to face the music.

Right, right, right — Emma, Candy. Looking back at the GhostOps posts, I found the one I was looking for. It showed the whole bust-up between Candy and Emma.

I went into the hallway and motioned Emma into my bedroom. Then, I called Detective Nakamura and told him about the GhostOps post and Detective Duke.

"Can you keep him away from Emma until I get a lawyer over there?" he asked.

"Of course," I said. "If he gets pushy, we'll eject him. I'm sure he doesn't have a warrant."

Going back into the living room, I found Skylar still defending Emma. Detective Duke was asking probing questions about Emma's past fits of jealous rage, of which there were a few. Did Skylar realize this guy might be a little more clever than he looked? He was prompting her to paint a picture of Emma that was not always pretty.

The detective nodded after Skylar's latest account and looked at me. Gesturing down the hall in Emma's general direction, he said, "The longer she delays, the more suspicious she looks. I hope you were encouraging her to cooperate?"

"Yes, of course," I said. "We're super cooperative here. It's just that at the moment, she's indisposed." I wasn't sure exactly what that meant, but it seemed to work in old movies.

Detective Duke's face scrunched up in a display of mock concern. He put his hand across his forehead. "Ah *do* hope she's not havin' a faintin' spell," he said with an accent that came straight out of Blanche DuBois's mouth in "A Streetcar Named Desire."

Watching the expressions play across his face, I longed for Detective Nakamura's stony look. Really? Had I gone completely around the bend? I blinked a couple of times and leaned against the wall to steady myself.

Detective Duke frowned. "You all right?"

"Yes, yes," I said. "Just thinking crazy thoughts."

Since Emma was indisposed for the time being, the detective asked me where I'd been at certain times and whether anybody could confirm that I was there — the usual detective stuff. My answers must have been reasonable because he didn't arrest me for anything.

After a while, the lawyer showed up for Emma, which didn't thrill Detective Duke. After Emma and the lawyer talked in my bedroom for two minutes, she came out and told the detective she did not kill Candice Longstaff. The lawyer announced that she would answer no more questions at this time.

The detective left, promising that he would get a warrant for Emma's arrest if she failed to submit to further questioning by noon at his office.

Skylar and I needed to go to work, but then Detective Nakamura arrived. Skylar pleaded with him to stop Detective Duke from persecuting Emma.

"He might prosecute Emma, but I doubt he'll persecute her much," Detective Nakamura told her.

There was his stony face, unchanging amidst the turmoil. It was kind of comforting.

"This whole thing is just wrong," Skylar insisted. "The guy should be out finding the crazy person who attacked Candy, not badgering Emma. Can't you do something?"

"You want me to interfere in a case where my daughter is the chief suspect?"

Skylar wanted to say yes. What she settled for was, "But it's all so ridiculous."

"For better or worse," Detective Nakamura said, "I said as much to my captain. And definitely for worse, I made a stronger comment about Detective Harris Duke."

"That's why," Detective Nakamura said, sitting down in a spare dining room chair that was parked in the living room, "I've been put on administrative leave."

His expression hadn't changed, of course, but his whole body said *I'm now useless.*

With a sleep-deprived brain, my first thought was: Does this mean I don't call him *Detective* Nakamura anymore?

While I was puzzling over this unthinkable problem, Emma hugged him briefly and told him she was sorry. She left with the lawyer.

Skylar looked distressed, though I don't think any of her distress was focused on Detective Nakamura. She had to go open the café and turn out vegan food on a schedule. I wanted to go to work too and was only staying home because I had to get some sleep. Otherwise, I'd be making bad decisions all day. I'm no perfectionist, but I do try to keep my bad decision ratio below 50/50.

When everyone else was gone, that left me with Detective Nakamura, who was still sitting in the spare dining room chair, slumped in a funk.

"Let's get on with it," I told him.

"I'm going. I'm going." He stood and put his hand on the front door knob.

"No, dimwit," I said in a very respectful, caring way. "Into the kitchen. You need a scone." That was fun, calling him a dimwit. Instead of Detective Nakamura, I could call him Dimwit Nakamura.

"I will be a detective again, as soon as this case is cleared up," he said, as though he was reading my mind.

"You haven't developed psychic powers, have you?"

"I thought you told me there's no such thing," he said.

"Yeah, I'm pretty sure. It's just that I'm so addled from lack of sleep that my thoughts might leak out."

In the kitchen, I loaded the coffee maker and turned it on. "Too bad about your layoff. Did you get to keep your gun?"

"Yes, so don't try anything." He sat at the kitchen table. "And don't tell anybody I said that."

"Your secret is safe with me."

"It's not funny."

"Got it." I opened the refrigerator to check the scone inventory. "We have carrot zucchini, jalapeño banana, and fig."

"Jalapeño banana, really?"

"Skylar's been a little upset lately."

"Understandable," he said, nodding. "Have you had the jalapeño banana?"

"Oh yes. I try them all, no matter how upset Skylar is when she makes them."

"And?"

"How about a fig?"

"Sounds good."

Sliding a fig scone into the toaster oven, I asked him casually if he'd heard anything about the FBI's attempt to track the killer zombie in the cemetery.

He didn't answer. When I turned around, he was looking at a watercolor of a hummingbird on the wall.

"You interested in art now" I asked.

"Has that always been there?"

"Every time you've sat at the table, that little bird has hovered on the wall next to you."

"Funny what you don't see when you're looking for something else," he mused.

"And I wonder if you heard my question while you were doing all this looking?"

"Tracking the zombie," he said. "Yes, I heard."

"Skylar and I saw a video of two agents following the tracks left by Candy and the killer. The tracker said the killer walked away like a normal person, while Candy walked away like a zombie."

"You told me the other day you didn't believe in zombies. Now you think Candy is a zombie?"

"Well," I said, "the first time you saw Candy, you thought she was a zombie."

"My captain noted that when he put me on administrative leave."

"Whatever's going on, we have to figure it out. At the very least, we have to clear Emma. Then, you can go back to work. Officially, I mean. You are going to figure out what happened, aren't you?"

I poured coffee in a mug and put it in front of him.

He blew on it and took a sip. "I'm certainly not supposed to be doing that."

"Detective Harris Duke is supposed to do it. We could leave the whole thing to him. You just relax and enjoy your time off. Do a little surfing."

"I don't have a board."

"I'll loan you mine."

Detective Nakamura took another sip of his coffee and didn't reply. He only had a sense of humor when he was making fun of me.

Taking a different tack, I tried to fill in a missing piece of information. "After the FBI guy followed Candy's tracks in the cemetery, the news reports never said where those tracks led."

"That's because the police haven't released that information."

"But you're going to tell me because you know I can help."

"What would make me think you could help?"

"Because I've been so helpful in the past, and let's just say I've had some adventures in that cemetery. I learned some things about the place that aren't obvious, things the police don't know."

"The Angelus-Rosedale Cemetery? What led you to have 'adventures' there, of all places? And what do you know about it?"

"The first thing I learned," I said, peeking at the scone through the window of the toaster oven, "was that scenes from *Buffy the Vampire Slayer* were shot there."

"Oh, for heaven's sake," he said.

Why had I started with Buffy? Sleepy squirrels had taken over my tree and were shaking out nuts.

"And then," I said quickly, "I learned that Dirk Condrescu — the guy who was murdered on the pier with a stake through his heart — was buried in the Angelus-Rosedale Cemetery."

"On purpose?" Detective Nakamura looked bewildered. His expression actually changed.

"No, accidentally."

"I mean, was Dirk Condrescu buried there *because* they thought he was a vampire and *Buffy* was filmed there?"

"Good question," I said. "That could be true. I found out about Dirk and *Buffy* from the Vampire Militia. Remember them? Dirk's wife might have chosen that cemetery on purpose, for all I know."

Sliding the fig scone out of the toaster oven and onto a plate, I put it on the table. "But all that vampire business has nothing to do with anything, really."

Detective Nakamura's expression reset to normal. This was probably his way of rolling his eyes. Why had I told him all that ridiculous vampire stuff? That was the reason I'd gone to the Angelus-Rosedale Cemetery in the first place. While I was there, I'd discovered the pool that led to the Waterway and met the three little blonde witches who could "walk" the Waterway. Was I going to tell the detective about any of that?

Nope.

What was I going to tell him? I had to give him some reason to reveal what the FBI had found out. While I thought this over, I made myself a pot of tea. As I put tea leaves into the steeper basket, I had a thought: Why would the police not release the information about where Candy's tracks led? If they found her body, they'd announce that a murder investigation was underway. If they didn't find her, why not? Did the tracks lead out of the cemetery? If so, wouldn't the police have a full-scale search underway to find her?

"You don't know where she went," I said aloud, more to myself than to Detective Nakamura.

He stared hard at me, but didn't say anything. Usually, he was the one interrogating me. Now the tables were turned.

"The police haven't released information about where Candy's tracks lead because they don't know," I said to him. "The FBI wasn't able to follow the tracks. They don't lead out of the cemetery. They don't lead anywhere, do they?"

Detective Nakamura shook his head no, his mouth full of fig scone.

"You're trying to hide what you don't know to begin with."

He shrugged a half-hearted yes and swallowed, glancing away and managing to look sheepish without changing his expression. "At a certain point, the tracks simply stop."

"As though Candy vanished into thin air," I said.

"Yes. It doesn't make sense."

"That's why I can help!"

He tilted his head. "I've always suspected that you're the expert on things that don't make sense."

"That didn't come out exactly the way I intended," I explained — or failed to explain, really. I didn't want to get into the magic with him. Did I? Even if I did explain, how much would he believe?

Detective Nakamura drank the last of his coffee and stood up from the table. "Thank you for your kind offer of help, but I've solved many cases that were more perplexing than this one, even if it is stranger than most. I don't need an amateur sidekick to assist."

"Like you didn't need anybody to help you find little Angelina Martinelli," I said.

"Glad you mentioned that," he said, leaning a little too close to my face. "Tell me again how you found that girl? Oh, wait, you never did tell me how you did that."

"What difference does it make?" I said back in his face, a bit louder than was absolutely necessary. "I found her. That's what matters."

"Did you stay within the law? That matters too, you know."

"Well, I littered the beach," I said in my most mocking tone. "Arrest me and throw me in jail if that's stretching the law too much for you. Oh, wait," I added with my hands on my hips, "you can't arrest anybody because you're on leave."

"And this is me leaving," he said. "Thanks for the scone."

When he was out the door, I shouted after him, "Let me know if you figure out where Candy's tracks go. Good luck with that."

For good measure, I slammed the door behind him.

I had a pretty good idea where Candy's tracks went and why they'd disappeared. But what could I do about it?

Chapter 10

My immediate plan was to take a nap, but as I stood next to the door I'd just slammed, I knew Detective Nakamura had ruined that plan. I was so wound up about his pig-headed refusal to accept my help, there was no way I could fall asleep. After changing into some slightly more presentable clothes, I drove around the block to the nursery.

When I got there, a woman was in the parking lot with the trunk of her Bentley open. My employee Ginger was standing next to the open trunk, looking into it, shaking her head doubtfully. She looked up when I arrived and was obviously relieved to see me.

Great. Sleep-deprived boss lady shows up just in time to deal with vexing customer problem.

The customer in question was standing with her hands on her hips but not in a belligerent way. It was more like a fingers-on-hips posture that suggested she always got her way, and the only question was how long it was going to take everyone else to realize that.

I grew up in a world of people who always got their way, and the only question was who was going to get her way *today*? Oh, and one other question was how long it would take for everybody else to get back at the person who got her way today.

Then fingers-on-hips turned my way, and I saw the big emerald dangling in the plunging neckline of her maroon blouse. It was Barb Vanderberry, celebrity chef, the woman who'd bought a bunch of plants for her new home in Redondo Beach. Looking into her trunk, I could see one of those plants would not be growing in her new garden because it was dead. I felt the soil in the pot. It was dry as dust.

"She murdered this bougainvillea," Ginger told me, putting her hands firmly on her hips.

Out of the corner of my eye, I noticed Barb's lips tighten at this murder indictment.

Ginger concluded, "Now she wants us to replace it."

"Not just this one," Barb corrected, as though she were speaking to a child. "All the bougainvillea you sold me and several of the Okuboi bamboo are inadequate. They must all be replaced. How soon can you pick them up?"

Figuring I might as well give it the old teapot along with the other two women, I put my hands on my hips. I looked at the withered bougainvillea in the trunk of the expensive car and then at Barb's fabulous haircut and the emerald nestled against her perfectly tanned skin. The women I'd grown up with would consider Barb's condescending tone crude and overdone in a matter as trivial as a few dead plants. My guess was, Barb had not grown up with the idea that she'd always get her own way. She was an amateur at this.

I felt the dry soil in the pot again and looked off into the nursery. "I believe we have enough plants to replace yours. Give me your address, and I'll see what you need."

Barb tried to hide her relief at getting her way, confirming my guess that she hadn't really expected to. Ginger, on the other hand, looked outraged. I was letting the bougainvillea killer go scot-free.

"I have some weeding to do," she said and stalked off.

I'd have to explain to her the fine art of throwing people off balance by yielding to their ridiculous demands. The technique proves especially effective on sleep-deprived days when you really don't have the will to resist, and you know with absolute certainty that if you oppose the demands, you'll say two or three things you'll regret.

Barb handed me a business card that had her home address on it. I thanked her and said I'd be in touch.

As I was walking away, she called after me, "Miss, could you get this dead plant out of my car?"

I was sure she knew my name was Hayley West. If you want Hayley the mule to do something, don't you at least say something like, "Hey, Hayley, let's get this stuff outta the trunk, all right?"

Lifting the 10-gallon pot out of the deep Bentley trunk, I admired the spaciousness of the luggage space. It was just about big enough to camp in.

As I was lugging away the sagging plant, Barb asked if I had a vacuum to clean the dirt out of her trunk. Before I could tell her that our auto detailing specialist at the Origins Café & Nursery was off that day (yeah, I was finally getting snarky), a BMW drove into the parking lot, and Candy's brother Landon got out of it.

Was he here to give me hell for not telling him where Candy was that day he'd come looking for her? Was he going to claim that she wouldn't have gone to the protest at the cemetery if he'd caught up with her? Was he going to blame me for her death? — *if* she was dead, of course. I kept assuming she was dead. If a zombie clobbers you on the head and drags you into a cemetery, you're a goner, right?

Or, wait a minute, what if Landon was the zombie who killed Candy? I put down the heavy pot I was carrying so I could think better. What if Landon had been so angry with his sister, he'd dressed up as a zombie and ambushed her? That didn't explain why Candy got up and walked away zombie style after she was clobbered, which might have had nothing to do with Landon — unless he was a sorcerer. What if he was a sorcerer?

While I was thinking these fuzzy, sleep-deprived, mostly paranoid thoughts, Landon was walking toward me. Like the first time I'd seen him, he was wearing a classy sport coat over a button-down shirt and a subdued tie. His eyes were still that amazing shade of green, but they weren't looking at me.

"Barb," he said.

"Landon," she said, closing the trunk of her car.

They knew each other? This would be a good opportunity for me to get away from Landon, just in case, but curiosity upstaged my sleepy paranoia. I stood a few feet away, holding onto the wooden stake that held up the dead bougainvillea, feeling invisible, taking it all in.

"You still owe me a hundred and twenty seven thousand and some change, Barb."

She fingered the emerald hanging against her chest. "And how is Blaise these days? Does he still favor a glass of Châteauneuf-du-Pape for lunch? Has he finished *Swann's Way*? Perhaps he's moved on to *In the Shadow of Young Girls in Flower* by now?"

"The Proust, yes," Landon said. "He brought it with him to that café on Silver Spur the other day. Wasn't that where the three of us met? I think it was. Alas, they serve no wine, remember?"

"Yes," Barb said, tugging on the gold chain that held the emerald.

"As for Châteauneuf-du-Pape, well, Blaise's tastes have evolved. When we do have wine, we typically opt for a decent Burgundy — a Dugat Py, Chambertin, or perhaps Jacques-Frederic Mugnier Le Musigny — nothing really extravagant, mind you, but a step above Châteauneuf-du-Pape. He's rather fond of the Dugat Py. I don't believe he'll ever again lower himself to the pedestrian vintages."

Barb flushed red at this and pulled the emerald chain until it dug into the flesh of her neck.

"And you still owe me a hundred and twenty seven thousand dollars," Landon said. "When might I expect payment?"

"Thanks to the protests by your obnoxious sister and her little friends, the property cost me far more than that in extra fees — environmental impact studies, Coastal Commission reviews, planning department requirements. I thought I'd never be able to build. So you can eat that little "finder's fee" as you called it. I'll wager you put your sister up to those protests. You enjoyed watching me struggle with it, didn't you?"

"Can't deny that I enjoyed it, Barb, but Candy's protests had nothing to do with me. I never encouraged that particular activity. She cost me far more than she ever cost you. And now she's been attacked, which is shocking."

"Oh, admit it, Landon. You're happy Candy was killed. With her out of the way, your life will be a whole lot easier — and more profitable. She might have cost you more than me over the years, but you could afford a few losses here and there. I was fighting to build the home I've dreamed of all my life. She tried to take that from me. And you took the love of my life. You've taken so much, and you still hound me for a few extra dollars."

"Barb, you have to deal with the facts. We both worked hard for what we have, and the fact that I have a lot more than you is just details. I also worked hard to win Blaise's heart, and I did win it, but honestly, he was so eager to get away from you, his heart was perched on the edge of a cliff, ready to fall into the arms of anyone who would catch him. You pushed him to the edge of that cliff, Barb. You need to face that truth."

The chain around her neck broke then, leaving a red welt where she'd pulled it hard into her flesh. With the chain and the emerald clutched in her hand, she shook in frustration for a moment, got in her Bentley, and roared out of the parking lot.

After watching her go, Landon turned to me. "Did not expect to find her here."

"What did you expect?" I asked.

"I'm hoping you've heard from Candy, you or Skylar. But I don't expect you have." He looked disappointed at my frowny face.

"What made you think we'd hear from her?"

"Nothing, except she was with you just before she was attacked. I'm not sure where she might go if she survived, and the police won't tell me anything."

"You've seen the news about the tracks in the cemetery?"

"Yes," he said. "Zombies. That's too strange to take seriously. You don't believe in zombies, do you?"

"No," I said. "Of course not."

He pointed at the former bougainvillea at my feet. "You seem to have a zombie plant there."

I was still holding onto the wooden stake in the pot. "Barb killed it," I said, poking the pot with my toe. "She wants me to give her a new one."

"You might want to give her what she wants. She tends to fight dirty, in a passive-aggressive kind of way. It's often simpler to keep her happy, however unfair it seems."

"*You* don't seem reluctant to wind her up."

He gave me a rueful smile. "Bad habit. Bear in mind that I have people to watch out for problems like Barb." He gestured toward a black SUV that had come into the parking lot after him. A big guy with a crewcut wearing aviator sunglasses sat at the wheel. His clone was in the passenger seat. "If you don't have Zalinski and Bobeck to cover your rear, don't give Barb a reason to come up behind you."

"Got it. I had a feeling she might have thorns, so I told her we'd take care of it."

He nodded. "If you hear anything, you'll let me know?"

I told him I would and dragged the zombie bougainvillea around the corner of the café where it was out of sight. Going further around to the back door and into the kitchen, I found Skylar, who was surprised to see me.

"I thought you were going to catch up on your sleep," she said.

"Detective Nakamura kept me awake."

"Men are like that." She kept stirring whatever she was making in a bowl. After tasting it, she threw in a pinch of salt.

"When you have that salty enough, could you look at a plant for me?" I asked, as I filled a bowl with water.

"Sure," she said. "Who cares about the lunch rush." She wiped her hands on a towel. "Where is this plant?"

When she saw the bougainvillea, Skylar said, "Oh dear." She put her hand on the plant and held it there.

I poured the bowl of water into the pot. "Do you think you can get it back?"

"Shhh." She held up her other hand.

As I watched, the vine quivered a little and writhed around the stake that was holding it up. The droopy heart-shaped leaves fluttered and greened. In a few moments, Skylar's magic coursed through the plant, and life came back into it from bottom to top. When a couple of blossoms had opened, Skylar took her hand off and took a deep breath.

"Should be all right now," she said, "so long as somebody keeps watering the poor thing." She put her hand back on the plant. "Somebody besides you handled this plant, somebody I know."

"Barb Vanderberry."

"Did she let this plant keel over?"

"Yes, and she has several more just like it and a few bamboo that I'm hoping you can save."

"That would be exhausting, and somehow I don't find myself wanting to help Barb Vanderberry."

"You'll be helping me, but before we get to that, do you know someone named Blaise?"

"Of course." She walked back to the kitchen door.

"Was he Barb's husband?"

"Of course. I told you about all that last year and left that issue of *People* on the coffee table for months."

"Oh, sorry. I thought you were telling me about something on *The Young and the Restless.*" Keeping up with my own life was hard enough without adding in a lot of other people I barely knew, some of whom weren't even real. I refused to feel like a dim bulb just because I failed to read all the issues of *People* on the coffee table. "Did Blaise leave Barb for Candy's brother?"

"Yes." Skylar went into the kitchen, and I followed close behind.

"So he's decided he's gay?"

"My goodness, you are firing on all cylinders today, Hayley West." Skylar went back to the bowl she'd been stirring and stirred it some more. "Why are you asking about this ancient history now?"

"Barb and Landon just had a little discussion about it in our parking lot."

"You mean right out there?"

"Yeah, you know, where our parking lot usually is."

"Why were they both in our parking lot at the same time?"

"I'd say it was bad luck. Killin would call it fate. Take your pick."

Skylar stopped stirring. "Let's address this one detail at a time. Why was Landon here? Did he have news about Candy?"

"He was wondering if we'd heard from her."

"Okay. And Barb? Why was she here?"

"She brought back the bougainvillea and wants me to replace all her dead plants."

"Only nearly dead," Skylar corrected. "But why is she buying all these plants when she lives in a high-rise condo?"

I drummed my fingers on her prep counter. "Skylar, I wish you'd stay up to date on these matters. Barb has built a new home somewhere in Redondo Beach. She bought the plants for landscaping."

"Where is this new home?"

I pulled out the card Barb had given me and frowned at the address. It was in the Redondo Beach Marina.

#

After closing the nursery, I threw the revived bougainvillea in the back of our old junk-hauling pickup and cranked her into life after only three tries. Skylar got in the passenger seat. She was wearing a straw hat and an old plaid work shirt we borrowed from one of my male gardeners. Skylar was eager to see Barb's new house but didn't want to give the impression that she did menial chores like move plants around. No, that was my purpose in life.

Skylar entered the house's address into her phone's GPS app, and we rattled and banged our way to the marina. When we made left turns, the door on Skylar's side tended to swing open. I'd been meaning to get that fixed. It was a bother when nobody was sitting on that side to tug it shut.

In the few minutes it took us to get there, we talked about ways to sneak into the cemetery despite the numerous police officers who were guarding the place. They must still think they could pick up Candy's tracks if they scoured every inch of ground. I knew they would be disappointed.

The easy way to get in was to cast my invisibility spell and walk right past the guards. We had one little complication that made that approach unworkable: Amelia, the little blonde witch, "walker" of the Waterway, insisted on going with me. I'd insisted to her father Sander that it was dangerous. Never mind the police, zombies were loose in the cemetery. Sander insisted that Amelia would be perfectly safe. She could call up a tiny lightning storm if anybody messed with her, and his three little witchy daughters were driving him crazy by telling him something was wrong with the Waterway and insisting that only a true walker of the Waterway could understand.

After all this insisting, I'd reluctantly agreed to take Amelia into the cemetery as soon as I could figure out a way to do it.

"You could see if the invisibility spell works on Amelia," Skylar suggested as we drove out of the nursery parking lot. "But what if you lose her when she's invisible?"

"Yeah, I have nightmares about that. The three of them have begged me to let them try it since they saw me do it."

"Or didn't see you."

"Even if we're not wandering around a cemetery with zombies, I worry about them getting into mischief when they're invisible."

"I know I would."

"Who could resist?" I said as I turned north onto Prospect Ave.

Skylar's door swung open, and she leaned out to pull it closed. "How about a spell that creates a dense fog?"

"Same problem. Might lose her. Might lose myself. How about if you create a diversion? Amelia and I could get in while the police look the other way."

"That would be easy enough. The only trick is making it big enough and long enough for you two to get over the fence and a ways into the cemetery."

"Then we just need a plan B in case the police see us in there. Here's the marina. Where do we go now?"

Skylar looked at her phone. "All the way down Marina Way."

Marina Way was a wide spit of asphalt that ran through the middle of the marina. When we got to the parking lot at the end of it, we found Barb's new house inside a new privacy fence.

"This is Moonstone Park!" I said in disbelief. "Or it used to be Moonstone Park. How did Barb Vanderberry get hold of it?"

"I wonder if Landon Longstaff had anything to do with it. He has some connections in local real estate dealings."

"Barb implied that he was involved, but that's strange if he and Barb don't get along."

"They used to get along better before Landon stole her husband."

We found the security door in the fence, and Barb buzzed us in. Skylar was carrying the revived bougainvillea, hiding behind the plant in her straw hat and tattered plaid shirt.

Barb met us at her front door. "Skylar, dear, how nice of you to help with the menial chores. And that hat is so *you*."

Skylar's face turned approximately the same shade as the bougainvillea blossoms, which are technically not blossoms but modified leaves called bracts, but never mind that. Barb pointed us to the south side of her new house, where the close-to-dead plants had been left to bake in the sun.

In case Barb was watching, I wanted to carry each plant back to the truck to revive it so we'd look like we were bringing in new plants. Skylar wanted to get out of there ASAP. She set to work reviving each plant on the spot while I watered.

Ten minutes later, Barb came around the corner of the house carrying a small plate. Skylar quickly picked up the plant she was reviving and headed in the opposite direction.

"Skylar, dear, put that plant down for a moment and taste this vegetarian hors d'oeuvre I'm testing for my cooking show. I think you'll agree it's divine, and you might want to steal the recipe for your little café."

Skylar walked five more steps, slowed, and then plonked the plant back on the ground. She wiped her muddy fingers on her pants. Picking up the tiny mound of green and red layers from the plate, she bit off half of it and chewed. I could tell from her expression that the morsel was, in fact, divine, and I was sure that Barb could see Skylar's appreciation, and I was equally sure that Skylar wasn't going to admit to that appreciation.

"It's good," she said, wagging her head from side to side to indicate her grudging approval. "The tart note might benefit from a little enhancement." She dropped the rest of the hors d'oeuvre in the waste bin next to the house.

"Any more lime zest and that bite would be turning your pucker out the back of your head," Barb observed. "Did you know I've started a new YouTube cooking channel? It's called Bites from the Beach. The show is all about seafood from the great Pacific Ocean."

She swept her arm westwards towards the water. We turned to look.

"Yes, quite a view, isn't it?" Barb said. "Oh, but I forget you're vegan. You won't be interested in seafood. In fact, I should have warned you that the okra in that hors d'oeuvre was flash fried in bacon grease. Don't you find it difficult to make decent hors d'oeuvre without saturated fat? I suppose you can use coconut oil, but it's not the same really. Well, don't let me keep you from your work."

With that, she walked away — sashayed would be a good description for her taunting exit — leaving Skylar with her fists clenched, completely furious. She chugged about a pint from the water bottle we'd brought, stuck her fingers down her throat, and barfed Barb's hors d'oeuvre onto the side of her new house. It made a satisfying splatter.

"Gross," I said.

When she'd finished spitting out the last of the divine morsel, she spat, "Bacon fat!"

We agreed that we needed to finish up and get out of there before Barb came back for another attack. Skylar grabbed two plants at the same time and induced both of them to grow fantastic new leaves and flowers in less than a minute. She went through all the plants like this and was quickly done with the lot of them. Skylar was exhausted, but now we could go.

It was only when we were walking away that I noticed the finely etched brown patterns on the leaves of the plants. On one shrub, each leaf had a "drawing" of a person on the rack. Another plant had iron maidens. The bougainvillea showed various small instruments of torture, from shackles to thumbscrews.

"How did you do that?" I asked her.

"Magic," she said.

When we were outside Barb's fence, we walked along the outside of it to the boulders at the water's edge and looked around at the marina and the ocean beyond. What a spot this was. The house's front yard was the Pacific Ocean. We stood there for a minute gawking at the watery prospect as the last of the sun was swallowed by the offshore fog.

Our friend Melanie Gosford, who was a regular on *The Young and the Restless*, had offered the harbormaster's son sexual favors just to get a slip for her boat in this marina. What had Barb Vanderberry given to get this whole chunk of prime real estate?

While we pondered that, we noticed something coming toward us through the water, around the corner of the boulders. In the fading light, we thought it might be a sea lion, but we realized as it staggered up on the rocks that it was a human being — a sodden, bedraggled man in a torn polo shirt and cargo shorts.

Skylar and I gasped and took a step back. The man saw us then and slipped sideways down the boulder he'd clambered onto and nearly fell back in the water.

Swaying from side to side, he said with a British accent fearfully slurred with strong drink, "Excuse me ladies. I was on my way to the gents. Would you be good enough to direct me?"

Looking around, we spotted the public toilets back on Marina Ave and pointed. He thanked us and weaved in that general direction, dripping water on the pavement as he went.

"I thought he was a zombie," Skylar whispered.

"Me too," I told her. "And I know how Amelia and I can get into the cemetery."

Chapter 11

Waist deep in the cold surf at midnight, I was shivering with misgivings about my great plan to get into the cemetery. Amelia, one of the little blonde witches, was treading water next to me. I looked up at the lights on the Hermosa Beach pier looming above us and then back longingly at the dim shapes of Skylar and Sander and his other two daughters standing on the beach. Why was Sander letting his little girl do this crazy thing?

The little girl in question was eager to keep going and asked why I'd stopped. She was splashing her way through the small waves rolling over us on this moonless night. The white dress she'd insisted on wearing billowed in the choppy water.

"Wondering why this water has to be so cold," I said, not telling the whole truth.

"The water flows down from the north pole," Amelia explained matter-of-factly. "Don't worry. We'll be warm enough when we get into the Waterway."

"Lead on, Amelia. You're the walker of the Waterway."

"It starts further out, but you can be in it as soon as you go into the water, if you know what I mean."

"Um, I'm afraid I don't know what you mean. Remember, I haven't done this before." Supposedly, I'd been granted the power to bridge the Stoneway and the Waterway, but I hadn't tested this power — until tonight.

"Follow me then. I'll make a light."

"Wait!" I shouted.

But she'd already ducked under a passing wave and was swimming quickly down into deeper water, surrounded by luminous green light. I grabbed a breath and dove after her.

If I hadn't been swimming hard, I would've been kicking myself for failing to ask sooner how we were supposed to breathe while we did this. Call me stupid, but in my own defense, I still hadn't caught up on my sleep. Everyone had insisted that we needed to hurry up and find out what was wrong with the Waterway.

Now, I was under water with no way of knowing when I might get my next breath of air. For that matter, I didn't know how we were supposed to get into the Waterway. To enter the Stoneway, I needed a magical incantation. Did the Waterway need something similar? Why hadn't I asked before we got in the water?

Amelia was swimming like a fish and zooming farther ahead of me by the second. Getting desperate for a breath, fighting a cross current, I tried a little harder, but it was no use. I had to go to the surface for air and wait for her to come back for me.

I'd just turned upward when something hit me. Or I hit something. The impact knocked my last little bit of breath out of me. Doubled over, tumbling in the surge of a wave, I lost track of which way was up. The surface was dark, everything was dark. I couldn't see what had hit me, and I couldn't even see the green glow around Amelia.

Then, I heard a voice asking, "What do you want?" The sound seemed to come from all around me.

All I could think of was wanting a breath.

The voice asked, "And what do you want from having that?"

This question left me speechless, not that I wasn't already, but I couldn't help thinking of everything I wanted in life like a movie flicking past my mind's eye in one second. Was this my life passing before my eyes before I died? But this wasn't the life I'd lived. This was the life I *hadn't* lived — a man to love, a man who loved me, brilliant children, a happy home with a wonderful family.

Then the lights came on. Amelia was drifting beside me in perfectly transparent water suffused with a blue-green glow. My lungs were about to burst. How was Amelia breathing? I sucked in a greedy breath. I needed to hold onto something solid, and the only thing handy was Amelia, so I clutched at her shoulders and pulled her into a tight hug.

"Here we are," she said. Her voice sounded like it was underwater except a lot clearer than that.

"I was afraid I'd drown," I said, releasing her from the hug.

"You have to hold your breath," she explained helpfully. "It's easier if you go in at the cemetery."

"I'll go in that way in the future," I said. "So, when you go into the Waterway, it hits you like somebody has run into you?"

"Yeah, blammo! That's only out here in the ocean."

"Also, someone asked me what I wanted. Did you hear that?"

She nodded yes. "I don't know what it means, but I usually say I want candy, because Daddy doesn't allow us to eat sweets. Don't tell him I ask for candy, okay?"

"Your secret's safe with me."

"Oh well, I never get the candy." She shrugged. "The voice just asks what I want after I get the candy. I mean, like, really? I want to be happy. Whoever's asking must have never graduated from kindergarten."

"So the voice always asks these questions when you go into the Waterway?"

"Yeah, and also at the cemetery."

"Speaking of the cemetery, how do we get there from here?"

"We need to call a fish, but it takes a lot of Wiza."

The little blonde witches called magical energy Wiza. Amelia's sister Anna had been trapped in the Waterway because she used up too much Wiza and didn't know how to get more. I knew how to get energy in the Stoneway. I was counting on my ability to connect with both the Stoneway and Waterway, even though I wasn't sure how that might work. Sometimes you just have to throw yourself at the situation and hope for the best.

Wait a minute! I wasn't just throwing myself at this situation. I had a little girl in this, too. If I couldn't figure out how to get enough energy, we were both up the creek without Wiza. Was I a complete airhead?

"We'll be fine," I assured Amelia. "How do we call a fish?"

"Like this," she said. "Here, fishy fishy fishy."

Okay. Who said magic was hard?

While we waited for our ride, I looked around. We weren't in the ocean anymore, and we weren't in a cavern. I'd imagined that the Waterway between the Hermosa Beach Pier and the Angelus-Rosedale Cemetery would be a long, dark, stony cave.

Instead, we were surrounded by walls covered in the patterns of Native American basketry, only they seemed to be woven of multicolor glass. Shimmering light shone through the patterns of zig-zag lines, blocky people and animals, and abstract forms that looked like buildings with columns.

Behind us was a dark opening maybe 20 feet in diameter, and through it swam a big fish — a very big fish — and as it swam past us and circled back around, I realized it was a shark. I'd had enough close contact with sharks recently to last my whole life. This wasn't a great white, so that was a tiny relief.

Amelia didn't seem worried about the animal's big teeth. As the shark made its second pass, she grabbed its dorsal fin, and I did the same from the other side. With a swish of its tail, the shark took us zooming along the passage. The shimmering glass patterns on the walls changed from abstract swirls of colored lines to herds of deer to families of human beings and back to abstractions again. They were all dazzlingly beautiful.

Fish of various types swam by us and along with us. We also passed side branches in the tunnel from time to time. I asked Amelia how we could tell which way to go, and she told me that the shark knew the way. How did the shark know we wanted to go to the cemetery?

Amelia shrugged. "He's a smart fish."

At one curve in the wide tunnel, we passed near the wall, and I stroked the glass with my fingertips — only to find that the wall wasn't made of glass at all. Each strand of the pattern was a liquid stream. The Waterway was woven of water. Some of the strands were dark, almost black, while others were the dun color of traditional baskets or any color of the rainbow. As I touched the watery strands, they flowed around my fingers like living things and rejoined the pattern, making a loud chiming sound as they rippled this way and that.

What was the purpose of all this? Magical people had gone to a lot of trouble to construct the Waterway. Surely they didn't do it just to have a watery subway from downtown to the beach, not that the city of Los Angeles existed at the time. I didn't suppose the three blonde girls had any idea about the purpose of this place.

I glanced at Amelia on the other side of the shark and found I was *not* looking at her. Amelia wasn't there anymore. I made a choking sound that had nothing to do with the fact that I seemed to be breathing water.

How long ago had Amelia dropped off?

Another few seconds went by while I continued to zip along, looking around, trying to grasp what had happened. I'd lost the little girl in a watery tunnel underneath the city. What did I do now?

I yelled at the shark to turn around, to stop, do anything different, and it ignored me. So I let go. The shark swam on into the far reaches of the shimmering tunnel.

Floating by myself, watching my ride disappear into the distance, I wondered how to find Amelia in this alien world of water. On my first forays into the Stoneway, I'd had a few instructions about what to do. About the Waterway, I knew almost nothing. I worried about losing Amelia, but who was most at risk right now? She was a native walker of the Waterway, while I was a stranger here. I didn't even know how to get around. Or maybe I did.

"Here fishy fishy fishy," I called into the water.

In less than a minute, back came the shark from the far end of the tunnel. I could tell it was the same shark by the smug look on its face. Now, how did I tell it where to take me?

Grabbing the shark's fin, I said, "Fishy fishy fishy, take me to Amelia."

Away we went toward the ocean end of the tunnel. Did this shark know how to find the little girl? At least I was going in the right direction.

In less than a hundred feet, the shark veered suddenly into a side tunnel. This passage was a lot smaller than the main tunnel and tapered as we went along, branching into narrow chambers and snug bottlenecks, some of them dimly lit or twisting off into complete darkness. Was this shark really taking me to Amelia? If not, I'd never find her in this maze, and how would I find my own way out to get help?

I'd worked myself into a frenzy of worry by the time the shark brought me to the little chamber where Amelia was tangled up in the arms of a huge purple octopus. Ever tried to scream underwater? It sounded like the kind of strangled noise you'd make in a dream. I let go of the shark and snatched at the tentacle wrapped around the girl's face.

"Oh, hi, Hayley," she said when she saw me and then yelped when I yanked the tentacle away.

"Ow, why did you do that?" She rubbed the side of her face, where a row of red welts testified to the grip the octopus had on her.

"Amelia, come to me sweetheart," I insisted, peeling off another tentacle that now had angry-looking beige and purple stripes rippling along its length.

"I'm comfy here," she insisted right back at me. "And please stop pulling on Bilbo. It hurts. And it bothers Bilbo."

Ever put your hands on your hips while you're floating in the water? It doesn't have quite the same put-out feel that it does on dry land. And I would have been more put out if this problem didn't have a cute name: Bilbo.

"Have you met this creature before?" I asked.

"This is my friend Bilbo," she said. "He's been all over the place and knows everything. That's why my sisters and I call him Bilbo. He's very friendly." She stroked the tentacle wrapped around her left leg. "If you don't yank on him."

"Okay, well, you gave me quite a fright when I noticed you had let go of the shark. We need to stay together down here. Do you think you can stay close from now on?"

"Sure," she said airily. "I only let go because I thought I saw a dead person. Then we passed Bilbo, and I decided to ask him why a dead person was in the Waterway and if that means my mommy is in here."

Oh dear, why hadn't I thought of that? Amelia's mother was buried in the Angelus-Rosedale Cemetery. If zombies were rising up out of that cemetery, could one of them be the girl's mother?

That would be horrible. Zombies were creepy in general, and what if one of them was your own mother? Amelia, on the other hand, seemed full of hope that she'd get her mother back. I wanted to tell her not to get her hopes up, but I had hazy memories of my own mother leaving me when I was a little younger than Amelia. I couldn't bring myself to tell her that she wasn't going to get her mommy back.

"What did Bilbo tell you about the dead person you saw?" I asked.

"He says dead people have been passing through for a while. He doesn't think any of them were related to me, but he'll keep a lookout from now on."

"All right, that's good," I said. "We'd better go. Tell Bilbo goodbye for now."

"Goodbye, Bilbo," she said and kissed him a little south of his eyes, which sent waves of purple, white, and beige stripes coursing across his entire body. Was this an octopus blush?

Bilbo unwrapped his tentacles from Amelia and eased her toward me. She called "Here, fishy fishy fishy" to summon a ride.

While we waited, I had an extremely terrible thought: What if the zombie that attacked Candy was Amelia's mother?

Chapter 12

The distance from the beach to the Angelus-Rosedale Cemetery is 14 miles as the crow flies. It's a little further as the shark swims because the Waterway isn't straight. Still, in no more than 20 minutes Amelia and I let go of the shark at the base of a vertical tunnel that went up to the pool in the cemetery.

For the past few minutes Amelia had been getting increasingly uncomfortable. Something was wrong with the Waterway, and she felt it on her skin like an army of spiders going "eedle, eedle, eedle, eedle." I couldn't feel the creepy pricking, but it gave Amelia the heebie-jeebies.

After we swam up to the surface of the pool, she quickly catapulted herself onto the stone platform and shook the water off like a dog. I climbed out a little slower, looking around the dark cemetery for roving zombies. From the sky glow of the city lights, I could make out the familiar shapes of the stone monument overlooking the pool and the gravestones across the rest of the cemetery.

Outside the Waterway, I shivered in the cool air. When I tugged on Amelia's sleeve to keep her close, I found that her white dress was bone dry.

"How did you do that?" I asked her.

"Magic," she said.

"Can you teach me how?"

"Put your arms out like this," she said, holding one arm up and the other down. "Then pretend you're spinning around, only stay in one place."

I was about to say that didn't make sense but stopped myself. Holding out my arms, I stood there pretending I was spinning around. Nothing happened.

"*Start* to move," Amelia suggested.

I jerked in place a little bit and began flailing uncontrollably. Amelia jumped backward as all the water flew off me, but I kept shaking.

"How do I stop?" I tried to say.

"What?" Amelia asked. "You need to stop now."

"How! Do! I! Stop!"

"Stop pretending you're spinning," she said.

I'd stopped pretend-spinning at least a minute ago, and I was still gyrating like an angry bull on Red Bull. I tried pretending I was spinning the opposite way, and my body froze in mid twitch. I vibrated for a few seconds on my tip toes. Slowly, I settled onto the ground and was still. And dry.

"It's works better if you wear a dress," Amelia said.

"So that's why you wanted to wear that dress."

"Well, I wanted to wear it because I look good in this dress. I don't know if you noticed. Anyway, the important thing is to look nice."

I looked down at my T-shirt and plaid shorts, not that I could see them very well in the dark. "I need to work on that, I guess."

"You don't need to worry about your looks," she assured me. "You're very pretty."

"Thank you."

"You would look nicer in a dress, though."

"Got it. And if I wear a dress, your daddy will notice me more?" Oh dear, I shouldn't have said that.

Amelia cocked her head to one side. "My daddy talks about you all the time. Is that like noticing?"

"He talks about me?" I asked, sounding like a little girl myself. I cleared my throat. "Anyway, let's see if we can figure out what's making the Waterway uncool. You said you could picture the problem in the pool?"

"Ha!" she laughed. "You just made a little poem."

"So I did. Do you have to be in the pool to make the picture?"

"No, you only need to put your hands on the water." She lay down in her white dress on the stone surface next to the pool. "It's a good thing we clean this place from time to time."

She stretched her arms over the water with her palms skimming the surface. Ripples spread across the water, and then the entire contents of the pool glowed with a spectral blue light. Yellow and green waves danced through like shimmers of aurora borealis. Over the next minute, the waves collected into forms — images of zombies, some male, some female, some indeterminate, all groaning. The glowing images rose up out of the surface of the pool to face us for a moment and then passed back into the depths.

"Yuck," Amelia said. "These are the dead people that got in."

"So they're warping the Waterway?"

"Bilbo told me they dirty it up. That's not the real problem. He said to look for someone who's alive, a man who isn't supposed to be in the water."

She kept moving her hands across the surface of the pool. The zombie images moved this way and that. Some of them didn't look entirely dead, maybe only recently dead. Would Amelia's mother be among them like a zombie ghost coming out to haunt the little girl? I'd seen photographs of Charlotte Nilsen. None of the zombies looked like her.

Then I caught a glimpse of someone I did recognize, a glimpse that made the hairs stand up on the back of my neck.

"Amelia, honey," I stammered, "could you go back to that man in the blue shirt? The one who was up here?" I gestured toward the upper right area of the pool, where a bearded zombie in a tuxedo was now carrying his head in the crook of his arm. The head was in bad shape.

"That one's bad-yucky," Amelia commented.

"Yes, he is! How about the one before that? Can you hit rewind on this thing?"

"Sure." She pushed her hands into the water and grunted "Uh" in disgust. "This part feels really pukey."

"Stop, stop," I hissed. "That's the problem right there."

"You know him?"

"Baldock Gunter," I told her. "I know him. He's an evil sorcerer."

"A sorcerer is like a witch, only bad?"

"Magic like a witch, yes, and very bad. He was in prison for killing a person and just escaped recently. This image of him means that he went into the Waterway?"

"I guess so," Amelia said. "Can I turn it off now?"

"Sure."

She yanked her hands out of the pool and did the pretend-spin to shake her hands dry.

"Can you tell if Baldock is still in the Waterway?" I asked her.

"I think he isn't. Bilbo told me he probably didn't get very far."

"That's good, except it means he could be out here in the cemetery with us. We don't want to run into this guy, believe me. He's a nasty piece of work. We need to keep our voices down, and if we see him, you need to run away as fast as you can, okay?"

"Okay. Then what do I do?"

"Um, run out to the street and find a policeman."

"Or woman?"

"Thank you, yes — a police officer. They should be posted around the cemetery, and they'll get you back to your father."

"Will you fight this guy, the sorcerer?" she whispered excitedly.

"Not if I can help it. I'll run away too. You need to run in a different direction, okay?"

"Sure."

"In fact, we need to quit jabbering and get out of here. But I need to check one more thing. Can you make your green light for me?"

"Only in the water."

"Okay, no problem."

Feeling around on the ground, I found a pebble and asked it to light up and hover in the air. The pebble explained patiently (rocks are nothing if not patient) that it could either fly through the air or lie on the ground, but it didn't know how to hover. I had it fly in a small circle a few feet above the ground in front of me as I walked around the magical perimeter of the pool.

It wasn't hard to find the place where the police had lost Candy's trail. They had her tracks marked by a series of orange cones with yellow police tape stuck to them. The last cone was at the edge of the protective barrier around the pool.

To the police, the tracks had simply stopped there, as if Candy had vanished into thin air, but I could see that her footprints continued through the magical barrier and across the weedy ground on the way to the pool. Even though she was walking like a zombie, zigzagging around a little, her path was definitely in the direction of the pool.

Wait a minute. How did Candy even get in here? Only magical people could pass through the barrier, and there was never anything magical about Candy. I had no way of knowing about the other zombies that were getting into the pool. They could be magical people — or were before they were buried in the cemetery.

If Candy got through, it must have been because of magic from something else — or somebody else. I had a bad feeling about who that somebody might be. We needed to leave. And I needed to make sure of one more thing.

While I'd been thinking, my flying pebble-light had started flying around and around my head. Snatching it out of the air, I told it to extinguish the light but not before it singed my hand. I needed a better way to make a light.

"Amelia," I said, "can we look at the images in the pool one more time?"

She huffed a little at that idea.

"Sorry, I know it's uncomfortable. How about if you teach me how to make the pictures?"

"Okay," she conceded.

We lay down on the stone platform again, and Amelia stretched out her hands. "Pretend you're drawing fish," she told me.

"Fish? Why fish?"

"Because that makes the pictures," she explained patiently.

Placing my hands in the pool, I pretended to draw fish. To my surprise, the blue light began to glow and the images of zombies rose up from the surface of the water.

"That one!" I whispered. "How do I rewind?"

"Draw the fish going the other way."

Duh. I hadn't even realized that all my pretend fish were headed to the left. I reversed course with a couple of fish, and the dim image of Candy rose up out of the pool, groaning. It was her all right. She'd made it into the water. And then where did she go?

"Is there any way to tell what happened to these zombies? Did they all pass through to the ocean?"

"We can only see who's been here at the pool," Amelia whispered. "Maybe we could try this at the other end?"

I was about to say that her idea was a good one when a foot crunched on the gravel behind us. Before I could whip around, a familiar voice made me break out in a cold sweat.

"Excuse me. Please don't be alarmed. I see that —"

"Change of plan," I whispered in Amelia's ear and shoved her into the pool.

As I was going in after her, Baldock caught my foot. "Just wait!" He pulled me toward him.

My heart pounding, I clung to the edge of the pool and strained against him, but his grip on my ankle was as firm as a manacle. I kicked at him with my other foot, and he seized that one, too. He dragged me back. My elbows scraped against the stone until my arms were at full stretch. The tips of my fingers clung to the rough rim of the pool. *This was good.* My face pressed against the wet stone. I kicked at Baldock and let the fingers of my left hand slip off the edge of the pool. *Swim, Amelia, swim.*

Of course, it was possible that he had no interest in Amelia. He had reasons to be upset with me. I'd put away both Baldock and his brother Lucan for murder. I'd prevented Baldock from getting his brother a new body to live in. Little reasons like that probably made Baldock a little touchy.

But had he even seen who I was in the dark? Did he realize whose foot he'd grabbed? And what did he want with the Waterway?

While these thoughts flashed through my mind, Baldock talked and pulled my legs. I was so busy with the thoughts-flashing thing, whatever he was saying was gibberish. And what he was doing made no sense either. He could easily pull me away from the pool. Baldock was no more serious about pulling me toward him than I was about getting away. And what *was* he talking about?

"...so as you can see, Ms. West," he was saying, "I have a problem that could possibly benefit from your help. The situation —"

I stopped struggling. "Are you *asking* me to help you?"

He let out a loud sigh. "Have you not been listening to anything I've said? This is why I find it so difficult to work with people."

"The last time I saw you," I said, turning over so I was sitting on the stone platform facing him, "you had just set the Minotaur on me. It sunk its claws into that ankle you're gripping and would have killed me if a tree hadn't throttled you. Maybe you can see why a friendly conversation wasn't the first thing on my mind when you grabbed me."

"Now, calm down. I did apologize. Obviously, you failed to hear that, too."

"And you continue to grip my ankle," I pointed out. "Which hurts."

To my surprise, he let go. I stood up cautiously and felt with my foot for the edge of the pool. Desperate to get away from this man, I could imagine Skylar and Killin shouting at me that this was an evil sorcerer, so run away immediately. Amelia should be safely away. Why linger?

Yet, I stood there. What could prompt Baldock to think that I'd help him with anything except going back to prison? The dark shape of his large frame loomed only a couple of feet in front of me. I felt for the edge of the pool again.

"To be clear," he said, "I didn't try to kill you per se. I simply needed your power to help my brother, which almost resulted in killing you — collateral damage, you might say. But returning to my main point, we both have an interest in preventing Fel Dinaden from bossing the world. We do not need to fight. I think we should work together."

"So you had a falling out with Fel, and you figure that puts us on the same side — opposing her?"

"As you would know if you'd been paying attention, it's more complicated than that, although that's not the worst place to start. Do you not want to stop Fel?"

"Sure," I said dubiously. I mean, I wasn't dubious about wanting to stop Fel the evil witch, if she was as bad as rumored to be, but would I team up with Darth Vader to do it? I was still wondering what kind of weed Darth was toking to make him think I would go in with him.

"We need to prevent her from obtaining, ah, certain powers," Baldock said.

"What kind of powers?"

"Well, one power, specifically: the Shuilong. That's Mandarin for water dragon."

"You think there's a dragon in there?" I half-turned toward the pool, which he probably couldn't see in the dark, but he knew what I meant.

"No, no, not a literal dragon. It's a type of magic that originated in China. Everything is a dragon over there. But this water could have dragons in it. How would you know? And what are you even doing here?"

"I might ask you the same thing. And how did you know it was me at the pool?"

"The scent of your magic is quite distinct to me, and as I keep trying to explain, I'm looking for a way to counter Fel Dinaden. The answer is here, or in there, rather. I need to know how to get it. Tell me what you know about this pool. What did you shove into it when I walked up? And what were those images? You're a walker of the Stoneway, so you're out of your depth in the water, aren't you?"

Now, we were down to the ultimate evil: bad jokes. I ignored his question about what I'd shoved into the pool. He apparently hadn't been able to see that it was a little girl in a white dress — not something he'd expect to see under the circumstances.

"I came to find out about the woman who was attacked here by a female zombie the other day," I told him. "You wouldn't know anything about that, would you?"

He laughed. "You know how it is with zombies. You can't know what they're up to because they're not up to anything. But I don't know about any attack. Is that why the police are all over the place?"

"Yes. Did you think they were after you?"

"At first I did, but the way they were looking made even less sense than the police usually make. What they're doing makes more sense if they're looking for a zombie. It's convenient also that they don't face the decision of whether to bring the perp in dead or alive, because, you know…"

The jokes were getting worse. I backed a half step away from him along the lip of the pool. It was about time to leave this cemetery comedy club, even though I still had a lot of questions. My biggest question was: How far could Baldock go into the Waterway? Next biggest question: Would he come after me when I jumped into it? Third question: What would happen if he caught me in there?

Oh, and one other question: Would he send the Minotaur in after me?

I was about to bet my life that the answers would be (in order): Not very far, no, not applicable, and no. To make sure that last answer was "no," it seemed like a good idea to let him think I'd work with him.

"Baldock, what do you want from me?" I asked him.

"First, I'd like to know what you know about this pool. My brother Lucan told me that the magic here can drown the Shuilong."

"The water dragon."

"That's right. What do you know about this pool?"

Had he heard about the Waterway? Nothing he'd said hinted that he knew any more than he'd told me about the water dragon, and he hadn't said what that dragon power was.

"I believe the zombies have been going into the pool. That's one thing."

"Well, yes," he said impatiently. "They have been. That doesn't tell us anything about the nature of the pool. That's what I want to know."

"It tells us that the pool attracts zombies."

"To hell with the zombies," he said angrily. "I don't care about the zombies. I want to know about the pool. You pushed something into it. What were you doing?"

"Trying to learn something myself," I lied. "A zombie attacked someone I know, and I want to find out what's going on."

"What did you find out?" he demanded.

"Nothing yet. It will take time."

"Eh, you're useless. Time is what I haven't got. I'm dodging the police and trying to counter a witch who's hell-bent on world domination. My brother is still in prison in the body of his murderer. Oh, and I'm living in a mausoleum." He raised his face to the city-glow heavens and shouted, "Damn it!"

"Well, the police won't find you if you're encrypted," I told him, joining the bad joke club.

Baldock let out a low growl of anger, which set my heart pounding again.

That was my cue to leave. I was about to step into the pool and swim for all I was worth when I thought of a slight problem. If Baldock didn't know that this pool was the portal to the Waterway, what would he think when I jumped in and didn't come back up? He'd know that I knew more than I was letting on. He might come after me to force me to tell him.

Oh well, I already knew he was after me on general principles. What else was new?

I stepped backward into the pool.

Chapter 13

The claw that clamped onto my toe as I swam away turned out to be a crab. I think it was just kidding around, but it gave me a fright. The shark that responded to my "fishy fishy fishy" call was a hammerhead, which spooked me a little more. The way those beasts look at you is unsettling. Then, all the way through the Waterway to the beach, I worried about finding Amelia.

She was sitting on a blanket in the sand with her sisters when I got to the beach, safe and dry. Skylar was absolutely beside herself with worry and indecision about whether to drive up to the cemetery to help me fight Baldock. She waited on the beach mainly because she didn't have a clear idea of how she'd fight Baldock.

Sander didn't seem unduly worried. He's just not a very excitable guy, or maybe he didn't understand how nasty Baldock was. He did give me a warm hug when I came up to him on the beach after I did the magical shake-off routine to dry myself. Was he only thanking me for getting his little girl back safely? I nestled my face in his neck. The hug went on for a long time.

It was two o'clock in the morning, and we wanted Sander and the girls to spend what was left of the night at our place, but the girls couldn't get through the protective barrier around our house. Sander insisted he was awake enough to drive home. It was the last little insistence we would have for this adventure, except for me insisting to myself that I sleep long into the morning.

# # #

I didn't, of course — sleep late, that is. My eyes popped open at first light, and I lay there thinking frantically about how stupid I'd been to risk the cemetery visit with Amelia in tow. She was the one towing me, really, but still: stupid. And when Baldock let go of my ankle, I should have immediately leapt into the pool.

Still wearing the clothes I'd had on the night before, I got out of bed, staggered into the kitchen, and put water in the kettle for tea. I thought dimly about brewing something without caffeine, maybe peppermint or chamomile. Then I could go back to bed, get some more sleep. I almost laughed out loud at that idea and heaped a spoonful of our strongest English breakfast tea into the strainer basket.

Skylar came into the kitchen as I was about to leave with my cup of tea.

"What are you doing up already?" she asked.

"I wanted to get an early start on the post-game analysis. Why did you let me take Amelia to a cemetery infested with zombies?"

"You said you didn't see any zombies. I'm going to make English breakfast. You want some?"

I lifted my cup. "Already made a pot. We saw zombies in the Waterway images, despite claims that they don't exist."

"I mean English *breakfast* breakfast. I made vegan bangers yesterday." She pulled a container from the refrigerator with several fat grey tubes in it.

Vegan bangers had the potential to be more ridiculous than my cemetery jaunt, but I said yes to the breakfast offer and sat down at the table with my tea.

"Did you find out if Baldock knows anything about the zombies?" Skylar asked, as she wrestled a skillet out of a low cabinet.

"Not his fave topic," I said. "The only thing I'm sure of is that he accepts their existence, unlike some people."

Skylar put a large tomato back on the counter and bent down to declare directly in my face, "Witches are real. Zombies are real. Aliens live among us. Google, Amazon, Facebook, and Apple have our best interests at heart."

Opening my mouth to reply, I found that I didn't know where to begin, so I sipped my tea and wondered if the part about witches could be true.

"How about the assault on Candy?" Skylar asked, going back to the tomato. "Does Baldock know anything about that?"

"He said he didn't."

"You believe him?"

"Hard to know what to believe these days," I said. "People make all sorts of claims." I drank my tea.

Skylar sliced two pieces of bread off the loaf she made yesterday and put them in the toaster. She cut the tomato into chunks.

"I followed Candy's tracks through the magical barrier around the pool and then saw her on the Waterway Jumbo Tron," I said. "That means she must have turned into a zombie."

I looked pointedly at Skylar, who just as pointedly ignored me. She dumped the sliced tomatoes into the skillet with the mock bangers.

"And if Candy turned into a zombie," I said, "that blow she took to the head must have done her in."

That part seemed to go without saying, but I thought we should get it out there. Candy's attacker had killed her. We were looking for a murderer.

Who was that murderer? It wasn't Baldock. The tracks of the killer belonged to someone much smaller than the sorcerer, who was built like a linebacker. Well, he looked like a junkie who just came out of a dark alley, but he was a big junkie.

Glancing over at Skylar, I saw her head bowed over the skillet. She was shaking a little. I got up and put my arms around her as two fat tears tumbled into the skillet and sizzled into steam.

"I'm sorry," I said. "It's sad to lose a friend."

She nodded and managed so say, "Even a difficult friend." She propped her flipper on the edge of the skillet. I released my hug so she could go blow her nose. Stirring everything around in the skillet, I figured it looked done. How could you tell when a mock banger was done? I divided the food onto plates and set them on the table.

Skylar came back with a box of tissues. "I knew from the first night that Candy hadn't survived the attack, but I couldn't let go of hope that she had."

"Yeah, I was 17 before I accepted the fact that my mother wasn't coming back. That only took 12 years."

"We're foolishly optimistic creatures."

"I was definitely foolish last night," I said. "And I'm optimistic that we can find the person who killed Candy Longstaff."

"Even if that person is no longer among the living? Somehow it won't be very satisfying to find a perp that's already dead. I don't believe in capital punishment, especially before the crime is committed. But let's don't think about that while we eat."

"These fake bangers are good."

"You sound surprised. And they're not fake. They're just not made of meat."

"I am surprised. Maybe that's why I sound surprised. It's not every day you run into a good vegan banger. You should package these things and sell them."

"You think vegans are a big banger market? I'll try them in the café and see how they go. In the meantime, I hate to discuss Baldock over food, but we need to talk about him. He must be behind the zombie outbreak. That's why he's touchy on that topic."

"He might be using the zombies as probes to find out how the Waterway works. He's trying to get some magical power out of the Waterway, and the zombies are attracted to the pool, for sure. He asked me to help him find this power."

"He's kidding."

"I'd like to say that Baldock doesn't kid, but he pasted me with a couple of jokes that were as lame as some of the zombies. He wasn't kidding about getting me to help him, though. He thinks we should work together to counter Fel Dinaden, because, you know, we're both on the same side with that."

"But he worked for Fel."

"Not anymore, and it's the usual thing with a breakup. You think everybody is going to take your side."

Skylar chewed her last bite of banger and chased it with a sip of tea. "Most of what we know about Fel Dinaden comes from an unreliable source — Killin Bardis. If we're choosing up sides, it would help to know what Fel wants. Is she really bent on world domination? And what does that even mean? Does she want to take over the governments of every country on earth and rule as Grand Poohbah of the planet? That's hard to imagine. Maybe she only wants to dominate magical people."

"Either way, I'm not really into the domination thing," I said. "Not a turn-on for me. How about you?"

She got up and put her plate in the sink. "What if Fel doesn't want to dominate anything? That could be just a malicious rumor passed on by your wayward boyfriend."

"He's not my boyfriend." I forked the last bite of banger into my mouth, hoping it was the last bite of vegan banger I would ever chew on this earth, and washed it down with a gulp of tea. "Your mother told us that Fel is an evil witch who's up to no good. You believe that, don't you?"

"Lots of witches are evil. Again, what Mother's heard are rumors. We don't know what Fel wants. We don't know what Baldock really wants, either. Did he give you a hint of what he wants you to do?"

"Like I say, he wants me to help him get some kind of power from the Waterway. It has something to do with a dragon, a water dragon. It has a Chinese name — like "shoe long" or something like that. We should ask your mother."

Skylar texted a question to her mother and said, "We should also ask the little blonde witches if they know anything about a water dragon. Amelia wasn't there when Baldock mentioned it, was she?"

"No, I sent her back into the pool as soon as Baldock showed up. Scared me half to death."

"Why didn't you go in with her?"

"He grabbed my foot, for one thing. Then, I was afraid that if I went into the pool, he'd come after me and get Amelia and me both. We'd already seen that he got into the Waterway. I don't understand how he did that, and I don't know how far he can go."

"We need some way to repel Baldock."

"Yeah, magical Mace would be handy."

"Or why not just use regular Mace? It works on anybody, doesn't it?"

"Sure, and then Baldock would invoke the Minotaur. I don't think Mace would slow that thing down. We could try it, I suppose. I'd rather not."

Skylar's phone rang, and she picked it up. "Mother, you're up early. Hayley's here. Let me put you on speaker."

"Hi, Hayley."

"Hi, Ms. Bemis. How are you?"

"Coughing from a cold I caught from Skylar's father. Hold on." We heard a short coughing fit in the background, and then she was back. "Otherwise, I'm fine. What's this I hear about dragons?"

"Hayley had a little chat with Baldock Gunter last night," Skylar said. "He wants her help with some sort of water dragon."

"The Shuilong," Ms. Bemis said.

"That's the one," I said. "You know about that?"

"My friend Madam Lee told me about that dragon. We call her Madam because she used to run a brothel, but never mind that. She said three witches in ancient China invoked the Shuilong after gunpowder was invented. I don't think it's a literal dragon, but they call it the water dragon because it drowns gunpowder — stops gunpowder from working."

"Remember that witch who was following me around last year, Alice Sharpe? The one who works at the human potential company? She mentioned something about stopping gunpowder," I said. "She told me Fel might use that power to stop people from fighting with guns and bombs."

"According to Madam Lee's story, the Chinese witches accomplished the same thing by threatening to use the Shuilong. That changed the course of history. China could have used gunpowder to conquer the world. Instead, they mostly shot it into the air to make pretty lights with fireworks. It was all because the witches promised to shut down the party if the booms hurt people. Madam Lee took the story as a whimsical myth."

"Well, my new whimsical buddy Baldock takes the story at face value and thinks the Shuilong lives in the Waterway. He wants to get the water dragon before Fel does. He kept saying he wants to counter Fel, which seems a little odd to me. Why doesn't he say he wants to defeat her?"

"And why now?" Skylar said. "His brother is still in the big house, and he's on the run from the police. You'd think those would be his most pressing concerns — unless Fel is about to make a big move."

We were all quiet for a moment, thinking about how bad that could be. It made the search for Candy's killer seem a bit less imperative.

"If Fel really is the big threat, does that mean I should take Baldock up on his invite to work with him?"

We were all quiet for another moment, thinking about how much worse that could be than the threat from Fel.

Ms. Bemis coughed several times. "Hayley, dear, I don't think that's a good idea. Let me ask Madam Lee if she knows any more about the Shuilong." She coughed a few more times and said goodbye.

Emma came into the kitchen then, followed almost immediately by the sound of the doorbell. When I opened the front door, Detective Harris Duke tipped his Stetson and said, "Good morning, ma'am. Sorry to disturb you at this early hour. I'm here to see Emma Nakamura, please."

"Again?" I said.

"I'm not here," Emma shouted from the kitchen.

"She's not here," I repeated to Detective Duke.

The door wouldn't close because his cowboy-booted foot was in it. As I opened the door to get a good swing at his foot, he said, "Phone records show that Ms. Nakamura was near the Angelus-Rosedale Cemetery at the time of the assault on Candice Longstaff."

Chapter 14

Using the tip of his forefinger, Harris Duke moved a small statue of Quan Yin, goddess of mercy, to clear a space for his Stetson on the end table next to his chair. Freed from the confines of the hat, his blonde curls sprang out around his head like party streamers. Anyone who thought he looked like a fun party (me, for instance) might be dangerously mistaken.

He put his phone on the coffee table in front of him, pressed the screen, and cleared his throat. Obviously, he was now recording everything. He leaned forward toward Emma, who was sitting on the sofa on the other side of the coffee table, working her fingers into a cushion she clutched in her lap.

"According to Verizon," he said, "your phone was visiting the Angelus-Rosedale Cemetery at the time Candice Longstaff was assaulted. Now, I suppose it's possible that your phone was there to pay its respects to a dearly departed iPhone 3 or Galaxy S that's now interred in that cemetery. Could you tell me if that was, in fact, the reason why your phone was there?"

Emma stopped kneading the cushion and scratched her cheek. She stared at the detective with her eyebrows squished together. She shook her head no.

"Phones rarely visit cemeteries on their own, do they?" the detective said reflectively, steepling his fingers. "No, the more likely possibility is that your phone did a ride-along with you to the cemetery when you went to assault the rival who was threatening your relationship with the woman you love."

Emma yanked the cushion out of her lap and flung it onto the sofa next to her. "I did *not* do that!"

"Well, thank you for clearing that up," he said, putting his hands on his knees. He lifted his hat from the table, moved Quan Yin back to her original location, and stood up. "Looks like I'll have to pursue some other line of inquiry."

Emma, Skylar, and I sat stupefied as he gathered his curls into his Stetson and stood with his thumbs hooked in his belt. "You've been more than cooperative," he said.

Relief flickered briefly in Emma's eyes before she realized it couldn't be this easy to get rid Detective Duke. Skylar's mouth was hanging open as she looked at him, which made me realize my mouth was hanging open. I closed it and rolled my eyes.

Looking at me, he said, "You're right. I shouldn't take the first answer I get, should I? Because often the first answer doesn't tell the whole story."

He moved Quan Yin, put his hat back on the table, and sat. "Let's see, where shall we pick up the story?" Tapping his chin with his forefinger, he looked off into the corner of the room and then looked at Emma. "I know. How about you tell me why you drove to the Angelus-Rosedale Cemetery the night Candice was assaulted."

"I didn't drive to the cemetery," Emma said. "I was driving around, and I guess I happened to drive near the cemetery. But I didn't drive *to* the cemetery."

The detective nodded, got down on all fours, and peered under the coffee table. "Nice shoes," he said. "Could I borrow one of those for a moment?"

Without waiting for an answer, he reached under the table and tugged off one of Emma's shoes.

"Cute," he said, peering inside the shoe.

It was a pink platform sneaker by Prada, and all the cuteness was on the outside. They looked like lace-up sneakers but you slipped them on (and off, as the detective had demonstrated) like loafers.

"Size 6. Let's see, where did I see something about a size 6 shoe recently?" He tapped his chin with his finger again. I rolled my eyes again.

"Oh yes," he said, smacking his forehead with the sole of the shoe, "Now I remember — tracks in the cemetery, the tracks of Candice's assailant. They just happened to be size 6."

"A very common size," Skylar pointed out. Her lips tightened into thin lines.

"Indeed," agreed the detective. "Could have belonged to anybody, really. Any smallish person. Any small woman. Who knows?"

He shrugged, leaned back in the chair, and crossed his legs. "I had a girlfriend who wore Prada knock-offs."

Emma got her Prada shoes and handbag through the shop where she worked on Rodeo Drive. They were real Prada, even if she bought them at a discount. She didn't object to the implication that her Pradas were fakes, which surprised me. She knew the detective was baiting her.

"In fact," Detective Duke continued about his ex-gf, "she had brand names all over her, all fake, of course, except for the underwear — genuine Frederick's of Hollywood. Said her father was in real estate. Turned out he owned a house in Tarzana that was long known to meth heads as a source. Location, location, location."

He put Emma's shoe on the coffee table in front of her.

She eyed the shoe and raised her little white-ankle-socked foot. "Back on, please."

Harris cocked his head and looked at her. He'd been jouncing us around in this interview, keeping us off balance. Emma was now nudging him back with her dainty foot.

"You took it off," Emma said, wiggling her toes. "You can put it back on."

The slightest smile tightened his lips. "Well, now, I reckon fair is fair."

He came around the coffee table and knelt at Emma's feet. Cupping her heel in his left hand, his right hand moved briefly under her foot, and she squirmed on the sofa. He had tickled the bottom of her foot. Skylar's eyes narrowed as Emma squirmed, but I don't think Skylar could see Harris's tickling fingers past the edge of the table. Emma didn't protest.

Now Harris picked up the sneaker from the coffee table and fitted it over Emma's toes, snugging it into place over her heel like an expert shoe salesman, except that he followed up by grasping her bare leg a little above the top of her ankle sock and rotating her foot with his other hand in a pantomime of making sure the shoe was on properly. He looked up into Emma's face. She met his eyes and looked away. Sitting back on his heels, he tugged at the lace top of her sock as though tidying up. When he released his grip on her leg, Emma let out the breath she'd been holding, which wasn't lost on Skylar.

"Thank you," Emma said, looking at the far corner of the room. When he didn't move away, she looked back down at him.

He winked at her and said in a near whisper, "Candice Longstaff was an annoying bitch, wasn't she?"

Emma's eyes went wide.

Skylar jumped up from the other end of the sofa. "Hey!" she shouted. "You can't talk about my friend that way — especially after she's been murdered."

Detective Duke regarded her coolly. "What makes you so sure she's been murdered?"

Skylar's face, already flushed with outrage, turned a little redder. "Uh, well, it seems obvious." She held out her hands and then pressed a fist against her thigh. "Doesn't it?"

Going back to his chair, Detective Duke didn't reply.

She turned to me. "Don't you think she's been murdered?"

I knew Candy had made it through the magical barrier around the Waterway pool, which meant she'd been a zombie at the time — definitely dead. Probably we shouldn't tell Harris Duke about that.

"We've talked about this a lot, as you can imagine," I said to the detective. "We don't see how she could have survived the attack and not be found. So we concluded she must have been killed."

"On the other hand," he said, holding out his right hand, "how could she have been killed and her body not found?"

Emma, Skylar, and I all shrugged simultaneously.

"Possibly," the detective said, looking at each of us pointedly, "someone killed Candice and hid the body. You wouldn't happen to know where it is, would you? The body?" He was looking at me.

Now it was my turn to blush, because I did have an idea where Candy's body went, and oh by the way, the detective was implicating me as an accessory to murder.

Before I could come up with a coherent objection, Detective Duke held out his left hand. This must be the other-other hand, which should really be a foot, my foot, and that foot would be in my mouth.

"Yet Candice Longstaff did survive the attack," he said. "We see her tracks leading away from the spot where her assailant left her. Granted she was walking like a zombie, but unless you believe she *was* a zombie, she wasn't killed by the person who hit her. Do you believe in zombies?" He looked at each of us.

As a general rule of thumb, when the police ask if you believe in zombies, always say no. We all did that.

Detective Duke nodded patiently and pursed his lips. "That leaves us with two unfortunate possibilities: number one is that Candice was alive after the assault and walked away oddly because she had severe trauma to the head. The person who hit her — or that person's accomplices — then finished her off and hid the body."

When he mentioned the accomplices, he looked at Skylar and me.

"Possibility number two is that whoever clobbered Candice on the cranium had accomplices who helped fake the zombie walk-away and then hid the body. Either way…" He held up both hands and shook his head sadly. "Either way, we're looking at a crime committed by multiple perps, and I will bring all of them to justice."

He stood and picked up his hat. "Thank you for your bountiful information."

Before he left, he asked Skylar where she'd been at the time of the assault on Candy. He'd already asked me to account for my whereabouts the first time he visited us.

"Convenient," he noted, when Skylar told him she was here with me. "The classic mutual alibi, home alone with each other. Very well then."

Before he left, he moved Quan Yin back to the exact position where she'd been before he moved her out of the way for his hat.

No sooner was he out the door than Skylar rounded on Emma for coming on to Detective Duke. "You were flirting with him!"

"No I wasn't! I don't even like men!"

"Exactly! And yet there you were all a-flutter on the sofa with him at your feet." Skylar made butterfly movements with her hands.

"Trying to charm him seems like a good idea," I ventured, for which I got glares from both parties.

Skylar stamped her foot. "Being coy is one thing, Emma. Wriggling around like a schoolgirl at a drive-in movie is too much."

From the look on Emma's face, I guessed she'd never been to a drive-in movie, but she understood well enough to take offense.

"You are so unfair," she hissed. "He's trying to pin a murder on me — the murder of that useless friend of yours."

"Useless?" Skylar shook her head in exasperation. "*Did* you kill my friend? Why did you drive to the cemetery? What's going on, Emma?"

"You heard what I told that detective. I didn't kill anybody, and the only thing going on is that you'd rather be friends with a loser like Candy than with me. Well, I've had enough."

Emma stormed out of the house, leaving Skylar feeling all wrong and indignant. After banging around the kitchen for a few minutes, Skylar left to open the café for breakfast. I got on the phone to my employee Ginger, who promised to take care of the nursery for a few hours. Then, I got some long overdue sleep.

# # #

That evening, Detective Nakamura came by to complain. I didn't let him in the house. He could do his complaining in the front yard.

"How could you let Emma talk to that detective without a lawyer present?" he demanded.

As I was wracking my brain for a good defense, my neighbor Georgina bustled over to complain. As usual, she was wearing an enormous flower-print shift. This one was covered in giant pink stargazer lilies that for some reason had little seahorses swimming among them against a pale green background. It was a beautiful outfit in which to complain.

She was targeting Detective Nakamura rather than me this time, saying, "Detective, oh detective." I was about to leave so they could complain to each other, when I heard what she wanted to complain about.

"This neighborhood is infested with zombies. When are you people going to do something about it?"

Normally, I don't think Detective Nakamura would take much interest in zombie infestations, but the assault in the cemetery had made him more attentive to the zombie issue.

"What makes you think this neighborhood is infested with zombies?" he asked.

"The two I've seen this week, for starters. Haven't you heard what's going on at that cemetery downtown? Don't you people monitor social media? The zombies are everywhere. They're attacking people, hitting people with rocks, breaking their heads, turning them into zombies — more zombies! Zombies multiplying from the center of the city, don't you see? They start from there and spread in all directions, infesting everything. Are the police just going to stand by and let the zombies move in and ruin the neighborhood?"

Detective Nakamura had held up his hand through everything after "The two I've seen this week" in an effort to get Georgina to stop talking. In all fairness, the sun had gone down, and it was getting hard to see his hand in the dusk. Just kidding; Georgina was never going to notice a shut-up hint as subtle as a waving hand.

"You saw two zombies with your own eyes?" he asked.

"Right here on our street!" she said. "They came staggering up from that way." She pointed in the direction of the beach. "It's probably because of the two women who live in this house." She pointed at my house, ignoring the fact that I was standing right in front of her, which was okay with me.

"Did you call the police when you saw these zombies?"

"Yes! That's the problem. They didn't do anything. This is how the zombie apocalypse comes to fruition, detective. The authorities don't take it seriously until it's too late."

"Just tell me exactly what you saw, please." Detective Nakamura said through clenched teeth.

"Zombies!" Georgina shouted. "What is it about zombies that you don't understand?"

"What did the first one look like? Tell me as many details as you can remember so we can send out a description to our officers."

"Well, shouldn't you be picking up all the zombies, whatever they look like? I didn't see only one. And if I saw two, there are undoubtedly lots more. Those are just the ones in this neighborhood. They're probably all over the place. Just arrest them all."

"We'll do that," Detective Nakamura said, taking a step away from her.

"And while you're at it," Georgina added, "please do something about these women. They're weird and strange. It's like living next door to a crack house, only spooky. I don't know why I should have to put up with this."

"We're on top of these women," he assured her. "I mean, we're on top of the situation. If you see any more zombies, give me a call, all right?" He handed her a card.

She held the card a few inches from her face, trying to read it in the dark.

"How do you know he's not a zombie?" I asked her.

"Zombies don't hand out business cards, do they?" she snarked back.

I think she stuck her tongue out at me, but it was too dark to be sure. She promised to get in touch if she saw any more zombies and toddled away to her house. As she approached her front door, a motion-sensor light turned on.

When she was out of earshot, Detective Nakamura asked, "Have you seen anybody that looks like a zombie around here?"

"Only Candy that day you pulled your gun on her. We've been busy with other activities lately; no time for zombie spotting."

I didn't tell him about the zombie I'd seen on the beach or the ones Killin had seen. The detective would have dismissed my sightings in any case. Why was he even asking?

He was turning to leave when I had a thought.

"Wait a minute," I said. "The GhostOps people left a camera on Georgina's front lawn. I think it's automated. I wonder if they got video of Georgina's zombies?"

He looked toward the house next door. The light was still on, and we could see the camera in the yard with various antennas and sensors poking in every direction. We could also see Georgina standing by her front door, looking at us.

"You mean I have to go talk to her again?" the detective said.

"No, the GhostOps people run the camera. If they get anything they consider strange, they post it on their web site and stream it on their app. In fact, we can look at that right now."

I took out my phone and pulled up GhostOps. Recent posts showed ectoplasm activities in Wisconsin and a haunting in Boise, but no zombies. Drat.

"Nothing?" the detective asked.

"Maybe Georgina saw Mr. Grundy and his wife from around the corner. They're not in good shape at all."

"If you see anything strange, give me a call, okay?" Detective Nakamura looked at Georgina, who was still standing by her front door. The motion-sensor light had turned off, so maybe she thought she was invisible. "When I say 'strange,' I mean something stranger than that woman. And please don't let Emma talk to Detective Duke unless the lawyer is present. Can you do that for me?"

"Sure," I said. "Sorry."

After he left, I went out to my car in the driveway and grabbed my laptop. I'd brought it home to take care of work issues that went critical while I was napping that morning. Back inside the house, I was closing the front door when Georgina started shouting.

"Stay away you!"

I stepped outside, trying to think of a snarky reply. Her motion-sensor light was on. She was standing by her front door, pointing a pistol at someone — or some thing.

Under the streetlight at the edge of Georgina's yard, a figure swayed and staggered. A terrible rot odor wafted on the breeze. Was this a zombie? Georgina thought it was a zombie; that was a sure bet. She held the pistol on it as it clumped closer.

As it swayed into her yard, she shouted again. "I said stay away. Stop where you are or I'll shoot."

The figure kept coming. It looked like a zombie and smelled like one, but the streetlight was behind it, and I couldn't see it clearly.

I took a few steps toward Georgina. If I interfered, would she shoot me? I whipped out my phone. Detective Nakamura had just left. He might still be close. My hands shook as I flipped through my contacts. He wasn't under D. Come on, Hayley; he's under N. I stabbed my finger at his name.

"Stop!" Georgina shouted. "You can't have my brain." She crouched with both hands on the gun, moving her head from side to side, squinting at the figure wobbling in the middle of her dark lawn. The thing let out an unearthly moan.

It had to be a real zombie. Did I care if Georgina shot a zombie? What difference would it make? For that matter, did I care if the zombie ate her brain?

"What now?" Detective Nakamura said from my phone.

The zombie tottered sideways and lurched straight toward Georgina, clomping fast now across the yard, coming into the light from Georgina's porch. The zombie was a woman. She had orange hair. Her head was shaved on one side. The light glinted off of metal rings and chains that hung from her ears, her nose, her eyebrow.

"No, no, no!" I yelled, running toward Georgina. "Not Candy!"

Five shots rang out, rapid fire. Candy jolted and stumbled backward.

Aghast, I froze in my tracks, staring at Candy's body sprawled on the lawn. "How could you?" I cried, dropping to my knees. But what difference did it make? Candy was dead before she got here. She was already a zombie. I knew that. I knew it. Yet, seeing her gunned down a few feet from me was more than I could bear. I wanted to go help her, and I was certain she was beyond any help, and what did I do now?

I got to my feet and looked at Georgina. She was pointing the gun at me, her hands trembling. Her eyes were crazy big.

"Georgina, what are you doing?" I whispered. "Put the gun down."

"You're behind this!" she said. "You sicced these zombies on me. You want them to kill me."

I backed away, holding both hands up in front of me. "None of us wants zombies here. We have to get through this together."

"I'm not going through the end of the world with *you*. How stupid do you think I am? I know what you're doing. You want to make me undead. Well, it won't work." She shook her head violently. "I'll stop them. I'll stop you."

"It's okay, now. Nobody's trying to make you undead. If we just take it easy, we can all be safe, and nobody will get hurt."

If Candy hadn't already been dead when she walked up, she'd have been hurt to death. I glanced toward where she'd been shot. She wasn't lying on the ground. A faint flicker of hope sparked in me and just as quickly went dark. She was a zombie. She'd gotten up and staggered away. How long would I be alive? Georgina was waving the gun as if it were some kind of brush that could paint over the parts of the world she didn't want.

"I'm so afraid," she said.

"Please, Georgina," I pleaded. "You don't want to get yourself in any more trouble here. Please put the gun down."

I moved my palms toward the ground to show which way down was, in case she was unclear about that. She was no good at following directions. I already knew that, and now she blinked rapidly and steadied the gun with both hands, her finger on the trigger.

"I'm not putting up with this anymore," she said, her voice shrill. "You've tried your last trick on me. No more year-round Halloween in this neighborhood. She squeezed her eyes half shut and tightened her grip.

Someone moved behind her   Detective Nakamura.

"You can't hurt me if you have the safety on, Georgina," I called to her.

She glanced at the side of the gun as Detective Nakamura ran up and tackled her. The gun went off as she went down — a shot that fizzed past my left ear.

Running to where the detective grappled with Georgina, I stepped on the hand that held the gun. She screamed and let go. I kicked the gun away. As Detective Nakamura yanked Georgina's hands behind her back, I sprinted toward the street to find Candy. She was nowhere to be seen.

Chapter 15

Detective Nakamura pretended to arrest Georgina for shooting Candy. Since he was on administrative leave, he couldn't arrest anybody, but she didn't know that.

She was pretty out of it with fear and outrage. She kept saying, "But what about the zombies?" I almost felt sorry for her.

When the police came, they had to read her her rights all over again, which didn't seem to confuse her any more than she already was. She was still mumbling about zombies, so they called ahead for a place in the psychiatric unit. We wouldn't see Georgina again for two or three days.

Since Candy's body was missing — again — they weren't charging Georgina with murder. The detective who was standing in for Ken Nakamura was completely baffled by the non-habeasness of the corpus, because Candy had clearly taken at least two shots to the heart. The GhostOps video showed it in more detail than I cared to see.

The next day, Detective Nakamura watched this video over and over, trying to figure out some way it could make sense without Candy being a zombie, which made no sense.

"It doesn't make sense," he told me. He pointed to his laptop on the coffee table where the GhostOps video was running on an endless loop.

"You're right," I said.

I'd let him into the house this time, and we were sitting in my living room. I hadn't forgiven him enough to offer him a scone and coffee in the kitchen, although I probably should on account of his saving my life.

"If you zoom in, you can see where three of those 9-millimeter slugs came out the other side of her body," he told me for the fourth or fifth time. "She couldn't possibly have walked away from that."

"And yet she did," I replied for the fourth or fifth time.

"Someone must have carried her body away," he said for the second or third time.

"Yet neither of us saw this person," I pointed out for the second or third time. "Unless you can find a trap door in Georgina's yard, you're going to have to deal with the zombie concept."

"You want me to believe that Candy Longstaff was walking around dead."

"Well, you know, it happens to the best of us. A long, frustrating, overworked day, and there you are: dead on your feet."

"It's not funny," he said. "We have to figure out what's going on."

"Yeah, I suppose we can't let Georgina take the heat for killing a dead person. Even Georgina doesn't deserve that. But at least we don't have to prove that Emma didn't kill Candy. As far as the law is concerned, Candy was alive and well when Georgina shot her."

"As far as I'm concerned, too. Until we get forensics on Candy, I'll continue to believe she's alive — or was until Georgina shot her. We need to find Candy, and you know how to do it." He gave me a knowing look.

"You mean the way I found Angelina Martinelli? No, no, no. You have no idea what I went through to do that."

The shark-dogs had been friendly that time. Would the next pod be as affectionate?

"Come on," he said. "It can't be that hard."

"Not for you, it isn't. All you have to do is clean up the beach."

"If we can't find Candy, we can't do anything," he said.

"Let me prepare you for a bigger problem if we do find her. What if an autopsy shows she'd been dead several days before Georgina 'killed' her?"

"No way that's possible."

"Well, just suppose for a moment that it *is* possible for a person to be a zombie. Can you suppose that?"

He screwed up his face with effort — a rare example of Detective Nakamura changing his expression. I was impressed.

"That's your supposing face?" I asked.

"Yes, but it didn't work. I can't believe in zombies."

"Try scrunching up your face more."

"Scrunching isn't going to do it. I need dramatic proof. I need to find Candy."

Trying to think of an alternative, I scrunched up my own face. I wasn't sure I wanted the authorities to get their hands on Candy because she might have carried magic out of the Waterway. Maybe I needed to use the shark-dogs to find her and not tell Detective Nakamura about it. The idea of finding her made me queasy. What would we do with undead Candy?

As much as I disliked the idea, persuading Detective Nakamura to believe in magic could be helpful. It could also be dangerous. At the moment, it would be helpful if he believed in zombies.

"What if you could meet a zombie?" I asked him.

He stared at me. "You mean like Internet dating?"

"Yeah, except in the cemetery."

"You're suggesting we go to the Angelus-Rosedale Cemetery to meet a zombie?"

"Are you willing to give it a try? You don't have to scrunch up your face. You just need to get close enough to believe the evidence of your senses."

"I'm willing to go, but the police still have the cemetery cordoned off, and I'm still on administrative leave for arresting Georgina."

"You got no credit for stopping her from shooting me?"

"Got a lot of questions about why I was involved in this case while I was on administrative leave, that's what I got."

"Thanks for saving my life," I told him sincerely.

"Georgina was shaky at that point. She probably would have missed."

"In any case, I enjoyed seeing you tackle her. Thanks for that."

# # #

When Skylar got home, I told her over dinner that we needed to revisit the question of how to get into the cemetery — this time without using the Waterway. "I can't get Detective Nakamura through there, and we can't make him invisible. Maybe we could use the diversion idea."

"That could work, but I thought of another way. Mother once mentioned that it's possible to stop time temporarily. I think the method is called the lull spell. Everyone and everything around you stands still for a couple of hours while you keep moving. Once we cast the spell, you can walk right past the police without them seeing you."

"That sounds like fun," I said. "Let's use it. I'll ask Detective Nakamura if he can go tonight."

"There's just one problem," Skylar said.

"The spell uses eye of newt," I guessed.

"Okay," she admitted, "two problems."

"Let's have the other one."

"There's a slight risk that the spell could rip the fabric of reality."

"Good heavens, Skylar. You mean like destroy the universe?"

"No no, more like ripping the hem out of one leg of the universe's pants."

"That still sounds bad. If it happens, can we fix it? Sew it up again?"

"I'll check with Mother. Are you sure you want to get Detective Nakamura in the middle of a magic spell? He's so determined to be rational. Don't you worry he might freak out?"

"Hadn't thought about it," I said. "What do you mean? He doesn't seem like a freak out kind of guy."

"I mean like putting LSD in somebody's coffee. Tends to make people think they're going around the bend. Magic is like that, and Detective Nakamura isn't a person I want to go around the bend with. Why do you want to get him into the cemetery?"

"I'm not doing it for fun." I put down the veggie wrap I was eating and wiped my hands on a napkin. "If he understands that the zombies are real, he can get on the right track with this case. It was nice of Georgina to distract everyone from the assault that actually killed Candy, but at some point they'll find Candy and discover she'd been dead for several days before Georgina shot her. Then, the focus will be back on Emma. While we have time, we need to find out who really killed Candy. Detective Nakamura can help us do that — I hope. If not, what do you figure we should do to find the perp?"

Skylar chewed a big bite of her veggie wrap longer than was strictly necessary. Eventually, she said, "I dunno. Maybe they won't find Candy, and Georgina will take the blame for everything."

"Are we okay with Georgina spending a few years in the slammer?"

We chewed on our wraps for several minutes, thinking about the tradeoffs of this outcome. It definitely had an upside.

"She did shoot a person," I pointed out. "It just turns out the person was already dead."

"And she tried to shoot you," Skylar said.

We chewed some more.

"I don't think she really would have shot me, do you?"

"Well, she probably doesn't even know herself. It's a good thing Detective Nakamura took her down when he did. Why was he even there?"

"I'd called him, and he heard me shouting to Georgina to put the gun down. He came to help."

"So, we're liking the detective a little more today," Skylar observed.

"Yeah," I agreed. "I might have to forgive him for — you know — being him."

# # #

A block from the cemetery, slides and climbing structures loomed out of the midnight darkness like scaffolds. Crickets chirped in the grass. The playground was deserted at this hour so far as we could tell by the dim city-glow from the overcast sky. A few street lights threw spectral shadows across the ground. Not wanting to draw attention to ourselves with flashlights, we stumbled around in the dark, looking for a spot that would be good for casting the lull spell.

After banging my knee on a bike rack and saying a couple of bad words, I wondered aloud, "Why do we always do these things at midnight?" I dropped the cat carrier I'd brought onto a picnic table, where I sat and rubbed my knee.

"It's the witching hour," Skylar said, drawing a circle on the pavement with chalk. "We're witches."

"That's such a cliché."

"Also, most sensible people are in bed at this hour, which leaves the world to us." She sat next to me at the picnic table.

"Us nonsensical people," I said.

"And here's Detective Nakamura, I'll bet."

A Jeep Cherokee had pulled up behind our car on the street. A black man got out. He pulled a small pack off the passenger seat and slung it over his shoulder.

We shuffled away from the picnic table and crouched behind a litter barrel.

The man looked up and down the street. He looked up at the moths circling the closest streetlight and then walked slowly up the short concrete ramp that led to the opening in the fence around the playground. At the opening, he paused and looked around. Then, he crept slowly toward a climbing structure with slides on three sides.

The cat we'd brought scratched at the inside of his carrier. He meowed. The man stopped. The cat carrier sat on a picnic table about ten feet from our litter barrel. The cat scratched some more and meowed again. The man turned. He came toward us.

I nudged Skylar and whispered in her ear, "Let's go."

"Hayley?" the man whispered.

"Detective Nakamura?" Skylar and I said simultaneously. We stood up.

"Why are you black?" I asked.

"Camo," he said, like that was obvious.

Now that he was closer, we could see he was wearing a camouflage shirt and pants, too.

"Camo, really?" Skylar asked.

"We don't want to be seen," he explained.

"And if you are seen, you want it to be obvious you're up to something?"

He huffed. "The whole point is to not be seen in the first place. You have some kind of diversion planned?"

"Uh, kind of," I said.

"Using the cat?" he asked.

"Kind of," I said again.

To avoid burdening Detective Nakamura's imagination with too much magic, Skylar and I were telling him as little as possible about what we were going to do, which was stop time for a couple of hours. We didn't think he'd be entirely comfortable with that concept. I certainly wasn't comfortable with it. Stopping time had sounded like fun at first, but spells had a habit of going sideways.

"To start with, we're going to read a little story. Then, you and I will go over to the cemetery while Skylar handles the diversion. We'll have about two hours to get in, find a zombie, and get out, okay?"

"Got it," he said. "You're showing an awful lot of skin. You want some camo paint? I brought it in my pack."

The night was warm, so Skylar and I were both dressed in T-shirt and shorts.

"What brand of camo paint do you use?" I asked him.

"What brand?" he echoed. "I think it's called Arcturus. What difference does that make?"

"I have sensitive skin. I only wear Clinique."

"Look," Skylar said, "it doesn't matter. Nobody will see you. You can go naked if you want."

"Not that you would," I added quickly. The conversation about dancing in the moonlight remained fresh in my memory. "How about let's stand in the circle Skylar drew over there on the pavement while she reads the story. Detective Nakamura, could you hold the cat?"

"Of course. I like cats."

It turned out that Cleveland, the cat we'd borrowed, did not like Detective Nakamura. Cleveland was a very mellow cat, but every cat reserves the right to dislike certain people. Cleveland wasn't violent about his dislike. He just did his best to squirm out of the detective's arms.

I placed a glass bowl inside the circle. In that bowl were a newt and frog we'd caught in the mountains east of L.A. In this lull spell, the eye of newt and toe of frog could stay in and on the little amphibians.

Skylar cleared her throat and brought up the story that powered the lull spell on her phone. "Everybody ready?" she asked.

"Ready for what?" Detective Nakamura asked, adding to the cat, "Come on, Cleveland buddy. Everything's okay."

"Just hang onto the cat while she reads the story," I told him. "Can you do that?"

"Ow. Yes."

Skylar read this story aloud:

> After my father brought shame upon our village, he spoke less and less, never to strangers.
>
> "Tend your cassava," Bokoman the neighbor would say, when he saw my father sitting by the river with a reed between his teeth.
>
> "Rebuild your kraal," Mbumo the goat man would say, when he saw my father drawing figures in the sand by the hut of old Ka'aksa, listening to her tales.
>
> My mother had gone away. She was here to see the dry season settle on the land like a serpent's hiss. She was not here to see the next to last goat die. She was not here to see the fig tree wither on the hill where the purple flowers wait for the moon. She was not here to see the lightning rip out water from the black belly of the sky.
>
> My father was here for the rains as a name more than a body. The rains fell all around this name, saying Tabombomula, Tabombomula. When the river rose, he sat in a new place, higher up the bank. I looked at him from a distance.
>
> One day, restless with too much rain, I asked old Ka'aksa to tell me a story. She said, "I am very busy, so I will tell you a very short story. Your days of being a child are coming to an end. In no time, you will be a man."
>
> That was the story she told me. "In no time, you will be a man."

I went to my father where he was sitting on the riverbank and asked, "Father, how long is no time?"

Father waved his gnarled hand toward the river and said, "Time is a cat."

"But how long is no time?" I asked again. "If time is a cat, what is no time?"

"To answer your question, you first have to know what the cat is doing. Is the cat sleeping in the shade of a knob thorn tree? Or is the cat chasing a jerboa? If the cat is waiting to pounce at a pangolin burrow, you might find that the world holds its breath, as only the tail of the cat twitches in the twilight lulling."

Thinking about this cat, I watched the river rush by, frothing at the edges, carrying all manner of fallen leaves and branches downstream. How long would this river take to carry away all the land and everything in it? I moved a little further up the bank.

"If the cat is waiting at the pangolin burrow," I supposed, "no time will end when the cat pounces."

"Then you will be a man," my father agreed.

He looked at the river. I looked at the river. In the green forest upstream, a cheetah coughed.

As Skylar ended the story, green light shone from the sky. The distant murmur of the city stopped. In the green glow, Skylar stood outside the circle with her eyes a little wide, her mouth a little open, a look of expectation frozen on her face.

For several long seconds I stared at her. The expression didn't change. She was in no time.

Next to me, Detective Nakamura was stuck in place too. Cleveland was now sitting at the edge of the circle, cleaning his face with his paw. He must have squirmed out of the detective's grasp before the story ended.

"Rats," I told him.

Cleveland stopped grooming and looked at me.

This spell lasted 2 hours they said. Please, please, please, let's have a restart in 2 hours. I listened to the hush, wishing for some noise, any noise, and looked around at the dim green world.

No moths fluttered around the street lights. The crickets were still. The cat was the only thing moving. The world was silent as a tomb.

Were Cleveland and I the only creatures in the entire universe with hearts still beating?

Chapter 16

The whole point of the lull spell was to get Detective Nakamura into the cemetery. Now, his hands were reaching out, paralyzed, forever trying to get the cat back — meaning forever until the spell wore off, and who knew how long that could be? What if the effects literally lasted until the end of time? I'd live the rest of my life alone in the world with Cleveland. Wait, was *this* the end of time?

I paced around the circle on the pavement, following the chalk line, engulfed in the green light from the sky.

What if we'd just pulled the plug on the time thing? Now the universe was stuck. Forever.

Okay, okay, calm down, Hayley. Don't go to worst case here. This isn't the end of time. You're still moving, thinking, feeling, freaking out. All these things take time. It's not totally busted.

I picked up Cleveland and hugged him. "Everything will be all right," I told the cat.

Witches had cast this spell before. Of course! This had all been done many times. Yeah, this spell couldn't end time, or it would have ended before we started — unless we did something wrong. What if we left out an ingredient that derailed the time train? Were we supposed to cast the spell on a riverbank? The story had a river in it. Maybe the newt and frog had to be in a river.

I was still pacing around the circle. When I came to the bowl, I squatted down to peer into the water. In the green light from the sky, the little creatures looked okay. Good. That doubled the number of living things still in business here.

What was I going to do with myself until the world started up again? If I could only get Detective Nakamura going. I lifted the cat into his outstretched hands, but that didn't unstick the man. To be included in the spell, the non-magical detective had to be holding the cat while we cast the spell. All we asked him to do was hang onto the cat, and he couldn't handle that one simple job. Now, of course, Cleveland was happy to curl up in the detective's immobile hands.

Well, if the detective didn't get included the first time, I would cast the spell again. Taking the phone out of Skylar's hand, I read through the story a second time. This time the sky glowed orange, and everything jittered a fraction of an inch in random directions, including Detective Nakamura. Cleveland leapt out of his hands. The jittering stopped after a second, except for the detective, who jolted back and forth long enough to get me worried that I'd messed him up.

After half a minute, he was saying, "Wha-, wha-, wha-" on and on, until he managed to say, "What's going on?"

"You were stuck in time, and now you're in no time. How do you feel?"

"Like I just drank six cups of Starbucks Blonde. Why is everything orange?"

"Not sure. Must be a side effect of no time."

"You keep saying that," he complained. "I have no idea what 'no time' means."

"You see Skylar?" I stepped out of the way.

"Why is she not moving?"

"You're not going to like the answer."

"Tell me anyway."

"We're in no time, and she's not."

He peered at Skylar's immobile face for a long time. Then, he looked around at the orange world. Was he going to freak out? We really should have prepared him for this, even if he wouldn't have believed what we told him. Even if we didn't know the world would be orange.

He looked at me. "What now?"

"Now we go to the cemetery to find a zombie."

"Let's go, then," he said, and sauntered toward the opening in the fence.

That was it? Just, "Let's go"?

"Hold on," I called out. "Let me get Cleveland in his carrier."

"You said we'd have a couple of hours for this operation. That's how long everything will stay on hold?" he asked.

"Probably. Our, uh, process didn't go entirely right. You were out of time for a while, and now the sky is orange for some reason."

"And why are my clothes so uncomfortable?" he asked. He walked back toward me, flailing his arms around and looking down at his camo outfit.

My T-shirt was tight against the front of my neck, now that he mentioned it. And my shorts felt funny.

"My zipper is in the back," he said. "Why is my zipper in the back? And the buttons on my shirt?"

He ran his hands up and down his back and then his front. "My clothes are on backwards. Why are my clothes on backwards? How could that even happen? Did you take my clothes off and put them on backwards when I was out of time? Why would you do that?"

"Calm down. I didn't take your clothes off. Mine are on backwards too. The process must have done it as a side effect."

"That's ridiculous!" he hissed. "I can't even unbutton my shirt to put it on right. What if someone sees me with my pants on backwards? I'll be a laughing stock. How could this possibly happen? What have you gotten me into here?"

"Take it easy!" I told him. "Don't get your knickers in a twist just because your pants are on backwards. I'll help with the buttons, but everything might reverse again when we come out of no time."

"There's no way I'm walking around like this!"

"People can't see you," I reminded him. "Everyone is stuck in time except us." I guided Cleveland into the cat carrier.

"Undo my buttons," he told me, turning around. "Why didn't you warn me about this?"

"It's a surprise to me, too, but it's not the end of the world, for goodness sake. Stand still."

He was shifting his weight from one foot to the other and kept on doing it. I managed to undo his buttons, despite the movement, and he shucked off his shirt like it was radioactive.

"Gaa!" he said. "That's maddening to feel trapped in your own shirt. Undo my pants."

I puffed out a little breath. Okay, then, so long as it's in the back. I fumbled at the button and pulled the zipper.

He jerked down his pants and tugged at his underwear. "At least my shorts are on straight."

"Yeah, if our underwear had been reversed I'd have noticed a lot sooner."

"Is magic always this unreliable?" he wondered.

"Pretty much, yeah."

With his pants hanging halfway to his knees, Detective Nakamura put his shirt on and buttoned up the front. "You need to get your act together with this stuff. It's irresponsible to go around messing with people's clothes when they're stuck in time. What if I were to go over to Skylar there and undress her while she can't defend herself?"

"I told you, nobody undressed you."

I turned around, pulled my T-shirt over my head, and put it on straight. Might as well be comfortable. I could live with my shorts being tight in the back, and for some reason I felt shy about dropping my shorts in front of Detective Nakamura. He obviously had no such problem. Sitting on the picnic table bench, he unlaced his boots and got his pants sorted out.

"You don't seem shy about undressing in public," I said.

"It's the idea of it," he shot back. "It's one thing for me to do it, and quite another to be taken advantage of while I'm frozen in place."

That was a good point. I wasn't going to say so. "Don't you want to mess with people a *little*?"

"But that's unethical," he protested.

"Even if they never know?"

"Yes!"

He gave me a lecture on ethics as we marched double-time over to the cemetery. I couldn't disagree with anything he said, but I was thinking about the times I'd turned invisible and snuck into the police evidence room. I'd "borrowed" magical objects that had no business being in there. My unethical actions had helped solve a couple of baffling murder cases. While I was invisible, I'd messed with a couple of people a little bit. Was I a bad person?

The yellow police tape on the cemetery gate looked white in the orange light from the sky. A police car sat next to the gate. In the car, an officer was frozen in place with a donut halfway to his mouth.

"Night of the living clichés," I said to myself.

"That's against regulations," he said, nodding toward the officer.

"Eating a cliché on duty?"

Detective Nakamura didn't reply. He swung the gate open a couple of feet. "They should keep this locked," he said officiously.

"They don't need to with donut guy guarding it," I pointed out. "Let's go this way."

I led him toward the Waterway pool. It had taken me many tries before I'd learned to find my way through the magical barrier that protected the pool. A non-magical person could never do it without help.

"You need to hold my hand," I told the detective.

"Hold your hand? Why?"

"Because you like me," I said with more than a little sarcasm. "Just do it, will you? Humor me." I held out my hand. He took it, complaining that it made him feel like a little boy. I walked us carefully around the granite gravestones and marble angels that marked the way. The dim orange glow made the cemetery garish and macabre, but it also gave us enough light to see what was around us.

When we got to the pool, Detective Nakamura was astonished that such a grave could exist in the middle of the cemetery. While he exclaimed about this place "of great historical importance," I realized that my plan for a zombie meet-up was flawed.

"Damn," I said.

"What's wrong?"

"I figured we could wait here until a zombie staggers in, since they're attracted to the pool, but now nothing is moving. Duh. We'll have to go find one."

"How do we do that?"

I shrugged. "Look for dead-looking people."

"Everything looks dead in this light."

He was right. The orange glow came from all directions, so everything looked flat. The trees and gravestones all seemed like cutouts. It was hard to distinguish one object from another, but the light was good enough to see Candy's "zombie" tracks. I showed Detective Nakamura the line of orange cones and yellow police tape that marked the zig-zagging tracks and how the markers ended at the edge of the magical barrier around the pool. That was where the police thought she'd disappeared into thin air.

We searched the cemetery for more than an hour, bending low so we might see zombies outlined against the orange sky. Detective Nakamura complained that I'd brought him on a wild goose chase. I was beginning to think he was right when I sniffed an awful odor.

"I smell a zombie," I said.

He pointed toward a black obelisk. "Someone is standing over there, next to the pointed stone."

It was a zombie all right. His face was bloated, and some of his features had slipped from their normal places. He was wearing a moth-eaten blazer over a shirt that was mottled black. It had probably been white once upon a time. Even though the zombie was frozen in place, I didn't want to get too close. The detective didn't hesitate. He walked directly up to the thing and poked at its chest.

"My God!"

"What?"

"My finger went right through."

Gross. That wasn't the end of the detective's disgusting zombie encounter. He pulled and shoved the thing, and little pieces came off, but the body was surprisingly tough for something that had been moldering in the ground for a long time.

"For a pile of dead parts you can stick your finger through, this thing hangs together rather well," he said. "I don't see how that's possible."

"Some are even sturdier than that," I told him. "I mean, I haven't tried to disassemble one, but the two I've seen looked fleshy. Candy was whole, except for the big divot in her head."

He stood with his hands on his hips, looking the zombie in the eye, or what was left of its eye. "It's hard to believe this thing could walk around on its own. It doesn't make sense."

"If it made sense, it wouldn't be magic."

"Let's look around some more."

"We need to get out of here before time starts again," I reminded him. "It's hard to know when that might happen."

Taking a circuitous route out of the cemetery, we saw no more zombies. Donut guy was still about to eat his midnight snack. Detective Nakamura closed the gate behind us.

Back in the playground, we sat at the picnic table petting Cleveland for a while. I kept glancing at Skylar standing there immobile. That was upsetting, and I was tired, so I got in the car and reclined the seat. The clock on the dashboard showed 12:34. I hoped I'd sleep and wake up, and everything would be back to normal, but I lay there awake for what seemed like hours. I opened my eyes and saw 12:34 again and again. The world was dead quiet.

Finally, I was so exhausted I dozed off. I woke, saw 12:34, and dozed again. After several frustrating rounds of this fitful dozing, I covered the clock with a shopping bag. Would the world ever go back to normal?

# # #

I woke with a start. The world was dark. Something was touching my leg. I jerked away from the touch and sat up.

"Hayley, it's me."

Skylar was back! I snatched the shopping bag off the dashboard and saw the clock — 12:36. The world had started again.

Leaning sideways to open the door, I tumbled out of the car. Skylar had already opened the door.

"So the spell failed?" she asked. "How did you get over here?"

"The spell worked," I said. "You've been frozen for hours. I was worried the world was permanently jammed."

"Really? I blinked, and you were gone. That's all I knew. Where's Detective Nakamura?"

We found him in his Jeep and startled him awake. He got out all groggy and stamped around on the sidewalk, unable to believe we were back in a world where it was still the middle of the night.

"We saw a zombie in the cemetery," I told Skylar, "but of course it wasn't moving, so he didn't get the full zombie effect."

"I got the idea," the detective said soberly.

"Why is your shirt on backwards?" Skylar asked him.

"Crap," he said. "Help me out, Hayley."

"I told you it would reverse when time started again."

"Wow, you're smart," he said. "Now get me out of this shirt."

I unbuttoned him and explained to Skylar that the spell reversed our clothes.

"Spell?" Detective Nakamura said. "I thought that's what you were doing. Why did you call it a 'process'?"

"Didn't want to spook you," I said.

"You stopped time, turned the world orange, and introduced me to a zombie. You didn't think that would spook me?"

"I figured you'd lose it," Skylar said.

"I'm tougher than that," he retorted.

"So long as your pants are on straight," I said, tugging on his zipper.

He pulled his pants down, and then pulled them back up. "I need to sit at the picnic table."

"Oh no," I said. "We left Cleveland in his carrier all this time."

"It's only been a few minutes," Skylar said to my back as I ran to the picnic table.

"It was a long time to him. We were in no time for hours."

Cleveland was curled up, asleep. I let him out for a stroll.

While Detective Nakamura got his pants on straight and put his boots back on, I asked him what he thought about a zombie being the perp who killed Candy.

"I suppose I have to entertain that possibility," he admitted. "You've shown me that magic happens, and that makes solving the case much harder. Now I have to think that anything is possible, even things that don't make sense."

"Welcome to our world," I told him.

He stood up from the picnic table and fastened his pants. "At the risk of making too much sense, let me pose a question. If a zombie killed Candy, wouldn't the zombie have eaten her brain?"

"Is that what zombies do?" Skylar asked. "We don't watch those kinds of movies."

"Yeah, brain feeders."

"Skylar says there's no such thing as zombies," I said.

"You know I walked back that statement," she said. "But I think it's safe to say that zombies haven't been known before now, so we don't really know how they behave, only we're sure they stink."

"I can verify that," Detective Nakamura said. "So zombies are out there as possible perps. I do have to note that it's still possible for anybody to dress up as a zombie. The perp could be a zombie, but the perp could also be a live person masquerading as a zombie. Could be anybody."

"For once, Detective Nakamura is right," Skylar said.

He got an astonished look on his face and raised his arms to the heavens. Then he did a victory dance around the picnic table, pumping his fists in the air and making breathy crowd noises, "Hurrah. Hurrah."

Now he was open to the possibility that a zombie was the perp. Did that put us any closer to finding out who — or what — the perp might be? We still couldn't prove that Emma didn't do it.

I looked down at the scuffed chalk line on the pavement. We'd let Detective Nakamura inside our magical circle. Would we come to regret that?

Chapter 17

I woke in my own comfortable bed and looked at the clock — 7:22. Good, I'd slept late. Morning light streamed in around the blinds. Closing my eyes again, I lay there for a minute. Thank goodness I was out of that ridiculous dream where the world was orange and people posed like manikins.

Wait, that really happened. A sudden chill passed through me as I remembered casting a spell that included Detective Nakamura. What was I thinking?

My eyes popped open. A shadow passed across the blinds, probably a bird. Or was it bigger?

I got out of bed and found I was still wearing the T-shirt and shorts I'd had on the night before. The T-shirt was on right, but my shorts were still backwards. Had I been through the lull spell twice? Yeah, it had been a long night.

Feeling like an idiot for not undressing the night before, I stripped off the T-shirt and threw it on the bed. I unbuttoned my shorts, let them drop to the floor, and was stepping out of them when I noticed another shadow on my blinds. This shadow was a person — someone on the outside trying to peep in, someone big, someone obviously male.

I scooted to the left and dropped to my hands and knees against the wall next to the window. Where was my phone?

The shadow man stood still for half a minute. A thud against the glass shook the window.

I crawled under the window sill, past my desk, and into the hall. I ran to Skylar's bedroom.

"Wake up," I whispered, shaking her shoulder. "Someone's outside. I think he's trying to get in. Where's your phone?"

She blinked several times and looked at her night stand. "It should be there. I always put it there. Where is it?"

We looked around her bedroom. Then I remembered I'd taken her phone out of her hand while she was frozen in time so I could cast the spell again. Where had I put it after that? And where was my own phone?

We crept back to my room. The shadow was gone, the room quiet.

My phone was on the nightstand where I usually put it, duh. I dialed 911 while Skylar peeked through the blinds. She whispered something. I ignored her and told the 911 dispatcher that a man was in my backyard trying to get in the house.

"You need to look," Skylar said.

I gestured for her to be quiet while I answered the dispatcher's question about whether I had a firearm, which I wished I had: "No, I don't have a gun."

The shadow of the man fell across the right side of the window and scraped against the screen.

"Hurry up!" I told the dispatcher.

Skylar opened the blinds.

"What are you doing?" I shouted as I dropped to the floor.

"Hello?" the dispatcher said. "Are you all right? Can you run away?"

From behind the desk, I peeked up at the window. Staring back at me wide-eyed was a zombie with gray hair and a nose newly damaged by scraping against the screen on my window. Skylar pointed toward the other side of the yard. I jumped up and looked. Candy!

"Cancel that!" I told the dispatcher. "Don't send the police!"

"Ms. West, are you all right?"

"Yes! Fine! Just don't send the police."

"Ma'am, the police are on their way, and you might be giving me a wave-off under duress, so you'll need to file a police report with them, okay?"

"Great." I hung up.

I dropped the phone on my desk and looked into the backyard. The gray-haired zombie lurched away from the window and staggered in a wide arc across the grass. Candy tottered more or less in one place and then veered off toward the vegetable garden. Another female zombie was shambling along the back fence. She reached up, grabbed the top of a plank, and shook the whole fence.

Funny I hadn't noticed the smell. Now that I knew the zombies were out there, the whole place reeked like a dump.

"What if that zombie back at the fence is the one that killed Candy?" I asked Skylar.

"Then the police can arrest her. Case closed." She shrugged, trying to look nonchalant.

"Not funny! They catch us with the perp zombie in our yard, and it's a verifiable undead person? They'll burn us at the stake for sure."

"Take it easy. We just have to keep the police out of the backyard." She paced in front of the window. "When they come to the door, don't let them in. Tell them the person in our backyard turned out to be a friend playing a prank. We're sorry to waste the officer's time. Please go away. Something like that."

"They're going to think I'm completely *duressed*-out. They'll never believe a word I'm saying."

"You need to lighten up. See the funny side. Zombies in the backyard, hahahaha."

"Hahahaha," I repeated.

"That's totally duressful." She looked out at the zombies milling around.

"Maybe we could think of a joke," I suggested desperately.

Skylar snapped her fingers. "Two zombies walk into a backyard! One says to the other, uh —"

"What if the cop insists on looking in the backyard?"

"Is that a punch line? You're totally not lightening up," Skylar complained.

The doorbell rang. How did they get here so fast? I pulled the Little Mermaid robe off the hook on the back of my bedroom door.

"Good morning, officer," I said as I swung open the door. I was about to tell him calling 911 had been a silly mistake when I noticed he was a total hunk. I mean, he was not like a bodybuilding hunk but more like a runway model with naturally wavy blonde hair and a body that fit in a police uniform more or less perfectly. Was that Kevlar or his actual pecs? They reminded me of that guy I'd hooked up with in Germany who looked like a young Brad Pitt. Something about those symmetrical features, the eyes, the not-quite smiling lips. They kind of dazzled your wits away. Yeah, I needed to look that guy up again, but really this guy at my front door would do as well, wouldn't he? And he had the advantage of being right here at my front door, right now, wanting something or other. I looked down at my Little Mermaid robe. It was too tight to close reliably and absurdly short. Why did I keep this thing? I looked up again.

"What did you say?" I asked the hunk.

"I said I'm Officer Whistler. Are you Hayley West?"

"Yes." I nodded and held out my hand. Did you shake hands with an officer who comes to help? "Pleased to meet you."

He shook my hand reluctantly. "You called about an intruder in your backyard?"

The zombies! I nodded yes. Then I shook my head no. "It turns out, Officer Whistler, that it was just a couple of friends who thought they'd surprise me by doing something nice in the backyard. They're early risers. I don't know what time you get up in the morning, not that it's any of my business, but I normally get up early, and this morning I slept in a little later than normal, and my friends were already out there, working away, being nice, when I woke up, so they surprised me. You know how friends are. Do you have friends? I mean, you know, I'm sure you have friends who sneak up on you and do random acts of kindness, like fixing your picnic table or something. My picnic table was broken. Or damaged, I guess you'd say, and needed a lot of kindness to get it up and running again. You know?"

I stood there in the doorway nodding like a complete idiot. But the hunk was smiling. I smiled back at him. Did he think I was a complete idiot? Maybe he thought I was cute? Did he like girls who babbled like idiots? Some guys did. If he was one of those guys, I didn't want him to like me, did I?

He gestured at my sleeve with his tablet computer. "Cute," he said.

"Not the kind of thing I'd buy for myself, of course."

A grown woman wearing a little girl's robe was a bit kinky, wasn't it? If this turns him on, I definitely won't like him.

Snugging up the robe's lapels so it was more or less closed in the front, I told him, "My boyfriend got me this. My ex-boyfriend, that is, because I don't have a boyfriend right now, really, on account of him cheating on me. But that's not important. Well, to me it is, not to you."

He looked up from his tablet. "Are you worried about your boyfriend? Is that who was in your backyard?"

"No, no. He's not in the backyard."

He was, in fact, walking up the driveway. My eyes widened in surprise, and Officer Whistler spun around to see what the matter was.

"Here's my boyfriend now," I explained, putting my hand on the officer's arm.

He yanked his arm away and spun back to face me. "This is the boyfriend you no longer have?"

"Not the ex-boyfriend who gave me this robe," I clarified. "Killin, what are you doing here?"

"Taking care of the mess in your backyard," he said.

"So you were in the backyard?" the officer asked him.

"Yes," Killin said. "Is that a problem?"

"Only if Ms. West reports an intruder to the police."

Killin's mouth formed a small oh. "Did she?"

The officer turned from Killin to me. "Are you okay with this man being in your backyard?"

Now that was a hard question, because the answer was yes and no, and I was already busy with another question. If Killin knew about the mess in my backyard, did that mean he put the zombies back there?

Killin walked closer and frowned at what I was wearing. "Cute outfit."

"Everyone thinks my outfit is cute," I said absently.

Killin glared at the officer, and the officer glared at me. "Ms. West, could you tell me if you're comfortable with this man being here so I can move on to other calls?"

"So long as he stays in the yard," I said. "Sorry you had to come for no reason."

"All in a day's work," he said with a tight smile. "And for the record, your robe struck me as cute because my husband and daughters are crazy about 'The Little Mermaid.'"

Looking at Officer Whistler's broad back as he walked to his patrol car, I thanked him for coming. Then, I shot Killin a what-are-you-up-to frown. He came as close as he could to the magical barrier around the house and said he'd meet me in the backyard.

"Not with the zombies back there," I told him. "Did you put them there?"

"Where else can I put them?"

"But what if they eat my brain?"

"They probably won't eat your brain," he said. "They didn't eat mine."

"Prove it," Skylar said from behind me.

He leaned over and showed her the top of his head. "Cranium complete. I may not have the full shilling, but it's not because zombies ate my brain."

"Well, they're too awful anyway," I said.

"And trampling the flower beds," Skylar said.

"You could at least have warned us," I said.

"Tried to. You weren't answering your phone last night. Where were you?"

"We took Detective Nakamura to the cemetery so he could meet a zombie."

"Janey Mack! Why'd you do that?"

"Well, I thought it was a good idea at the time. He needs to prove that Emma didn't kill Candy, and to do that he needs to know that the perp could have been a zombie. We also want to prove that our neighbor Georgina didn't kill Candy, since Candy was already dead when Georgina killed her."

"You noticed Candy wandering around your backyard, right?" Killin asked. "You could turn her over to the police. They'd find her pretty well perforated, but she was definitely dead when that happened. Georgina would be off the hook."

"Great idea," Skylar said.

I grimaced. "I already feel queasy about bringing Detective Nakamura into this. Can you imagine if the police get their hands on the zombies? All hell will break loose. I'm surprised they haven't nabbed one already."

"They're wily buggers — the zombies, that is. I don't know how they do it, but you see them one minute, and then you can't find them again. They are first-class wanderers."

"How on earth did you corral them in the backyard?" Skylar wondered.

"They're attracted to magical barriers. Took me a while to figure that out. You've got a barrier around your house, so the zombies have been wandering this way on their own. I cast a spell that put a barrier around me, and that attracted the zombies. They followed me into the backyard."

"You might be the first person in history who wanted to attract zombies." I observed.

"And these might be the first actual zombies in history — which aren't even actual zombies. I wonder if your friend Baldock didn't create them."

"See?" Skylar said. "I told you there's no such things as zombies."

But a light bulb was flashing in my brain. "Baldock was trying to find the pool in the cemetery, so he made zombies that gravitated to the barrier around the pool."

"Bang on."

"They're magical, but they're not alive, so they pass right through magical barriers."

"Baldock is a clever melter, isn't he? Now, he can get to the pool."

"Whatever he wants it for can't be good," Skylar said.

"It's not good for the Waterway, that's for sure," I said. "The zombies pollute the magic, but they also carry away part of the magic when they come out. We need to put that magic back."

"So I'll keep collecting them in your backyard," Killin said cheerfully. "You're welcome."

"What good does that do, when we don't know how to get the magic back in the Waterway?" Skylar protested.

"Get the three blonde witches to help."

I shuddered to think how close Baldock came to getting his hands on little Amelia.

# # #

Seeing Candy stagger around the backyard was disconcerting, to say the least, and having zombies thud into our house from time to time wasn't fun. Also, they smelled.

Skylar's mother came up with a brilliant zombie containment scheme. We created a super-powerful magical barrier around a little patch of grass at the back of our yard, slightly screened from the house by a few wispy bushes. Drawn irresistibly toward the "protected" area, the zombies wandered through it, wheeling around, and then wandered back through it the other way, endlessly.

Now that we had them, what were we going to do with them?

Chapter 18

Skylar's car kept stalling when she took her foot off the gas. We took it to the shop for repairs, and a few hours later, our mechanic Zheng called to ask Skylar if she'd been cheating on him. She told him no, he was the mechanic of her dreams. He insisted that another man had had his hands on her car, and "This man is no good for you."

"What makes you say that?" she asked.

"He is stupid," Zheng said. "He put your parts on backwards."

Skylar was about to object that that made no sense. Then she looked at me wide-eyed. We were at a little table in the corner of the café having a bite to eat after the noon rush. She put her hand over the phone.

"He says my parts are on backwards."

"I knew that," I told her.

"On my car."

"Oh." I brought a forkful of arugula to my mouth and put the fork down again. "Oh no!"

Skylar nodded and grimaced. To Zheng she said, "Can you put the parts right?"

"If anybody can do this, it is your man Zheng."

Skylar and I chewed our salads for a minute, looking at each other, wondering how much of the world had woken up with its pants on backwards after our spell. Then, Emma called to ask if she could borrow Skylar's car.

"Sorry," Skylar said. "It's in the shop. What's wrong with your car?"

"Had to loan it to my father," Emma said. "His car is in the shop. Why is everybody's car in the shop?"

"Good question," Skylar said, even though she had an idea what the answer was.

I called Detective Nakamura on speaker. He answered briskly, "What?"

"Did you find out what's wrong with your car?"

"Parts on backwards, but I have a bigger problem. Harris Duke has an arrest warrant out for Emma."

Skylar's fork clattered onto her plate. "But he already arrested Georgina," she protested.

"He can't arrest two people for the same murder," I added. "Can he?"

"Apparently, Georgina can be held a couple more days for psychiatric observation, which leaves him free to arrest Emma. She's not at home, and she's not answering my calls. Do you know where she is?"

"I just talked to her," Skylar said, "Hold on."

She hit the Emma button on her phone and waited. And waited. And went to voice jail. "Emma, Detective Duke is out to arrest you. So —"

"Tell her to get with her lawyer," the detective said from my phone.

"Go to the lawyer's office. He'll know what to do."

"I already left five messages like that," Detective Nakamura said. "When you talked to her, she didn't say where she was?"

"I think she was in a public place. Little noises were happening in the background."

"Little noises like traffic? Or inside noises like voices?"

"More like voices, rustling of objects, that kind of thing."

"Maybe she took an Uber to work. Could you drive me up there?"

"I thought you had Emma's car," I said.

"Confiscated as evidence."

"I'll pick you up in ten minutes," I said.

"Let's just call the store," Skylar said.

"Already tried that," the detective said. "They won't give information about specific employees, and employees are not allowed to use the store phone."

"Well, I won't be shopping there any time soon," Skylar said.

"You wouldn't be caught dead with that lux stuff unless it's on Emma."

"We're wasting time, ladies!"

"Ten minutes," I said.

# # #

Nine minutes later, Skylar and I picked up Detective Nakamura in front of his house.

"Maybe we should check places around here before we drive all the way to Rodeo Drive," Skylar said as he got in the car.

"That's okay if you know the local places where she's likely to be. I think she's probably at work."

"Riviera Village has a couple of places she likes," Skylar said. "Let's try those."

"Or the South Bay Galleria?" I said.

"That's huge," Detective Nakamura said. "Even if she's in there, how would we find her?"

"We can split up and cover it in a few minutes if we each take a floor," Skylar said.

"When you talked to her on the phone, did she sound like she was at Riviera Village or the Galleria?" he asked.

"How would I know what those places sound like?"

"You have ears. You've been to those places. You must know what they sound like."

Skylar pretended to hold her phone to her head. "Is that the ambient buzz of Coffee Cartel or Hotdog on a Stick? Let me think."

"She's not going to be at Hotdog on a Stick," the detective said dismissively.

"I just used that as an example," Skylar said. "I know lots of places Emma likes. I can help you find her if you let me."

"If you want to help," he said, "get on your broom and fly up to Rodeo Drive."

"How about you go sit on a broom," Skylar said.

"Girls! Girls!" I said. "Let's focus! The good news is, Detective Duke will have a harder time finding her than we will."

"Unless she's at work," Detective Nakamura said. "He's a lot closer than we are, and he'll check there first."

"Then it doesn't matter," I pointed out. "He'll get there before we could. We have to hope she's somewhere around Redondo Beach. Let's start with Riviera Village, since we're just about there already."

"How did Detective Duke suddenly decide to arrest Emma?" Skylar asked.

Detective Nakamura cleared his throat. "Purely accidental circumstances. I went to lunch with a friend of mine in vice, and we stopped at a grocery store afterward to pick up a few things. I grabbed a couple of shopping bags out of the trunk of Emma's car. When I checked out, the cashier dumped a zombie mask and raggedy clothes from one of the bags."

Skylar groaned. "The other detective just had to be there to see that?"

"As I say, purely accidental circumstances."

"It wasn't accidental that Emma had a zombie outfit in her trunk, was it?" I snapped.

That didn't make me very popular in the car. Nobody said anything until I found a parking space near the Coffee Cartel.

"Obviously, somebody's trying to frame Emma," her father said.

I turned around and looked at him in the back seat. "She drove to the cemetery the night of the murder. Nobody framed her into doing that. She needs to come clean about what she was up to that night."

"That's why we need to find her," he said. He rubbed his hand across his eyes as though he'd had a vision of his daughter that he had to wipe away at all costs.

Skylar looked from him to me and put her hand on my arm. "You don't believe she did it."

"Of course not," I said. But as I got out of the car, I didn't feel as certain as I hoped I sounded. "When we do find her, what then?"

"We get her to come clean, as you say." He slammed his door shut. "And we make sure she talks with the lawyer before Duke arrests her. She needs to surrender herself with a complete story that makes sense."

"And then we need to find the real perp," Skylar said.

# # #

By 5 pm, we'd looked every place Skylar could think of and couldn't find Emma anywhere. Detective Nakamura checked with an officer in Hermosa Beach, who said the police hadn't found Emma, either. Nobody knew where she was, and she wasn't answering her phone.

"Did someone kidnap her? Who would do that?" Detective Nakamura asked for the umpteenth time. He slumped into a chair at our kitchen table. We'd tried to get him to go to a restaurant with us, but he begged for one of Skylar's scones. She told him he'd have to eat proper food before he could have a scone. He sat at the table with his head in his hands while she whipped up vegan tacos.

I started a pot of coffee and sat across the table from him. "Let's talk about who could have a reason to kill Candy. Besides everyone who ever met her."

Detective Nakamura raised his head. "That's about the size of my suspect list: everyone." He took out his little notebook. "Candy's obsessive hobby was protesting. Figuring out all the real estate developments and other activities she opposed could take many weeks."

"The last thing she protested was that wall at the cemetery," I said. "Could someone have reason to kill her for that?"

"Seems far-fetched, but I did look into it," Detective Nakamura said. "The city has two companies contracted to demo the old wall and put up a new one. They both have lots of business, so nobody takes a huge financial hit if the wall stays. One other possibility is that someone felt the protesters were desecrating the cemetery."

"Kill somebody for desecrating a cemetery?" Skylar said. "That does have a certain symmetry to it."

"Symmetry isn't usually a motive for murder," the detective mused. "People can get touchy over issues that offend their beliefs, but why target Candy?"

"She was the only one who walked through the cemetery after the protest," I pointed out.

"Yet protesters had been on the wall without Candy several times during the previous week, and nobody walked through the cemetery. Someone who wanted to kill a random protester couldn't count on having the opportunity inside the cemetery. But here's a key fact: Candy joined the protest once before. She walked through the cemetery after that protest, and a news report showed her doing it."

"That only means *someone* could have known in advance that she might walk through the cemetery," I said. I got up and brought the coffee to the table. "The person could be a whack job who wanted to hurt a random protester or a person who had a grudge against Candy in particular."

"Exactly right," the detective said. "But we can say the attack *could* have been planned by a person who saw that news report and knew Candy would be protesting again that night. If we figure out who could know about that, we can narrow the list of suspects."

I poured coffee and looked over at Skylar. She'd stopped stirring the ingredients in her skillet, and I knew what she was thinking. Emma had known Candy would be at the cemetery that night.

Skylar dropped her stirrer with a clatter and put her hands on the table next to Detective Nakamura. "Here's another fact for you: Candy announced her upcoming protests on her social media feeds. She had lots of followers on Instagram, TikTok, and Twitter. Make sure all those people are on your list."

"Got 'em," he said morosely, holding up his little notebook. "Not that I wrote them in here, and not that I have their actual names. In most cases, I can only get user names. Comparing those against a list of people she protested against might reveal a connection."

"Tedious," I said.

"Welcome to police detective work."

Skylar plopped tacos on plates and set them in front of us. "Have you found any possibilities that are worth following up?"

Detective Nakamura eyed his taco. "I eat this, and I get a scone, right?"

"That's the deal," Skylar said, sitting down at the table. "Clean your plate."

"Okay." He took a bite and chewed. "Not bad at all," he said when he'd swallowed.

"You're welcome," Skylar said.

He was always surprised when vegan food tasted good. "Any possibilities worth following up?" I prompted him.

"Candy's brother Landon had lots of reasons to be vexed with her. Did you get the impression he could kill?"

"Yes," Skylar said at the same time I said, "No."

I waved at her to run with it.

"Over a number of years, Candy opposed three big beachfront developments Landon worked on — condos that would have sold for millions. The Coastal Commission denied permits for two of them, which must have hurt. She said he seemed like a decent person, but he was really a scoundrel. He had shady deals going all over the place."

"Shady, as in illegal?" Detective Nakamura asked.

"Maybe." Skylar said. "She didn't give many details. She did think he was bribing a couple of people on the Redondo Beach Planning Commission."

"Why didn't she report that to the police?"

"I got the impression that even Candy had limits on the wrath she was willing to incur. She was a little afraid."

The detective turned to me. "But you don't think she had reason to fear her brother?"

"She feared him. She started off talking about him killing her, but after she got drunk, she confessed that she wasn't really afraid he'd kill her. She had an odd idea that he saw her as his conscience. She'd oppose one of his developments, and in the end he admitted that it probably wasn't a good idea."

"That's a rosy view of their relationship," Skylar said.

"It's a view I heard from Candy," I insisted.

"Sometimes she felt that way but not always."

"And yet she spent years working for her brother, and he was willing to employ her. Why would Landon give her a job if he was angry enough to kill her?"

"So he could keep his eye on her? I don't know. That never made sense to me, that she worked for him."

"It only makes sense if he wasn't really bitter about what she did," I concluded. "And anyway, he couldn't be the perp because that was a woman."

"The oldest disguise in the book is for a man to dress as a woman," Detective Nakamura said.

"In a size 6 shoe? Not very many men can do that."

"Ah," the detective said. "Landon Longstaff has unusually small feet, judging by the photos I found online. I haven't been able to nail down the exact size yet."

"Okay," Skylar said, "Landon Longstaff stays on the list. What else do you have?"

"These were Candy's targets for protests in the past two years, companies and individuals," the detective said.

He handed his little notebook to Skylar. "Well, that's interesting," she said, pointing to the page. "Barb Vanderberry."

"You know her?" Detective Nakamura asked.

"Everyone knows her," I said before Skylar could. "Celebrity chef? Chain of big-deal restaurants? Wildly popular YouTube channel?" I looked at Skylar. "Is that everything?"

"Millions of followers," she said.

"Millions of followers," I repeated. "And there's a connection between Barb Vanderberry and Candy's brother."

We told him about Landon Longstaff wooing away Barb's husband.

"So, both Barb and Landon had motives to murder Candy," Detective Nakamura said. "But Barb also has a reason to murder Landon, so it seems unlikely that those two would conspire to kill Candy."

"Right," I said. "When they met at the nursery the other day, Landon said she owed him a hundred and twenty-something thousand dollars. It was part of a deal for a nice little piece of property that used to be a park in the marina. How Barb got her hands on that I don't know, but she mentioned Candy's protests complicated the deal and cost her a lot of money."

Skylar handed the notebook back to Detective Nakamura.

"Aren't you going to ask if we think she's capable of murder?"

"Well, do you?"

"Yes," we both said at the same time.

"It's unanimous," he said and put a star next to Barb's name. "We have two suspects with motive and opportunity. And we have Georgina Clark-Whyte in custody who had no motive to commit the actual murder in the cemetery. Then, we have a long list of possible suspects that will get longer if we work on it."

"Shouldn't Detective Duke have a team doing that?" Skylar asked.

"Like in TV mysteries? That would be good. Here in reality, he might have one person assisting him. But since he's got video of Georgina shooting Candy and strong circumstantial evidence against Emma, I doubt he's bothering to compile a thorough list. That's what I hear from people who've worked with him. He'll be certain that Emma assaulted Candy in the cemetery, and Georgina finished Candy off in Redondo Beach."

"So," I said. "if they prosecute the case like that, Emma could only be found guilty of assault."

Skylar stood up from the table. "But that's true only if nobody finds out Candy was dead when Georgina shot her." She took two scones from the refrigerator, put them in the toaster oven, and banged the oven door closed. "We've got to keep Candy under wraps."

I shot Skylar a don't-go-there look, but she was getting vegan butter for the scones. When I glanced back at Detective Nakamura, he was gazing at me with his usual implacable expression.

"Keeping Candy under wraps is possible only if we find her before the police do," he said. He continued to look at me intently before saying, "And then, the ethical thing to do would be hand her over to the police."

"Even if that means Emma is charged with murder?" Skylar asked.

The detective's lips tightened a bit. "It's still the right thing to do."

"And how will they react if they get their hands on Candy?" I demanded. "Here's a person who's clinically dead, who's still walking around. What will they do with her? Put her in a cell? They can't put her in the morgue. And what do they tell the public? Will they issue a press release — 'Hey, we caught a zombie'? Your ethical move would either make the police a laughing stock or set off public pandemonium, probably both."

He put his elbow on the table and bumped his fist against his mouth. "We have to find the real perp."

Chapter 19

In the fading light of evening, five zombies wobbled and lurched across the little patch of grass near our back fence. It was like an undead disco out there. A new female zombie in a scarlet dress had both hands gripped around the neck of the gray-haired zombie who'd tried to look in my window. They were twirling together across the yard while the others floundered this way and that, their arms waving like scarecrows on a carnival ride. When two zombies thumped together, they groaned, and little parts of them fell away onto the ground. At the rate they were clumping around and knocking each other to pieces, neither the grass nor the zombies were going to last long.

I closed the shades. At the moment, the zombies weren't my biggest problem. Let's see, what was trending today on my problem checklist? Was it finding Emma? Her father and Skylar were worried that something bad happened to her, but I was pretty sure she was hiding. She'd turn up eventually and get arrested.

In the meantime, what about the effects of the time-bashing spell we'd cast in the playground? The magic must have leaked out of the circle we'd drawn. What else had reversed besides the parts in our cars? Did nearby houses have their front yards in their backyards and their toilets on wrong? Did sewer lines still run in the right direction? And what could I do about problems like that? Go door to door and say, "Sorry my spell trashed your hood?"

Flopping onto the bed, I hugged a pillow. How about Killin? What was I going to do with him? Anything? He was a first-class problem, and not just because he'd convened a zombie rave in my backyard. He was a cheater. Like hell he needed to couple with the cutest young skirt in Redondo Beach to cure his magical wound.

Several groans erupted from the backyard. All the zombies must have bashed together. I threw the pillow against the wall and sat up.

Another man problem was Baldock. He was up to no good at the cemetery, but what did he want with the Waterway? The water dragon thing? If Skylar's mother finds out how the water dragon works, am I going to share that knowhow with Baldock? When the Waterway freezes over, I might do that.

I couldn't possibly cooperate with that villain, but I needed to know what he was up to. Also, I needed to stay away from his Minotaur. I shuddered. The grip of that thing's claw on my ankle cut at my memory like a knife. If being a superhero meant I had to face that nightmare again, did I want to be a superhero?

That left the murder case. Finding the perp had to be my biggest worry, the apex predator in my problem jungle. Detective Duke didn't seem likely to bring down that beast. Detective Nakamura said his fellow detective was too certain of his conclusions, and "Certainty lies to the eye of the beholder."

Detective Duke was certain that Emma had assaulted Candy in the cemetery. Was I certain he was wrong? In a way, this was my most vexing problem, the one that kept gnawing at me. Try as I might to push the possibility away, the specter of Emma dressed as a zombie came at me, grabbing at me like a Hollywood monster. The image was horrifying. I betrayed Emma every time I conjured it in my imagination. The only way to purge the horror was to find the real killer.

If only I knew how to do that. If only I knew how to take one step toward that goal.

I had to do *something*.

Flipping open my laptop, I checked Action News. They had no updates on Emma, but they did have an announcement that the police would allow the Angelus-Rosedale Cemetery to reopen starting tomorrow.

# # #

The night was cool, the cemetery silent — not the tomb-like silence of stopped time but the bug-chirpy calm of a summer evening among trees and shrubs and granite headstones. Donut guy was no longer guarding the cemetery gate. I climbed over and looked around, letting my eyes adjust to the dark. The police had given up on finding more evidence here. If we'd waited one more day, Detective Nakamura and I could have come in without stopping time.

I left the entrance road. The headstones that marked the way lay up ahead along a dark path. Pale marble angels lifted their wings on one side. I walked on. A black obelisk loomed on the other side, invisible until its polished surface reflected the faint light from the overcast sky. I turned, walked all the way around a headstone with an urn on top, and continued on a weaving course through the oldest part of the cemetery. The Waterway pool was still, reflecting the dim sky. I sat on the stone platform around the pool and waited.

Crickets chirped around me as the city murmured in the distance. Tiny wings beat overhead; bats were hunting. I crossed my legs and looked up. Down the hill, car horns blared. A motorcycle whined along the 10 freeway, going east. My left leg rocked up and down. I made it stop.

A red light glinted through the trees and headstones, brakes squealed. A truck engine roared and passed away into the distance. I tapped my foot. Off to my left, a scrape and a crunch in the gravel silenced the crickets. I stood up, my heart pounding. Drat, what if this was a zombie? I tiptoed along the edge of the pool and put one foot down on the stone path that led away.

The crunch of footsteps in gravel came closer until a dark form passed in front of the gray headstone at the far end of the pool. Silence returned. The crickets chirped.

"Baldock?" I said.

"It is you," he said. "You smell different."

"Um, thanks, I guess. You mean magically different?"

"Of course magically. You think I'm sniffing your alluring female hormones?" He laughed. "Silly girl."

He walked around the edge of the pool. I stepped back onto the stone platform.

"I thought you might have left when the police went away," I said.

"Did they leave? I've been busy. Something strange fell over this place 24 hours ago. The night was much longer than it should have been and orange."

"Oh?" I said using my innocent voice.

"For pity's sake, Hayley West, you're not fooling anyone." He straddled a fallen headstone and sat down. "That was a dramatic get-away you made the other night. I confess I worried you were drowning for a moment until it dawned on me that there's far more to this pool than I realized. And you know all about it, don't you?"

"Tell me what you want with it." I sat at the edge of the pool. Might as well have a comfy chat.

"I already told you. I want a way to extinguish the Shuilong."

"But the Shuilong is about extinguishing gunpowder, so what does it mean to extinguish the extinguisher? I don't get it."

"Ah, well, it's simple, really. Let's say someone has the Shuilong. This person could snuff out gunpowder, and that would stop guns from firing. Fel Dinaden craves this power, by the way, and you might agree with her that muzzling gunpowder is a nice idea, but think about it. The police would be powerless to stop criminals. Armies couldn't repel invaders. The world would fall into utter anarchy. If I can extinguish the Shuilong — drown the dragon, you might say — I can save the world from chaos. We can."

"Sounds good." I dangled my fingers in the pool. Who's this guy trying to kid?

"So you'll help me?" he asked.

"Sure. Why not. But tell me, what do you get out of this? A Nobel Peace Prize? MacArthur genius award?"

"I'm trying to be a better person," he said, using his innocent voice.

"Mm hmm," I said, trailing my fingers across the surface of the water. "And where does this Shuilong currently live?"

"It's not an actual dragon. I thought you'd figured that out."

"Thanks, you're right about that," I said in my thank-you-for-man-splaining voice. "Let me ask in a slightly more literal way. The

Shuilong is a power, right? And a person has this power? Who is that person?"

"We're not talking about a person here," he said impatiently. "We're talking about a concept, a potential calamity." He stood up, sat back down again. "We need to make sure that doesn't happen."

This guy is wigged out about a *concept*? "So Fel doesn't have the Shuilong and can't get it?"

"No!" he cried. "I mean no she does *not* have it, and she must not *ever* get it. I can't let that happen. You do see that, don't you?"

"Absolutely. Gotcha."

My fingers were swirling around in the pool, and the water was trying to tell me something. I held my hand still. The water was wanting to know why I was thinking about the Shuilong. I pulled my hand out and dried it on my T-shirt.

"Honestly, Baldock, I don't know how I can help you. I never heard of the Shuilong before you mentioned it. I don't have any idea what this pool can do about it."

"You could find out, I'm sure. But just tell me this. Is it possible to merge with this water using a spell? How did you get in there?"

"Through the Stoneway, and I was afraid of losing my life when I did it."

Even in the dark, I could see him slump. "So you have to be a walker of the Stoneway." He kicked at the ground. Stones clattered across the gravel between us. "Once again, you're the key to everything."

"That's me," I said brightly. "Key to everything."

I stood up and stayed tight to the edge of the pool. "Tell you what, Baldock. I'll see if I can find what you want. The Shuilong snuffer might be in there for all I know. Any idea how I might find out?"

"Look for it? I don't know." He slapped his hands on his thighs and stood up. "You can talk to stones. Perhaps you could *ask*."

"If I find out anything, where will you be? You're not going to stay in the crypt, are you?"

"I fixed it up," he said a little defensively. "You want to see?"

Great idea; take a little tour of the sorcerer's lair. "HGTV will probably do something on your remodel. I'll wait for that."

"I don't even know what that means, but it's amazing what a little magic can do for a cold, damp place. The biggest drawback is the zombies. They keep thumping against the door at odd hours, making me think the police have made it through the barrier I put up."

"Your barrier is a zombie magnet, right? What keeps them from piling up at your door?"

"How did you know that, about the attraction?" he asked.

"Just, ah, figured it out. Did you create the zombies?"

"Yes," he said, walking toward the big headstone at one end of the pool. He leaned against the stone. "I needed a way to find this place. The zombie spell worked great, but now I don't know how to turn them off, not that they're really on, if you know what I mean." He laughed. "I guess eventually everyone buried here will rise out of their graves and walk into this pool. Could get crowded in there."

Great. That included the mother of the three little witches. "Do you know if it was one of your zombies who attacked a woman several days ago?" I asked

"One of my zombies? Nah, these aren't real zombies, like in voodoo. They're dead, sure. They shuffle around and stink. But they wouldn't *hurt* anyone. This isn't Hollywood, after all."

"No, we're four miles south of there. You didn't happen to see a live person dressed as a zombie, did you?"

"As a matter of fact, I did," he said. "I only noticed because she stripped off her zombie clothes and put them in a bag. None of my zombies would do that."

I took a couple of steps toward him. "Did you get a look at her face?"

"Then I'd get up on the witness stand and point her out to the court? Fat chance. I didn't see her face anyway. I was hiding, you know? But I could see her feet, and I did see a gold glint from one of her shoes — a Gucci logo. I think she was wearing Gucci loafers."

# # #

Jumping in behind the wheel of my car, I looked in the back seat for zombies and then locked the doors, started the engine, and dashed around the block, checking the rearview mirror every two seconds. I parked in front of the playground where Skylar and I had cast the no-time spell and allowed myself a sigh of relief. Baldock hadn't followed me.

Houses were farther from the playground than I'd remembered, and the church across the street looked okay — except for the fence. Weren't the pointy bits supposed to be on top rather than the bottom?

In the playground itself, a few features were wonky. Yellow caution tape was draped around a double set of slides that were on backwards. A ladder on another slide had moved to the back of the structure, where it was impossible to get off the top of the ladder. I went in to use the restroom and found one of the sinks on backwards.

Skylar and I needed to find an undo spell.

# # #

When I woke up the next morning, Skylar was already in the kitchen chopping veggies for breakfast. I told her about visiting Baldock and figured she'd be upset with me. I should have waited until she put down the knife.

"Are you brain dead?" she said, wheeling around from her cutting board.

The tip of her big chef's knife caught my left forearm and sliced a neat furrow a little more than two inches long. The burning pain seared up my arm as blood spurted to the floor.

Excellent. Now she'll be all contrite and apologetic.

"And you sneak up on me with news like that when I'm using a knife? For heaven's sake, Hayley, have a care."

"You cut me!" I said, still looking for the turn toward contrition and apology.

"Sorry!"

She clonked the knife onto the counter, pulled a packet of herbs out of a cabinet, and slapped green stuff on my cut.

"Ow! Take it easy."

"Be still." She rested her hand on the cut. "*Sana hoc vulnus sine misericordia.*" She walked backwards around me, carefully stepping over the blood on the floor.

The cut burned worse. "Is that supposed to heal me or hurt me?"

"Yes and yes. What if Baldock had locked you in one of the crypts up there so you two could be neighbors? I wouldn't have the faintest idea where to find you."

"I left you a note, just in case."

"Well, *that* was thoughtful. How about telling me what you wanted to do so I could go with you? Or better yet, talk you out of it?"

"Exactly," I said, sitting down at the table. "You were all upset about Emma. I knew you'd argue about talking to Baldock. I needed to do something that felt like progress. Make it stop hurting." I held up my arm.

Skylar pressed her hand on the cut — much harder than was absolutely necessary — and said, "*Sana hoc vulnus.*" She walked backward all the way around me and the table.

"That's better. Thank you," I said. "I'm sorry I went without arguing with you first." At last, we'd reached Apologyville, or I had anyway.

"I forgive you, so long as you promise never to do that again. I apologize for slicing you open, but *honestly.*" Shaking her head, she went back to her cutting board but didn't chop anything. "Also, you got blood on my knife."

"Sorry. Want me to wash it for you?" I asked.

"I'll take care of it. You can clean up the mess you made on the floor."

"Yes ma'am."

"And don't pout." She washed the knife and chopped furiously at her veggies for a minute. Then, she put the knife down and was quiet for a minute. "Goodness," she said quietly.

She came to where I was sitting at the table feeling hurt and stupid. She put her arms around me. "Please, please, please, Hayley West, take better care of yourself and know that as much as I might love Emma or anybody else, I will always love you so much more."

That choked me up a little. And made me feel a little more stupid. Sometimes I forget I'm not in this alone.

Skylar cleaned up the mess on the floor and made me a vegan omelet with frilly mushrooms I'd never seen before. She assured me she wasn't trying to poison me. Breakfast was delicious.

She was not surprised to hear that Baldock had created the zombies and that they would never conk anyone over the head with anything. On the other hand, she was surprised to hear that Baldock had been aware of the no-time state, when the night was orange and lasted much too long.

She couldn't account for how that might happen but observed that I'd been lucky he hadn't noticed me in the cemetery while time was stopped. "That meet-up could have been a problem — you and Baldock and Detective Nakamura, all alone in the world."

"Would the detective have tried to arrest Baldock? That could have been interesting."

"Baldock would have turned him into a toad and walked away," Skylar said.

"I asked if he'd seen a fake zombie, and he had. He didn't see her face, but he thought she was wearing Gucci loafers."

"You mean, the perp was wearing Gucci?" Skylar asked, her eyes wide.

I shrugged. "According to Baldock."

"Yes!" Skylar pumped her fist in the air. "Wild horses couldn't drag Emma into the Gucci store."

Chapter 20

The front door was hardly open a foot before Detective Nakamura asked if we'd heard from Emma.

"If we had, we would have let you know on that little light-up thing you carry around," I told him. "Why don't you use your phone instead of driving all over creation?"

He walked in and shrugged. "The element of surprise is important in my line of work."

"I'm never surprised when you show up," I said, closing the door. "We're just finishing veggie omelets. How about a scone?"

"Do I have to eat a proper breakfast first?"

"Let's see what the chef says." I gestured him toward the kitchen.

"What happened to your arm?" he asked.

"Skylar sliced me open with a knife."

"On purpose?"

"Just about. I chatted up an evil sorcerer last night, and she thought that was taking too big a risk, which is correct."

"Does this evil sorcerer know Baldock Gunter by any chance?"

"Ah, not very well." That wasn't entirely untrue. "Anyway, I found out a couple of things." While I made coffee, I told him about the Gucci loafers on the perp and the reason why the zombies were harmless.

He sat down at the table caddy corner to Skylar, who was eating the last bite of her omelet. She swallowed.

"I did not cut her on purpose," she said.

"No problem," he said. "I'm off duty."

Skylar clicked her fork on her plate a couple of times. She got up to put her plate in the sink. From the refrigerator, she said, "Cranberry cucumber or orange thyme."

"Cranberry cucumber, please," he said.

"Excellent choice," she said with surprise. She put the scone in the toaster oven and sat back down at the table. "I'm worried about Emma."

"Yeah," he said. "I hardly slept last night. Yoshiko and I called all our relatives and anybody who might know Emma. No luck."

"Same here. I don't know what else to do."

"You guys found that little girl," he said. He took a sheer pale-green shirt out of his jacket pocket, unfolded it, and spread it out on the table. "I got this out of the laundry. You can use it. You know how to find her."

Skylar glanced at me. "You don't know what Hayley went through to find that girl."

"Look," I said, sitting across the table from him, "even if we find her, she'll just get arrested. She's probably staying with a friend, exactly the way Angelina Martinelli was. Would you rather have Emma sitting in a cell?"

"At least we'd know she's all right," he said.

I looked at Skylar. She pulled a face and shrugged.

"How about this," I said. "If we don't find Emma by midnight, we can cast the spectral bloodhound spell."

"Ooo, sounds scary," he said.

I got up from the table, keeping my clinched fists behind me. He didn't have to wonder whether the shark-dogs would be friendly. He didn't have to put his life on the line. I poured coffee, bonked the cup onto the table, and left the room.

Skylar found me in my bedroom half an hour later. "I chewed him out for you," she said, sitting on the bed next to me.

I put down the rock I'd been talking to. "If you want me to find Emma, I'll do it for *you*."

"We can't do it in broad daylight. Regular people can't see the shark-dogs, but they'd see you flying through the air. Besides, it takes a lot of prep work."

"So you want to do it tonight?"

She puffed a big breath through her lips. "No, not really. I want to find her, but I can't imagine anything's happened to her. She's just hiding, but it's nerve wracking whether we know where she is or not. Her father's worried sick about what'll happen to her."

"You suggesting I cut him some slack?"

"Uh, I'd never recommend cutting a man too much slack. He might be a little more reasonable now that I've read him the riot act. You want a raspberry scone?"

She knew that was my fave. "I thought you only had cranberry cucumber and orange thyme."

"One raspberry left. I wasn't going to give it to *him*."

When I walked into the kitchen, Detective Nakamura stood up and said he was sincerely sorry for presuming on my powers. "I had no idea you risked so much to find that little girl. You really are a hero."

The aw-shucks feeling I got from that made it impossible to be angry with him, which was infuriating. "Thanks," I said. I sat and looked at my phone.

Skylar slid the raspberry scone into the toaster oven, turned the selector dial, and pushed the start button. The oven beeped. She opened the refrigerator and rustled around in there with bags of vegetables or nuts or who knows what.

Detective Nakamura cleared his throat and shifted in his chair. "I want to interview a couple of Candy's friends, and I'm wondering if you'll go with me."

I looked up from my phone. "You want me to interview people with you?"

"Please. I can't do it officially, and if you take the lead, Candy's friends might be more willing to talk."

"It would be better if you take Skylar," I said. "She might know some of those people."

"I'll be late opening the café as it is," she said, glancing at the clock on the microwave. She put the scone on a plate for me and dashed out of the kitchen.

"When do you want to do these interviews?" I asked the detective.

"As soon as you finish that scone."

# # #

Anjani Kanu lived in one of those cookie-cutter L.A. apartment buildings that have two stories of units enclosing a small central courtyard. Anjani was at the back of the building on the bottom floor. After I knocked, she opened the door on a chain and began listing the kinds of people she was not willing to open the door for.

"Candy!" I said.

"What about her?"

"We're looking for clues into her murder."

"You're detectives?"

"No." Well, it was half the truth. Or since Detective Nakamura was on administrative leave, it was three-quarters of the truth.

"The police already arrested a woman in Redondo Beach."

"Yeah, well, we think that shooting in Redondo was faked. The police are still looking for the woman who assaulted Candy in the cemetery."

"Why haven't the police come to talk to me? Shouldn't they be the people looking for clues?"

"The police aren't doing a thorough job, I'm afraid."

"Well, no surprise there," she said, sliding the chain off the door. "Those guys are idiots."

I glanced at Detective Nakamura. His lips were a little tight. He didn't say anything.

"This is Ken. I'm Hayley," I said as we entered the apartment and looked around. "Wow."

The living room was lined with shelves of books and African art of the most dramatic kinds — carved wooden figures of people and animals, colorful woven baskets, metal plaques, and ritual masks. Some of the masks were terrifying.

"This is spectacular," Detective Nakamura said, turning slowly to take in the entire room.

"Thanks," Anjani said. "I'm writing my doctoral thesis on the influence of the Sahel figures on the southern masks. I'm afraid there's no place to sit in here. Let's go in the kitchen."

She made coffee and gave us each a cardamom seed to crush in the bottom of our cups. The effect was fantastic. I'd have to tell Skylar about this.

"We want to find out who Candy might have angered with her protests," I said. "One of those people might have killed her."

"That's going to be a very long list," Anjani said. "Have you looked at her Instagram?"

"We have that list," Detective Nakamura said, holding up his little notebook. "We're wondering if Candy mentioned anyone in particular that she had problems with. It might help narrow the search, especially anyone in the past month or two."

"Her brother Landon, certainly," Anjani said. "She was always moaning about him, and she must have been a thorn in his side."

"A big enough thorn to motivate him to murder?"

"Mmm." She studied the ceiling with one eye scrunched closed. "I wasn't around him all that much, but I did see him go ballistic about something she did at his apartment complex."

"When she let those units flood?" I asked.

"Before that. A tenant who worked for the city had a problem with his disposal, or was it his refrigerator? Maybe both those problems. Candy ignored him because she didn't like what he was doing in his job. I was with Candy in her car when Landon caught up with her in the parking lot. I thought he was going to flatten her right then and there."

"You mean, hit her? With his fist?"

"He had a cricket bat. He plays on a local team with some Brits, and he swung the bat right next to her head and smashed the rear-view mirror off her car. I was in the passenger seat. It's scary to have a guy smashing parts of a car you're sitting in, you know? He opened Candy's door, and she pulled back to close it. They tussled like that for a few seconds until Candy started the car and shot it into reverse with Landon hanging on. He let go, and we drove away with him shouting until we were too far away to hear him anymore. He was saying the tenant she ignored was important, and she was ruining his business. Like, a lot of money was at stake."

"This tenant worked for the city of L.A.?"

"Redondo Beach. Somebody in the planning department, or something like that. Candy said the guy was corrupt scum. She said that about a lot of people."

"Okay, and this bust-up happened recently?"

"Two? Maybe two and a half years ago? But about a month ago, Candy reminded me of it. She told me the tenant she ignored was doing some kind of deal for that local celebrity chef who thinks she walks on caviar. The one who wears the big emerald? That stone's got as many carats as her bra size." Anjani made a sizing-up-the-big-ones gesture around her own sizable breasts. "You know her?"

We nodded. "Barb Vanderberry," I said.

"That one. Candy was outraged by the underhanded dealings for Barb's house."

"Illegal dealings?" Detective Nakamura asked.

"Yes, some kind of scam involving the tenant who worked for the city and Candy's brother."

"Did she go to the police?"

"Candy wasn't a go-to-the-police kind of person." Anjani stood and poured a warm-up in our cups. "As I say, the police tend to be dolts, so there's no point. But she was pleased with herself for getting back at Vanderberry by vandalizing her house. Candy was cackling about it, saying, 'That great house of hers is going to be her own private hell. I guarantee it.'"

I put down my cup with a thunk. "Right! Barb told me someone was vandalizing her landscaping. So that was Candy."

"That was part of it. I don't know what all she did. Anyway, Barb Vanderberry should definitely be on your list."

"How about the tenant at the apartment complex who was part of the scam?" Detective Nakamura asked. "Do you recall his name? Any details about him?"

"She didn't mention a name. She usually described people as 'That jerk who did this or that' rather than names. She did say her brother was giving this guy his apartment rent free. It was a nice unit too, at least when the disposal and refrigerator were working."

On our way out, the detective and I gawked at the masks and figurines in Anjani's living room. She showed us a mask from West Africa and said she'd found evidence that the zombie concept might have originated there, long before it showed up in Haiti.

I pointed to a bizarre carving of a cat mounted on the end of a tree branch. The cat seemed to be going in two directions at once with an array of tiny creatures jutting out of it. Anjani told me it was from Ethiopia. "According to a tale from there, time is a cat."

# # #

Detective Nakamura and I talked to three more people that day. Two of them were regulars at the protests Candy organized, and all of them pointed accusatory fingers at her brother and Barb Vanderberry, as well as several others. No one knew the name of the apartment tenant who worked for the city of Redondo Beach.

"This is exhausting," I told the detective as he drove to our last interview. "How do you keep all this stuff straight in your head?"

He patted his breast pocket. "It's all in the little notebook, but don't you see the facts lining up in your little gray cells?"

"My brain, you mean?" I wobbled my head around. "I can feel the facts sloshing back and forth. They're not lining up, except for the two suspects we started with — Landon Longstaff and Barb Vanderberry. I'm hoping Barb is the perp, because I don't like her. That kind of thinking is probably frowned upon in the detecting biz, eh?"

"Generally considered bad form, yes." He stopped at a red light.

"How are the facts lining up in your little gray cells?" I asked.

"Barb seems like a good bet because of the perp's small footprint. We need to know Landon's shoe size. If it's much bigger than size 6, we can rule him out."

"How do you usually check a thing like that?"

"Get a search warrant and look in his shoes. Barring that, we might find a place where he walks and leaves clear footprints."

"Or I could sneak into his house."

The light turned green. The detective looked both ways and drove through the intersection. "People like that have alarm systems and video surveillance. You're sure to be caught."

"Oh, I don't know about that," I said.

"If you do the orange no-time *procedure*, I'll go with you."

"No, that one scares me. And all we need is a look at the guy's shoes. I can do that in a few minutes with another *procedure*."

"The orange one isn't terribly scary, once you understand your pants will go bass-ackward," he said. "And a trained eye might find other clues."

"Don't forget about the parts on your car, and that's not all." I told him about the other reversals I'd seen around the playground. "I need a way to put those right, and next time the effects could be more extreme. What if your head did an about face? So to speak?"

He drove in silence for a minute. Then he said, "That couldn't happen, could it?"

"The problem is, anything could happen, absolutely any crazy smash-up. Killin used to play me an old YouTube video of a guy jumping off a barn with wings on his arms. I didn't pay any attention and went ahead with whatever spell — excuse me, *procedure* — I wanted to try. The fact is, the outcome could be much worse than crashing into the barnyard. Magic could twist the world's pants around backwards or turn heads the same way. You can't know."

"Wouldn't it work better if you used a wand?" he asked. He put on his directional signal for a left turn.

I studied the side of his head as he made the turn. "You find me a wand. I'll wave it around and see what happens. In the meantime, I'm going to sneak into Landon Longstaff's house."

Chapter 21

Invisibility was my favorite spell, partly because I knew the ways it could go wrong. Skylar and I cast the spell in our backyard. Then, we jumped in her car, which was running again after $334 worth of repairs, and drove the couple of miles to Landon Longstaff's fancy house in Redondo Beach. Our plan was for Skylar to ring the doorbell, Landon to answer the door, and me to slip in and check his shoe size. I'd be out again in minutes.

Our plan did not include the possibility that Landon might be throwing a big party that night. We had to park half a mile away and walk past the Maseratis, Ferraris, and Teslas parked on the street. When we got within a hundred yards of the house, we could hear the music thumping. From the sidewalk in front of the house, we saw throngs of people through the windows, waving their drinks in animated conversation, dancing, or chasing one another through the house.

"I don't know if this is a good idea," Skylar said.

"Should make it easier. If I make noise, no one will notice."

"But with so many people milling about, they're bound to bump into you."

"Even sober people don't react much when they bump into me. I mean, do you ever expect to find an invisible person in the room with you?"

"Well, actually," she said, "when I toss a bad tomato at the compost bin and mysteriously miss or lose a bottle of olive oil that I just set down, I think you're messing with me."

"Nah, just Murphy's Law messing with you. Ready?"

She walked up the flagstone path to the front door and pressed the lighted button. We couldn't hear a bell over the thumping music — "Oo, oo, oo, oo, stayin' alive, stayin' alive."

"Nobody's going to hear the doorbell over the Bee Gees," I shouted in Skylar's ear. "Open the door, and I'll slip in."

"I'll wait on the sidewalk," she shouted back as she turned the knob.

At that moment, the door jerked open, taking Skylar along with it. Two extremely hunky guys in short-shorts came rushing past her, one chasing the other, both of them squealing with laughter. I stepped out of their way and then walked through the doorway, rubbing Skylar's arm on my way past. She closed the door behind me.

The foyer was frantic with people darting this way and that. Flattening myself against the wall, I edged into the enormous living room, where the scene looked like a freewheeling party from a Hollywood movie. Most of the people here were male. Taking a closer look, I could see several of the partiers who looked like women were also male, and vice versa. A couple of buff men wearing only thongs and bowties carried little trays of champagne glasses around the room, colored lights playing across their oiled bodies from a disco ball rotating on the ceiling.

Next to me, a staircase curved upward, crowded with people going up and down and leaning over the polished wood banister, shouting at the dancers below. I steeled myself and headed up the stairs behind a woman in purple heels with straps that wound halfway up her muscular calves. Besides the high-heeled sandals, she was wearing an orange hoodie and not much else. I stuck close behind her until she reached a couple of men in black silk pajamas who were making out against the banister. One of them reached his arm around to include the woman in the make out. She stepped backward to evade him, which put her left heel squarely in the tender part of my foot.

I yelped and pushed her forward. She clutched a double handful of one man's PJs. He grabbed for the banister but got his make-out partner's arm, and they both rotated sideways, taking the woman with them. As the three of them wavered on the steps above me and then slowly gyrated my way, I planted my right foot down a step, gripped the banister with my left hand, and leaned into the woman with my right hand on the step above me.

Skylar was right. This wasn't a good idea.

We tottered, halfway up the staircase, my face mashed into hoodie woman's panty-clad cheeks as I shoved upward with all my might. As we swayed there, the woman looked over her shoulder to see who was barging into her nether parts and saw no one. She shouted the F-word and did a little flamenco move up and down the steps to get away from the empty space that was butting into her. In the middle of this dance, her right heel stabbed into my right hand. I jerked my hand away and let out an F-bomb of my own.

We avalanched downward then, taking several other people with us. In the crushing pileup at the bottom of the stairs, I was sandwiched between the hoodie woman and an older gentleman in a blue tuxedo. As we untangled ourselves, the woman did the only sensible thing — she accused the tuxedo gentleman of groping her. Nonplussed, the man said he hadn't had the pleasure but would be delighted to grope her. She slapped him and immediately said she was sorry. He said it was no problem, could he get her a drink?

I made my getaway up the stairs, shoving past people recklessly. They didn't seem aware of anything except the person they were talking to, the rhythm of the music, and the drinks they worried about spilling as I jostled them.

At the top of the staircase, a broad hallway led left and right. Several people were gathered off to the right, enveloped in a cloud of funky-smelling smoke. I went left.

The searing pain in my hand was starting to throb, and my foot wasn't far behind in the unbearable hurt sweepstakes. I sat on the floor against the wall and felt the heel-sized hole in the back of my hand. It felt sticky. If any crime occurred in this house, my blood would be all over it. In a couple of hours, the blood would gradually become visible.

And what if I got seriously injured? No one could see what was wrong with me. I couldn't even see myself. I could bleed to death. Great. But not tonight. I wasn't going to bleed to death tonight.

Wrapping the bottom of my shirt around my hand, I stood up. Pain shot up my leg from my punctured foot. Tonight, I'd only hurt like hell.

Leaning my left hand on the wall for support, I hobbled to the first bedroom on the right. It was huge and dark. I reached for the light switch and stopped. A moan of pleasure or pain — I couldn't tell which — drifted from the bed. Why had they left the door open?

Across the hall, the door was halfway open, the light was on, and several people were writhing in the bed. A high-pitched voice kept saying, "Ow, easy now." I looked the other way as I gingerly went around the bed to the walk-in closet. Okay, to tell the truth, I was moving so slowly I had plenty of time to *glance* at the bed more than once, because what fun is being invisible if you can't spy on people? To be perfectly honest, if I hadn't been in so much pain I would have stopped and studied how that many people had gotten so tangled together. They must have used Google Maps to find their way into that.

By the time I'd labored slowly to the closet, I still wasn't clear how many people were in the bed, but I'd be coming back this way in a moment — a brief moment, it turned out. The closet was half full of cardboard boxes. Two shirts hung there, both pink. No shoes.

Five people, that's how many were in the bed. They'd need more than Google Maps to get out of that. Sometimes I feel like a babe in the woods.

I wobbled across the way to the first bedroom again, but the moans were still drifting out of the dark, so I struggled further down the hall and found an empty bedroom, or what I thought was an empty bedroom. When I flipped on the lights, I saw a man sprawled on the bed. He raised his head and blinked at the light, and then let his head drop and his eyes closed.

In the closet were shoes, lots of them, all arranged neatly on slanted shelves. None of them had shiny gold logo medallions on them, but they were all small. A pair of Nike running shoes was a size 5, likewise a beautiful pair of brown wingtips. Who wore wingtips anymore?

I looked around, pretending I had Detective Nakamura's trained eye. The blinding pain in my hand and foot made it a bit harder. All the clothes looked like what I'd expect in a gay guy's closet, all neat and tidy. Then, I spotted a two-drawer file cabinet in the corner. I rotated my good hand upside down to grab the handle and get my thumb on the latch. Is this what lefties had to do all the time? With the drawer open, I looked at a bunch of hanging folders and closed the drawer again. I'd make a mess of these papers poking through there left-handed, possibly with blood on me. Besides, I was in need of serious pain killers. I got up from looking in the file cabinet, and a spike of pain shot through my left side.

When I staggered back past the bed, two men sprawled there. I turned off the lights and let them sprawl in peace. People still packed the staircase, standing at the bannisters on both sides. My right foot howled in pain when I put weight on it, and my left side thundered with pain when I put weight on my good foot. I leaned heavily on people's shoulders as I limped down the stairs. Nobody seemed to mind, and I didn't care if they did.

Out the door as fast as I could hobble, gasping with every step, I asked Skylar to bring the car around and leaned against a tree in the front yard to wait, afraid that if I sat down, I wouldn't be able to get up again. The party raged on in the house behind me. I'm not really a Bee Gees fan, but it's hard to sit still with that stuff pushing at you. If only I'd been able to boogie. As it was, I twitched in place to the pounding beat while every movement pounded me with agony. Why not move? Standing still hurt about as much.

As soon as I fell into the car, I asked Skylar to cast a healing spell.

"I can't fix it if I can't see it," she said.

"Why not?" I demanded. "What's seeing it got to do with anything?"

"It's got to do with the way the magic works. I have to aim the magic at the problem."

"Aim it at heel-sized holes in my hand and foot," I said. "Just picture what that looks like, or you can feel the punctures with your finger if you want. And I think I broke a rib or two. You can't imagine how much it hurts."

"Sorry, you'll have to wait. Why were you crawling on the floor, for goodness sake?"

I told her what happened on the stairs. "You were right. Going into that crowd was a bad idea."

"And you could have done it without being invisible," she pointed out helpfully.

An hour later at home, I was woozy with pain and finally becoming visible again, starting with my clothes.

"Jeez!" Skylar said when my bloody shirt became visible. "Were you gored?"

"I wrapped my hand to keep from getting blood on everything," I said.

"You certainly got it on yourself."

When my flesh finally came into view, she said, "Wow, what a mess. Your hand is ripped up. Next time somebody heels you, don't pull your hand away."

"Just sit tight until they step off? That's your advice?"

"Well, look what you did!" She held my hand up to my face.

I fixed my eyes on the ceiling. "Looking at it isn't likely to make it hurt less, which is my main goal in life at the moment. Please fix it."

"You might need professional help. Definitely stitches." She made distressed noises as she dabbed at my hand with washcloths she'd wet and "sterilized" in the microwave. The growing pile of red washcloths didn't make me feel any better.

"Can't you do stitches with magic?" I asked. "I don't want to go to the ER."

"Putting in stitches is easy enough. It's knowing what to stitch that's the issue here. Your hand has lots of moving parts that you probably want to keep moving. Have you tried wiggling your fingers?"

"I could try giving you the finger," I gasped as she moved my hand around.

"Move your thumb," she commanded. "Now the first finger..."

She went through each finger in turn, and I moved them all with the aid of extreme swearing. Then, she made me grip her hand. She's a cruel person with no mercy, and I told her so.

"All the moving parts are still moving, pretty much," I concluded. "Just close it up, okay?"

"Do you mind if your pinkie ends up attached to your thumb?"

"Not really."

She didn't bother me with any more questions for a while — a long while in pain minutes. When she'd closed everything up and cast a spell to put a small dent in my pain, we called Detective Nakamura. I told him Landon's shoe size.

"That's awfully small for a grown man," he said. "His feet would be a bit tight in a women's 6, but it's possible. Landon Longstaff could be our man, especially since he lied about where he was the night of the murder. I'll tell you more in a minute."

We waited for him to continue. After half a minute, Skylar looked at her phone and saw that Detective Nakamura had hung up. Half a minute after that, the doorbell rang.

"Who could that be?" I said in mock bafflement as Skylar got up to answer the door.

"Well waddayaknow, it's Detective Nakamura," she called from the front door.

"What happened?" he said in alarm when he saw me on the sofa, bandaged hand and foot, mostly visible.

"I got walked on at Landon's party." I told him the whole story. Well, I ran through it as quickly as I could, and it wasn't quite the whole story. I didn't include the part about being invisible when it happened. If he was looking at me closely, he must have seen a few gaps in my ears and fingers, but he didn't say anything.

He rubbed his hand and grimaced when I got to the part about the heel coming down on me. Apparently, that kind of injury was a valid reason for moving his face into a different expression.

"That must hurt," he said.

"All in the line of duty," I said. "Skylar put some herbs on it."

"You should apply for Workman's Comp."

"You said you'd tell us more about something. Landon?"

"Yes, a detective with our local department interviewed Landon just after Candy was attacked," Detective Nakamura said, still rubbing his hand. "A friend in the department told me the alibi Landon gave for the night of the murder. You must not repeat any of this — ever — understand?"

Skylar and I nodded yes.

"Landon said he was home with his boyfriend the entire evening. But here's the interesting part. I just talked to a woman who saw the boyfriend at a concert that night."

"So the boyfriend lied about Landon being home," I said.

"Nobody ever bothered to confirm Landon's alibi, so the boyfriend didn't even need to lie. That's how well run this case is."

Detective Nakamura's face turned a distinct shade of angry red. "Anyway, Landon's alibi is no good. He could have been anywhere, and no one bothered to check. I asked someone to look into it — do not repeat this either — and Landon's phone records show he left the house and then turned off his phone."

Skylar pumped her fists. "So he must be the perp! We got him!"

"Steady on," the detective said. "We have him in a lie about where he was. That's all. People lie for all sorts of reasons."

Skylar put her hands down. "Well, he must be up to no good. That's what I think."

"And if I were handling this case, I'd confront Landon Longstaff with his lie to see if I could find out what he was up to. As it is, we're stymied unless I can convince someone in the department to take this on. They've stuck their necks out for me already, so I hate to ask."

"What if Skylar and I talk to him?" I suggested. "He told us he wants to find out what happened to his sister. We could strike up a friendly conversation about it and then pounce on his false alibi."

"Which you can't mention to anyone!" Detective Nakamura reminded me. "Besides, you don't look like you'll be doing a lot of pouncing any time soon."

"Oh, yeah," I said, holding up my bandaged hand and foot, which sent pains shooting up my arm and leg and all through my rib cage. Laying back down hurt more. When would I be able to walk again?

Skylar got up and paced in front of the window. "I'm willing to talk to Landon. I can't guarantee it will be a friendly conversation."

"If you can't let on that you know his alibi is fake, what will you say?" Detective Nakamura wanted to know.

"I could say somebody I know was at the concert where the bf was seen. What concert was this?"

"Red Hot Chili Peppers, but you still can't know that blows his alibi, because the alibi is part of confidential police info. I can't emphasize that too much."

"Anyway," Skylar said, sitting back down again, "nobody I know would go hear the Chili Peppers."

"What do we do then?" I asked.

"Please figure out where Emma is," he said. "I'm following up on several other people who might have motives to go after Candy."

He stood up and took a step toward the sofa. His hand came up, and I thought for a moment he was going to pat me on the head. The hand went back down again.

"Hope you feel better," he said.

"Thanks."

Starting toward the front door with Skylar, he took out his phone and said to her, "The Chili Peppers are a good band."

Skylar looked over her shoulder at me and shrugged.

At the door, Detective Nakamura made a choking noise.

"What's wrong?" Skylar asked.

Facing the other way, he leaned against the door. Was he having a heart attack? I swung my legs off the sofa and leveraged myself up on my good foot.

"What is it? What's wrong?" Skylar asked again, her hand on his arm.

"No," he choked out. He held up his phone, looking at it in disbelief. "This, this message. It's encrypted. From a detective downtown. He got her."

"The detective found Emma?" Skylar asked. She tried to look at his phone, but he was holding it in the air, up and away from him.

"Duke found her, arrested her."

"Oh," Skylar said. "That's too bad. It was only a matter of time, though. We'll just have to deal with it, keep on dealing with it. Don't worry."

"But." He was pale as a ghost. He held the phone toward her, his eyes wide, lips trembling. "She confessed."

Chapter 22

Skylar and Detective Nakamura went to find out where Emma was being held, leaving me on the sofa with a broom. The broom wasn't very good company, but neither was I. When the broom was bored senseless, I used it as a crutch to tilt myself off the sofa and hop to my bedroom where I threw my laptop and then myself on the bed. I'd meant to lower myself gently, but for some reason, it's hard to remember that your cracked ribs are going to seize up with pain halfway through the lowering.

After a minute, I was able to focus my eyes again and see my laptop screen. Skylar's mother had emailed photos she'd taken of a grimoire that might help with the zombie problem. She said the symbols on the blackened leather cover meant "awakened death." She figured it was about either resurrecting people from the dead or dealing with zombies, which was kind of the same thing while being totally different. Either way, she hadn't gotten around to translating this book into English because she wasn't eager to deal with dead people.

Me neither. Unfortunately, my backyard was filling up with them — a dozen at last count.

The spells in the grimoire were in multiple languages, by which I mean multiple languages simultaneously. A sentence might start in Latin and finish in Old English with a few words of Medieval German or Gallic dialect in the middle. Pasting these sentences into Google Translate gave me worse gibberish than what I put in.

I had to search for each word's meaning and then make sense of the zoo of definitions I ended up with.

As Skylar had taught me, if it made sense, it wouldn't be magic, so I was wasting my time trying to make sense of this stuff, wasn't I? But what good is time if you can't waste some of it? What did it even mean to waste time? Time is money. Who decided that? Why can't time be something else? Time is a cat.

Time was slipping by. The grimoire was waiting.

An hour later, I hadn't heard from Skylar and Detective Nakamura about Emma, but I had "translated" parts of spells for reviving dead apple trees, chestnut trees, and basil plants. I wasn't holding out much hope for a zombie cure, but if we ever needed to perk up wilting basil, we were set.

An hour after that, I still had no word about Emma. The grimoire was now giving me animal revivals. If you suspected your squirrel was dead, you could "draw the buzz up out of a hive and the curl from the fiddlehead" to spring your squirrel back into the acorn-gathering biz. After that came spells for reviving dogs and goats.

By the time Skylar and Detective Nakamura came back, I was woozy with pain. Words and animals brought back from the dead were rampaging around the inside of my head, beating thunderous torment into my temples.

Emma was held at a downtown lockup after being arrested in Redondo Beach — at home. Her mother had been hiding her. While we'd been searching all over, most of that time Emma had been sitting in her own bedroom. She'd confessed that she went to the cemetery to confront Candy but not to harm her.

"The lawyer will get her out some time tonight," Detective Nakamura told me. "But listen to this. When I was asking around about Emma, a detective mentioned he was investigating a guy on the Redondo Beach planning commission, and this guy has ties to Landon Longstaff."

My head was spinning and trying to think about this news didn't help. "That's nice," I said, looking vaguely in the direction of my bandaged hand. "Did you see Emma?"

"They wouldn't let us see her," Skylar said. "They're questioning her. The lawyer is in there."

She turned my head with her hand so she could search my face. She frowned and left the room.

Detective Nakamura sat on the corner of the bed. "Finding out about the planning commission guy is important because Landon might have been with this guy the night of the murder."

I tried to focus on him. "So Landon might have a real alibi to replace his fake one?"

"Exactly. This could make or break one of our main suspects. We need to check it out."

"Hayley's not checking out anything right now," Skylar said as she came back into the room. "She's going to sleep and leave all her hurt behind for a while."

"But I'm not done translating the book," I protested without enthusiasm.

"The book will wait." She draped a white cloth over my head that smelled of sage and fenugreek and placed her hands on top of the cloth. "Morpheus, son of Hypnos, this child has entered the temple of night to be led onward past the clamor of waking."

"Will she step through the white gates?" asked a voice from the air.

"What's that voice?" asked Detective Nakamura.

"Shh," Skylar hissed.

Almost inaudible, a deep tone resonated out of the distance. My eyelids drooped and closed.

"She has her foot upon the white threshold," Skylar said.

"Does she heed the tolling bell?" the voice asked.

The deep tone pealed again, closer now.

"Until dawn," Skylar said.

"How far will she follow the whims of Morpheus?"

"Into oblivion," I answered slowly.

"Now, she may drowse," Skylar said, laying me back onto the bed, "and slumber in the arms of Morpheus."

My body felt weightless and then drawn upward. The last thing I remember before losing consciousness was Detective Nakamura's voice.

"Can I get some of that?"

# # #

At first light, I woke from a dreamless sleep to find all my pain waiting for me. I struggled out of bed using the broom as a crutch. Skylar had wound an ace bandage around my rib cage, but my side stabbed with burning pain at every movement.

As I was working slowly along the hall to the bathroom, Detective Nakamura came out of the guest room in just his pants.

"Sorry," he said, gesturing for me to go ahead. "Skylar knocked me out last night with that Morpheus routine. Marvelous."

"Great while it lasts." I limped into the bathroom, leaning on my broom, gasping with each agonizing step.

While the detective and I had been reposing peacefully in oblivion, Skylar had tossed and turned, worrying about Emma. She'd gotten a text from the lawyer a little after midnight saying he couldn't get Emma released until morning at the earliest. The idea of precious Emma sitting in a jail cell all night was almost unbearable.

Standing next to the kitchen table, Detective Nakamura was incandescent with rage. "Harris Duke just wants to lean on her. All he has is circumstantial evidence, and he's hoping she'll give him more." He kicked the table leg.

"Easy, Dad," Skylar said from the stove.

"It's only assault!" he shouted. "He has no reason to hold her for that."

He thumped himself into a chair and put his face in his hands.

I wanted to put my hand on his shoulder and tell him everything would be okay, but I was anchored to a chair on the other side of the table by a heavy load of hurt. "Everything will be okay," I said without the hand on his shoulder. "We just need to find the perp."

He lifted his face from his hands and wiped at his cheeks. "How can we find the perp when I can't do proper detective work? I need to put Landon Longstaff in an interview room and get serious with him. Same for Barb Vanderberry. What was she doing the night of the murder? Nobody knows. Nobody's interviewed her at all. Nobody's doing proper detective work!" He pounded his fist on the table.

"How about if we sneak into Barb's house? We can at least find out what size shoe she wears."

"If I'm caught breaking and entering somebody's house, they'll lock me in the big house for years, and my career as a detective will be over." He drummed his fingers on the table. "Of course, that would be better than having Emma on trial for murder. Maybe I'll do that. Yes." He pounded his fist again. "I'll do that."

"Look, you don't have to risk being caught," I said. "We can stop time, and no one will know."

"I thought you decided that was too dangerous. It must push us into a parallel universe or something. Who knows what effect that might have on the real universe?"

"I don't know about a parallel universe. The time thing does mess up the playground, but we might be okay if we keep the magic circle intact."

"Yeah," he said, as the concept of a magic circle sailed over his head. "In any case, you don't look fit to sweep the floor with that broom you're going around with. You'll be out of action for weeks."

We sat in hopeless silence for a minute until Skylar put breakfast in front of us.

"Risking your career to find out Barb's shoe size hardly seems worthwhile," she said as she sat at the table.

"So, the only option for moving forward is a really bad one," I pointed out in an effort to make sure the situation seemed hopeless to all of us. Judging by the hangdog looks on the faces of Skylar and Detective Nakamura, they were clear on that. "Sorry," I added.

Nobody said anything for a few minutes while we shoveled vegan breakfast into our mouths. They ate, anyway. I tried eating with my left hand and watched every forkful fall back onto the plate. Switching to my bandaged right hand, I held the fork sideways and got one excruciating bite into my mouth. Skylar and Detective Nakamura started arguing about the identity of the murderer. I put my fork down and told myself not to cry. After a couple of minutes staring at my food, I gave up trying to hold it back. I was such a loser. The tears fell onto my uneaten breakfast.

The next thing I knew, strong arms came around my shoulders from behind, gathered up my arms gently from the table, and enfolded me in a comforting embrace. I cried harder for a couple of minutes. What a miserable situation this was. I hurt all over. I couldn't do anything to help Emma, who was locked in a cell. Some hero I turned out to be. I was useless. My body shook with sobs.

When I was tired of crying — What good did crying do? — I patted Skylar's arm to say thanks for the hug, only to hear Detective Nakamura's voice in my ear, whispering, "Everything will be all right." He released his embrace, gripped my shoulder for a moment, and sat down.

I wanted to leave the room and go hide until I stopped hurting, but I hurt too much to get up. I hung my head over my food and saw that my plate was gone. In its place was a bowl of breakfast with a spoon.

"See if it's easier to eat with the spoon," Skylar said.

It was. I felt like a child spooning my food with my left hand, but unlike a lot of things at the moment, it worked.

Detective Nakamura ate a scone and then left for downtown to find out if he could see Emma. Skylar helped me to the sofa in the living room and cast a spell that was supposed to reduce the pain. It worked about as well as an ibuprofen. She left for work, promising to call and see how I was doing, but two hours later she was back home.

"What's wrong?" I asked in alarm. "Why aren't you prepping for lunch?"

"Detective Nakamura called. He said we both need to come see Emma."

"No way," I told her. "I hurt enough just sitting here. In fact, before you go, how about knocking me out for a few hours."

"Can't run the Morpheus spell until 24 hours after the last time, and Detective Nakamura said specifically that you have to come. He said it's important."

Why was it important to torture me? Skylar told me he wouldn't say, but he gave instructions for us to bring Emma's mother. We hadn't seen Yoshiko since we got clues that she was probably a witch. The idea made her uncomfortable, Emma told us. Yoshiko didn't want to talk about it.

On the way to the downtown lockup, we didn't talk about much except Candy's murder. Every bump we hit jarred my foot, and after we passed an old truck, I had a coughing fit that drove daggers of pain through my ribs.

By the time we got to the lockup, I was done with this expedition. No way was I hobbling into the jail. Skylar and Yoshiko went in without me, and a few minutes later, Detective Nakamura came out with a wheelchair.

"Get in," he ordered.

"No."

"I have a couple of friends in uniform here. If I ask them to, they'll arrest you."

"For what?"

"Being obstinate on public property."

"Look who's talking," I said.

"Just please trust me on this," he pleaded. "Emma wants you to do something for her."

"Something? Could you be more specific? You're not wanting me to stop time in there, are you?"

"No, no," he said. "That's an outrageous idea."

"Wouldn't solve anything."

"Yes, we have to leave Emma in there and solve the problem out here, and that's why you need to come in for 20 minutes. Just give me that. Please."

I huffed a couple of times at this nonsense and let him pull me out of the car onto my good foot. He sat me gently in the wheelchair and rolled me into the building at a trot. When we were inside, he whispered, "People will be watching, but the microphones are off."

He nodded to an officer, who rolled me to an interview room and parked the chair at a small table. Looking into the big mirror to my left, I saw myself looking back. As Detective Nakamura said, people were watching. What a sorry sight I was. Why was I doing this? When could I go home? Why did I let myself get talked into these stupid ideas, like I could do anything for Emma by being here.

The door at the end of the room opened. I fidgeted in the wheelchair. Then, a guard led Emma through the door. She was wearing an orange jumpsuit. Her hands were cuffed. She sat down across from me. She looked like she hadn't slept in days. I opened my mouth to speak and couldn't think of anything good to say.

"You look awful," she said.

"So do you," I said. "Orange is not your color."

"It's not the new black as far as I'm concerned. Thanks for coming. I know it's painful."

"Your father said you want me to do something for you? Something like find the perp?"

"Yes," she said. "And you can't do that if you're laid up with these injuries. So, I want you to give them to me."

I stared at her blankly. What was she talking about?

"Since I was a little girl," she said, "whenever I've skinned my knee, or cut my finger, or come down with a cold, my mother has taken away the hurt. I've never suffered pain or illness for more than a few hours in my entire life."

"Your mother is a healer. That's wonderful. We thought she was magic." I shifted in the wheelchair, trying and failing to get comfortable. "Wait a minute, did your father know your mother was doing this?"

"Yes, he did," Emma said with a half smile.

"So despite your father's hard-headed denial of the 'irrational,' he knew all along that magic is possible."

"It upsets him to admit it. He tries to explain it with weird physics principles he sees on Nova. But yeah, he knows a little about magic."

"That explains why he didn't totally freak out when we stopped time, although finding his pants on backwards did upset his world view. Nova couldn't sort that one out. Had to be magic. Your mother's magic sounds like the best kind of magic."

Emma chewed her lip for a moment. "It is wonderful, but there's a catch."

"Of course," I said. "There's no free lunch with magic. It always comes at a price."

"Well," Emma said and stopped. She glanced at the one-way glass next to us. "The price in this case was that my mother took on my injuries and illnesses. She took them from me, and gave them to herself."

A mother's love. That's what a mother would do — take her child's suffering — if she could. Except for my mother, who abandoned me when I was five. What kind of cosseted child was this in front of me, a girl who'd hardly ever known pain in her life because her mother took it upon herself? I sat looking at her with my mouth opening and closing, forming words that emerged soundless. And why was she telling me this? Then the reason dawned on me.

"You want your mother to take my injuries." I shook my head. "I can't possibly let her do that."

"No," Emma protested, blushing. She glanced at the one-way glass again. "I know what you must think of me. And you're right. I am a spoiled child. But I don't want my mother to take your injuries. She can transfer them to anyone. I want her to give your wounds to me."

I shook my head. "Emma," was all I managed to say. This girl, wholly unused to pain, wanted to take all my pain.

"You have to do this for me," she said.

"But I've got broken ribs. Any movement hurts. A cough sends daggers through my body. Any weight on my right foot is unbearable. My hand is torn up and useless." I waved my bandaged right hand.

"That's why you have to give all these problems to me," she insisted. "I'm stuck in here. I can't do anything. You can help me, but you have to be able to move. I need you to help me. Don't you see?"

The door opened at the far end of the room, and the guard stepped in. "Two minutes," he said.

Emma leaned forward. "When I walk away from the table, I'll fall down. If you agree to let me take your injuries, look into the mirror and nod yes. My mother is on the other side. She'll do the rest."

She stood up and pushed her chair back. The guard opened the door at the far end of the room.

"Please," Emma whispered and took a step away from me and another step and crashed to the floor.

I stared at myself wide-eyed in the mirrored glass, undecided. The guard let the door close and rushed to help Emma up. If it was this hard for me to let go of my wounds, how hard would it be for Yoshiko to give them to her daughter? Yet Yoshiko was willing. I looked back into the mirror and nodded yes.

The briefest of violet flashes lit the room. The guard looked at the ceiling, puzzled. Emma groaned on the floor, and said, "My hand. Help me."

The guard crouched next to her. He lifted her arms, still joined at the wrist by handcuffs. Blood was pouring from her right hand.

"How did this happen?" he asked. "Wait here."

He ran out of the room. I stood up and felt no pain. Emma looked at me and mouthed, "Thank you." She lifted her face and looked toward the ceiling, her eyes shining with tears in the harsh white light.

The guard came back with a woman carrying a first aid kit. Someone behind me put a hand on my arm and pulled me away.

Chapter 23

Half-eaten vegan tacos lay abandoned on our plates. Detective Nakamura paced around the kitchen table. He clutched a green cloth napkin in his hand and waved it when he made the same point he'd made three times before.

"Landon Longstaff is our top priority," he said.

Skylar and I nodded agreement for the fourth time.

"So, you need to interview Landon," Skylar said. "But you can't, and we haven't figured out a way to get anyone else to do it. I don't see what else we can do to check him out."

"We can search his office," the detective said. "He might have records about what he did the night of the murder if he was involved in some financial deal with the planning commission guy. Really, the best we can hope for is to eliminate him as a suspect so we can focus our efforts elsewhere. It's all we can do."

"You want to stop time so we can get into his office?" I asked. "That's risking big problems just on the off chance we might find some little clue in filing cabinets that probably don't exist. The important stuff will be on computers, and none of us knows how to hack into them."

"I took a class on reading spreadsheets," Detective Nakamura said.

Skylar looked at me. I shrugged. "Okay," she said to him. "You're in charge of data forensics, including the step where you have to guess the user's password. Hayley and I will be in charge of stopping time."

"We need a newt and a frog for that," I told him.

"And a cat who's willing to let you hold her," Skylar added.

"Yoshiko already said she's willing to go find the amphibians if you tell her where to look. She needs something to do."

"I can't imagine how hard that was for her, giving Emma my injuries," I said.

"She didn't realize how bad they were," he said. "That was because I didn't realize how bad they were, and *that* was because you were so stoic about the pain you were in. You should have been sedated in the hospital, and there you were translating some book." He threw his hands in the air in exasperation.

"Excuse me for not complaining enough," I said.

"I thought you complained more than enough," Skylar said.

"Thanks," I said.

"All right," Detective Nakamura said. "It's done now. Yoshiko will forgive me in a day or two, and by then we'll have made progress on solving this case."

He stood up and looked at his phone. "I'm having coffee with the detective who's investigating the connection between Landon and the guy with the planning commission. Maybe he'll have info for me."

"I'll tell Yoshiko where to look for newts and frogs," Skylar said. "Then I need to make sure the café has food for tomorrow."

"Wait a minute," I said, standing up and balancing on my newly painless foot. "I'm all healed up with no place to go. What can I do to help?"

Detective Nakamura put his phone back in his pocket. "When we have the parts for stopping time, you and I can go into Landon's office. Until then, I don't know. Find a cat."

"Keep working on that book," Skylar said, pointing behind her hand at the backyard.

At last count, we had 18 zombies milling around back there. They'd worn out the grass in the little area they were crisscrossing. I was starting to think they might walk themselves back into the ground if they kept on. Wishful thinking.

"I'll take the book with me to the nursery. Might as well catch up on some work while I've got the chance."

# # #

The chaotic state of the nursery made me feel like I was useful for something. Without me, my employees put new plants in random places, labeled begonias as petunias, and let the purple fountain grass dry up. It's not that they didn't know better. They simply felt overwhelmed by all the little tasks that needed attention. I understood that feeling really well.

In only an hour, I got a lot of problems sorted out while helping several customers. (Mrs. Jenkins: "These are the most unusual petunias." She was disappointed to learn they were begonias but bought them anyway.)

I was ringing up a customer at the front desk when Detective Nakamura drove into the parking lot. He gestured for me to come to his car. I waved the customer's MasterCard, and he gave me the hurry-up signal.

Some customers get through checkout with nary a word. Other customers want to discuss the fascinating world of plants at some length or tell you about the surprising behavior of their Aunt Sally. While Detective Nakamura tapped his foot impatiently, I listened to my customer rattle on about how her Aunt Sally had put nasturtiums in the luncheon salad, except that the aunt had accidentally plucked azalea blossoms, and everyone got a tiny bit poisoned.

When I was finally free, the detective asked if I wanted to listen in on an interview with the guy on the planning commission who was under investigation. I said I did, and the detective asked if we could do it "where the scones are."

"You're going to interview this guy at my house?" I asked, getting into the car.

"No, I'm going to eat a scone at your house. The interview is at the station, and we're listening in on the phone."

"You can get a scone here at the café. All we've got at home is the cranberry cucumber."

"I like those, and we need to keep this strictly private. A buddy of mine, Detective O'Neil, is going to leave his phone on while he interviews the planning commission guy, and that's kind of against the rules. We don't want to broadcast this in the café."

He pulled out of the parking lot. "I just had coffee with O'Neil and found out he had a casual chat with Landon's boyfriend this morning. So listen to this. O'Neil said to me, 'That guy has the smallest feet I've ever seen on a grown man.' And I go, Landon Longstaff? And O'Neil goes, 'No, his bf. Nice looking wingtips, though. Just awful small.'"

"No!" I said. "You mean I was looking at the shoes in the boyfriend's closet?"

Detective Nakamura didn't bother to confirm my mistake. He turned at the corner my house was on and drove into the driveway.

"Does that mean the boyfriend is a suspect?" I asked as I got out of the car.

"If we knew some reason why the bf might want to kill Candy, he could be a suspect."

"He might have been doing Landon a favor," I pointed out. "I think the bf should be an honorary suspect. Otherwise, I got injured at that party for nothing." I unlocked my front door.

"All right, the bf is on the list. Hold on." He put his phone to his ear. "Yeah, okay, good. Will do." He touched his phone's screen a couple of times and said to me, "O'Neil's going into the office of the planning commission guy now. The guy's name is Dominic Dettmer. I'll keep my phone on mute, but O'Neil is wearing one earbud so I can ask a question if we really need to know something."

While I was making coffee and warming up a scone, we listened to Detective O'Neil putting questions to Dominic Dettmer about his role with the Redondo Beach city government and his relationships with various people. These questions went on and on. Dettmer's answers were brief and to the point.

"This is all basic stuff," I complained. "Why take all this time for such basic, boring questions?"

Detective Nakamura swallowed a bite of scone. "All part of the strategy. You ask a series of questions you know the person will answer truthfully. You get them accustomed to answering truthfully and specifically. You learn what the person looks like when they're doing that. Then, you slip in a challenging question. That will happen any minute now."

From the phone, we heard, "And what was the dollar amount you got from Longstaff Development last year?"

"I got... nothing. I — what do you mean?" Dettmer stammered.

"Classic," Detective Nakamura said.

"The $95,990 you paid on May 16 of this year for a Tesla Model S?"

"Why would you question that? It's, it's an environmentally sound investment." Dettmer went on to cite climate change and Redondo Beach's low-lying vulnerability and several other issues.

"See how his answers are beginning to wander?" Detective Nakamura said. "O'Neil doesn't know that the Tesla money came from Longstaff, but putting those questions together makes Dettmer feel like the connection is known. O'Neil suspects that Dettmer got payoffs in Bitcoin. We can't trace those, so people think the money is safe and get careless when they take it out of crypto."

Detective O'Neil calmly asked about a series of financial transactions, and Dettmer got increasingly defensive in his rambling answers. The detective then began asking about occasions when Dettmer met with Longstaff. Dettmer explained that his job involved interactions with developers.

"Your last meeting with Landon Longstaff was June 27? In the evening?"

That was the evening of Candy's murder. Dettmer didn't say anything for a moment. We were starting to wonder if the phone connection had dropped out, when he said, "Yes."

"Do you typically have your interactions with developers in the evening, commissioner Dettmer?"

"Sometimes." He was silent for another moment. "Sometimes they are."

"And that particular meeting lasted several hours. Is that right?"

"Yes."

"Lots to talk about." Detective O'Neil said.

"Yes," Dettmer conceded.

"Commissioner Dettmer, we're investigating Landon Longstaff for a series of questionable transactions stretching back at least six years. One transaction in particular is the acquisition of a piece of property in the Redondo Beach Marina that used to be Moonstone Park and is now the home of Barbara Vanderberry. Are you familiar with this property?"

"Yes. Yes, of course. Look, look, I can help you with this. I can fill you in about Longstaff's tactics, the way he pressures people, coerces people, the way he works his business, if you just keep my family out of it. Keep me from, you know…"

"You're help is much appreciated," O'Neil said. "I can't make any promises about an agreement, of course, but cooperation will usually put you in a much better position. Let's talk about a few more specifics that we can take to the DA's office for their input, shall we?"

Detective Nakamura picked up his phone, touched the mute button, and whispered, "Perfect." He disconnected and put the phone down. He looked at me. "There it is."

"Why didn't Dettmer ask for a lawyer?" I asked.

"He is a lawyer, but yeah, he has a fool for a client. He should have asked for counsel. He'll probably claim that Landon blackmailed him."

"But *he* was getting the money. Isn't the blackmailer supposed to get the money?"

"In this case, the blackmailer gets favors and pays money that ensures the blackmailee has to continue providing favors. Once they start, they're locked in. In any case, implicating Landon in this deal gets him off the hook for murder. Good alibi."

"Good/bad alibi," I said. "We don't need to sneak into Landon's office any more, unless you want to do a favor for Detective O'Neil."

"Nah, he can handle his own case. We need to focus on Barb Vanderberry."

# # #

While we waited for Yoshiko to get back with amphibians, I took care of business at the nursery. It was good to get back into my regular routine for a while. After a couple of hours, I took a break at my desk, and my laptop reminded me that the grimoire pages were on there, waiting to be translated. That didn't seem like much of a break, but the overpopulation of my backyard was getting worse by the hour. The zombies were battering the cedar fence at the far end of the yard. That fence separated my yard from the back of the nursery. If the zombies knocked it down, they'd be visible to any customer who walked all the way back there. I opened the laptop and got to work.

Before I'd made much progress, Ginger, my best employee, stuck her head in to tell me Barb Vanderberry was outside.

"Just give her whatever she wants," I said.

"She wants to speak to you," Ginger said.

Our main suspect had come to pay me a visit — handy in a scary kind of way. Should I call for backup? No, she didn't know I suspected her of murder. She was here for some annoying plant problem.

I closed the laptop. "What's her problem?"

"She's an extreme narcissist."

"No, I mean, what does she want to see me about?"

"She doesn't say. She's standing out by her car." Ginger headed in the opposite direction.

Barb was talking at her phone when I got out there. Without slowing the barrage of words she was ralphing into the phone, she gestured me over and pointed toward the trunk of her Bentley. Inside was a nearly dead bougainvillea, but it was not like any other nearly dead bougainvillea that had ever grown on earth. At the end of each twig where a leaf should be, the plant had miniature green shackles, thumbscrews, iron maidens, racks, and a few items I didn't recognize, except I was pretty sure they were instruments of torture. Skylar had asked the plant to grow them, and the plant had done a beautiful job — if you were the kind of person who finds instruments of torture attractive.

Finished dictating to Siri, Barb hit send, dropped the phone into her purse, and turned toward the bougainvillea. "Why is it," she said, putting her hands on her hips, "all the plants from here die?"

"No water?" I ventured.

"My yard boy takes care of everything. He says no matter how much he waters these plants, they dry up."

Did she call her "yard boy" that to his face? Probably. I could imagine he was treating Barb and her plants about as well as Barb treated him. There was no point arguing about it.

"Aren't you going to plant these in the ground?" I asked

"As soon as Mauricio prepares the soil, he'll plant everything. It's a good thing he hasn't put these plants in the ground if they're only going to die."

"I'll bring you new plants," I told her.

"I don't want new ones," she said. "I want you to save the ones I have. These are the most amazing plants I've ever seen. These little bracelets and mummies are hilarious. What kind of bush is this?"

She thought the shackles were bracelets and the iron maidens were mummies. She might win my Dimwit of the Week award. "It's a rare variety of bougainvillea cultivated in Syria," I said.

"Those desert people are so whimsical. Can you save it?"

"Probably," I said. "How about the others? Are they like this?"

"Most of them. When can you pick them up?"

"How about tomorrow afternoon?"

"All right, but not before three. I have a hair appointment after lunch. Take this bougainvillea out now and see if you can revive it. I think it needs minerals or nutrients in the soil."

I walked around Barb to the other side of the trunk and grabbed the edge of the 10-gallon plastic pot.

"Try not to spill any dirt in my car this time." She pulled her phone from her purse and tapped on the screen.

With one hand on the pot, I lifted the wooden stake holding the bougainvillea and tilted the plant vertical. I was about to hoist it out when I noticed a pile of old clothes at the back of the trunk. Was that a rubber mask underneath? I glanced to my left. Barb was scrolling through stuff on her phone. I leaned inside the enormous trunk and nudged the clothing aside with my finger. Underneath was a pair of Gucci loafers. They had mud on them.

"What are you doing?" Barb said behind me.

"Just cleaning up a little dirt," I said, wiping my hands around on the carpet. I ducked out of the trunk and pretended to drop dirt into the pot. Had she seen me looking at the shoes? I slapped my hands together to get off the imaginary dirt and kept my eyes glued to the bougainvillea. But as I lifted the pot out of the trunk, I couldn't help glancing at her. She was gazing back stony-faced, her eyes glinting in the afternoon sun. She slammed the trunk and drove away.

Chapter 24

"What was I supposed to do, yell 'citizen's arrest' and wrestle her to the ground?" I asked Detective Nakamura.

"You let her drive away with the evidence," he complained. "She's probably dumped it somewhere already. How can we ever prove she's the perp?"

"Can't I testify that I saw the loafers?"

"Yes — your word against hers — and tell me again how you know Gucci loafers are a clue to whodunit?"

"Um, yeah, an evil sorcerer who's hanging out in the cemetery saw the perp wearing them." I switched the phone to my other ear and sat down at my desk. "But by the same token, Barb could never guess that I know the significance of those shoes. Maybe she won't throw them out. If she didn't get rid of them a long time ago, maybe she feels safe."

"You saw a rubber mask under the clothes? The significance of that would be clear."

"Not sure," I said. "When I moved the clothes and saw the loafers, that kind of captured my attention. I didn't notice anything else except Barb asking what I was doing in her trunk."

"You have a ways to go before you'll be a first-rate detective," he told me.

"That's not even on my list of personal goals." What did I want to be when I grew up? In high school, I'd told my father I wanted to be a veterinarian. He laughed at me. He laughed at most things I wanted. I'm sure he'd guffaw if I told him I wanted to be a first-rate detective. Or how about a witch, Daddy? That one's the funniest of all, isn't it? What if I could become invisible and stop time? Would you stop laughing if you knew that?

"Hello?" Detective Nakamura said.

"What?" I said.

"Thought I lost you. Sorry if you're disappointed about the detective gig."

"Oh, that's okay. You can be the detective, and I'll be the one who solves the case."

"All right," he said. "Just bear in mind that solving the case and nailing the perp are two different things. In this case, we need the evidence in the back of Vanderberry's Bentley, or we need some other evidence, whatever that might be. Otherwise, we know she's the perp but can't prove it. Do you have magic for getting in the trunk of a car?"

"Borrow the keys?"

"Could work," he said. "So, we need to sneak into her house tonight, find her car keys, and hope she hasn't ditched the evidence."

"I'll let Skylar know we're on for tonight. Do you have any cats in your neighborhood you're friendly with?"

"Why would I be friendly with neighborhood cats? They use my yard as a poop box and chase away the birds."

"We need a cat you can hold for a few minutes. Cleveland is the mellowest cat I've ever met, and he didn't want to hang with you. Our cat Stella lets all kinds of people pet her but hides under the bed when you visit. Can you suggest some way to find a cat who'll put up with you?"

"I'll go to a pet store and test drive whatever they have until I find one," he said.

"Pet stores don't have mammals. Go to the animal shelter and ask to see full-grown cats. Don't get a kitten."

"Yes ma'am."

When I came out of my office, Ginger asked if someone was working on the nursery's back fence. "It sounds like lots of people are in your backyard thrashing around at something," she whispered. "Lots of groaning, like a big orgy?"

"A big orgy?" I said. "And nobody invited me?"

Ginger didn't laugh. "Whatever's going on, I'll leave it to you."

"Sorry," I said. "Skylar has some sort of acting thing going on. I think they're rehearsing the zombie apocalypse."

Ginger nodded and looked away. She could tell I was hiding something. Yeah, it was the zombie apocalypse all right. This had to stop. I went straight back into my office and got to work on the grimoire. This time I searched for words in each spell that looked like they might refer to a type of plant or animal. That gave me a clue that the spell was for reviving a particular creature, and I could ignore it. On a hunch, I flipped to the last spell in the book. That was the logical place for an undo spell.

An hour later I had it. The last spell was for cleaning up "diverse torments of vexing vital sparks unwanted." The book had a lot more verbiage like that. I was pretty sure this was my fix. Unlike any spell I'd run into before, this one called for a couple of minerals as well as eye of newt and an herb called Asp of Jerusalem. Today it's called Woad, and I had some growing in my garden.

I ran to the café kitchen and found Skylar frying up strips of yam and laying them on a towel.

"Try this," she commanded, pointing to the yam strips.

"Ow," I said as I dropped the yam.

"Careful, they're hot."

"Thanks for the warning." I blew on my fingers. "Listen to this. I found a spell that's probably for laying down zombies that you've raised up. And we have all the ingredients except eye of newt, as usual, but we can probably substitute Tannis Beltane without major mishap."

Skylar dumped another bunch of yam strips on the towel. "This spell won't zombify us all — probably?"

"Right," I said.

"Let's go for it," she said. "If we don't do something soon, the entire clientele of the Angelus-Rosedale Cemetery will be stomping around in our backyard. Do we cast the spell here? Or do we have to get the zombies back to the cemetery first?"

"We can probably lure the zombies into a truck and drive them up there."

"Probably," she said.

"They came here through the Waterway. I wonder if they'd go back the same way if we cast the undo spell on the beach? How can we figure that out?"

"We could cast the spell on one zombie and see how it goes."

"That's a great idea," I said, snapping my fingers. "All we need to do is cut one zombie from the herd and get him to the beach."

"Sounds like a job for a cowboy," Skylar said. She dumped the last batch of yams onto the towel.

I picked up a yam strip from the previous batch. "These yams are really good, by the way."

"Thanks. Secret spices. Do you know any cowboys?"

"Let me check my contacts." I pulled out my phone. "Nothing under C."

"Try K," Skylar said.

"Kowboy Killin." I touched his mobile number.

"What's happening?" he answered in a groggy voice.

"Zombie roundup," I told him. "Sorry if I woke you. It's almost four in the afternoon."

"I've been sleeping during the day and rounding up zombies at night. I don't think your back fence will stand much more of their bashing. I'll have to move them closer to the house, but we really need to figure out how to get them back in their graves."

"That's why I'm calling. I think I have a spell that'll undo zombification."

"You *think* you do?"

"The spell is in an old grimoire that's a mashup of languages. I'm pretty sure what the spell is for. The only problem is, it calls for eye of newt, which we don't want to use, but Tannis Beltane usually works instead."

"I showed you that video of the guy jumping off his barn, right?"

"Do you have a better plan?" I asked.

"I'm asking around," he said. "So far, hardly any of the magical people I talk to are willing to believe zombies could exist. I don't know where Baldock came up with this spell."

"So you don't have a better plan," I concluded.

"How about we try your spell with a single zombie and see how it goes?"

"That's a good idea," I said. Skylar and I gave each other thumbs up. "Can you separate one we can use as a guinea pig?"

"Um, how would I do that?" he mused. "If I find a new one tonight, I can bring that one."

"We'd like to cast the spell near the Waterway. Can you take the zombie to the beach?"

"Difficult. They come out of the water and want to boogie away from there."

We agreed that he'd bring the zombie to the house, and we'd cast the spell in the front yard. The GhostOps people had moved their equipment elsewhere, and Georgina was still in the psych ward. How many other neighbors would notice a zombie in our yard?

As I pushed open the front door of the café, Detective Nakamura was getting out of his car with something furry in his arms. It was furry in a demented way, like the animal had stuck all its paws in light sockets at the same time it was hit by a tornado. Some of the fur around its head had gone missing, and the rest was sticking out in every direction. The creature's teeth were protruding, and one eye was much bigger than the other."

"What is that?" I asked.

"Fluffy," he said.

I'd never seen the detective so happy. He held the animal up. It had the general shape of a cat — four legs, two triangular ears (though one was on sideways), and a long mostly furry tail.

"Isn't she something?" he said, and snuggled her against his cheek. The cat purred. "She likes me."

"She's something, all right. If time is a cat, it definitely looks like Fluffy. Now, we need the newt and frog, and we're set to get into Barb's house. Have you heard from Yoshiko?"

He plopped the cat onto the front seat of his car and slumped against the door. "Not good news on that front. Somebody dumped a load of garbage where you got the frog last time. She couldn't find anything alive in that pond. She sat on a stack of paint cans and cried."

"Poor Yoshiko." I closed my eyes for a moment and held onto the car door. "Poor frogs. She needs to try the other places."

"That's what I told her. She has to keep going. I should have gone with her."

"You still have time. We don't want to sneak into Barb's house before midnight, do we? And it's easier to find frogs in the dark."

He dashed off to the San Gabriel Mountains with Fluffy, and I went into my office to double-check my translation of the zombie undo spell. It would be nice if I had all the details right. We needed to finish our trial run on the zombie in time to stop time so we could sneak into Barb's house. It was going to be a long night.

# # #

Killin brought a new zombie into the yard about an hour after sundown. Wearing a double-breasted pinstripe suit that had probably been blue eight decades ago, this zombie didn't have a lot of face left, so he was hard to look at.

"Let's call you Jack," Killin told the zombie.

Jack stalked back and forth through the magical area we'd prepared for him while Skylar walked around the yard in a big circle, sprinkling white lime powder. The spell would shroud everything within this circle in moonlight, according to the book. How you can shroud something in light was a mystery to me. I was hoping none of the neighbors would walk their dogs past the house while we were casting the spell. I didn't want to introduce our new friend Jack.

We set out a chunk of granite, an iron nail, a Woad plant from my herb garden, and a few leaves of Tannis Beltane. Skylar began reading the story that powered the spell from her phone:

> All the rooms were taken at the Inn of the White Raven. Stephanie Bledsoe stood in the rutted dust at noon outside the broken plank that served as the inn's front door. She stared up the road first in one direction and then down the other. She stepped aside as the char woman thundered out of the broken door with the publican in close pursuit, berating the sooty woman for using the front door of the inn. The two went up the road arguing until they were out of sight.

Hugging her cloth bag to her chest, Stephanie gazed at the upper windows of the inn. An unshaven man in a dove-gray waistcoat peered back at her from the middle window. As he leaned out of the window, his bald pate shone like the full moon. She looked quickly away and walked 11 steps up the road in the direction in which the publican and char woman had disappeared.

Killin and I walked 11 steps away from Skylar, toward the edge of the lawn. All along the perimeter of the yard, the lime sprinkled there began to flicker with blue light as though the white powder was releasing gas that sparked into flame. The blue flame grew brighter and extended upward until the fire was arching over our heads. Heat prickled the skin of my face. Were we about to be engulfed in an inferno? I looked at Killin.

"I've seen this kind of thing before," he said, not entirely convincingly. "It's all right."

The blue fire grew from all around the edges of the yard, hissing as it rose. The blazing wall curved overhead. We trotted back to the center, where Skylar was standing with her phone, near the zombie. The sheet of flames closed over us, and when the fiery vault was complete, it snuffed shut at the top with a whoosh and turned pale yellow. The glimmering dome shone like the moon.

"I hope the neighbors are all watching TV," I said.

"If this is like other enclosures I've seen," Killin said, "no one on the outside can see anything unusual. They can't even see us now, unless they step through the enclosure. I think."

"Hope you're right," I said.

Skylar continued reading the story:

This was the way to her father's house. She stopped and glanced back at the inn. The man in the second floor window was watching her. He beckoned. She turned and ran past the bend in the road that brought her to the local burying place.

Pushing open the iron gate, Stephanie trudged along the dirt path between small markers, most of stone, a few of carved wood. Two laborers stood by an open grave. One of them was taking handfuls of lime from a sack and throwing the white powder carelessly into the gaping hole. Stephanie did not look into the grave. The two men touched their caps as she passed but did not take them off.

She stayed straight on the path, as straight as she could, until she came to the edge of another rectangular hole. Sunlight glittered from puddles far down at the bottom. She read aloud her father's name from the rough-cut stone at the grave's head. He should lie there, but he would not. He refused to be still.

She stood at the grave's foot and watched sparrows come and go among the green stems and yellow flowers of Woad growing next to the open grave. Behind her, the laborers shoveled dirt into the tenanted hole. They exchanged not a single word between them and clanged shut the iron gate when they left. The world fell silent except for the birds.

The shadow of the Woad and her father's stone marker grew a little longer on the dirt. At the cry of a hawk, the sparrows went still. Stephanie went out of the iron gate and up the road to her father's cottage. She was halfway along the path to the front door when the man in the gray waistcoat came out of the cottage with his hat in his hand.

"You are his daughter," he said.

"Yes," she said, drawing back from him.

He bowed slightly. "I am sorry for your loss. As your father's lifelong friend, I share some small measure of your grief. I am Arndt Zaadowald, Professor of Motives at the academy in the city."

"He spoke of you. You gave him a painting."

"Yes, my poor effort to capture the light from the sky." He looked back at the cottage and then met her eyes. "I must apologize for bringing your father back from the far country."

"You!"

"On one of his visits to the city, your father and I heard a woman bellowing in what we took to be the language of the dead. Your father urged me to pull him back when he had passed. 'Discover the mordant morphology of this language,' he told me." The professor shook his head.

"My father is not pulled back. He is gone yet wakeful. This is only death made more plain."

At the end of the driveway, another zombie appeared, just inside the moonlight dome. This one looked to be female and was even uglier than the one who was staggering around next to us. I nudged Killin and pointed.

"Probably drawn by the magic enclosure," he said. "If the spell doesn't take care of that one too, I'll put her in the backyard with the others."

The zombie in the driveway swayed and took a step backward.

"She should gravitate to the same area Jack is pacing around. Let's call her Jill."

Jill lifted her arms and stamped toward us like a classic movie zombie. Killin was right. Jill was coming to join Jack.

A few yards behind Jill, another zombie walked into the driveway, this one wearing a cowboy hat. We were drawing them like flies. Except this one was a lot better looking than our other zombies. In fact, this one didn't look like a zombie at all. This one looked like Detective Harris Duke. What was he doing here?

"We've got to stop," I said.

"We can't stop," Killin said.

"Never kill a spell," Skylar said, "or it might kill you."

"You're the storyteller," he reminded her. "You're adding stuff to the spell." To me he said, "Skylar is right. If we stop the spell now, the whole thing could blow up. We have to keep going. You go distract him."

"What am I supposed to say? We're doing early Halloween, want to join in?"

"Talk about the weather," Killin said. "Doesn't matter. Ask him what the hell he's doing here."

I started toward the detective. Skylar carried on with the story:

> The professor held up his hand. "I was foolish to undertake this venture. I have traveled to the southern coast to procure a remedy and returned to apply it."

The new zombie — Jill — was a few yards from us now, cutting across the yard. I trotted sideways around her and she veered toward me.

Behind me, Killin said, "Oh no."

Skylar stopped reading the story.

Jill froze in her tracks, and so did I. Out at the end of the driveway, Detective Duke stood dumbstruck, his eyes wide.

"Keep on with the story!" Killin shouted. "We're close. We've got to finish."

Jill and the detective stared at me, and I stared back at them — but what were they looking at? They weren't staring at me.

I spun around. The zombies in the backyard were pouring through the gate at the side of the house. They were moving fast, and Candy was leading them.

Jill turned and took a step toward the street. She saw Detective Duke and stopped in her tracks, and I could see the back of her head. It was a normal head of hair, nicely coifed, and across that hair was a strap. She was wearing a mask. Jill was no zombie. She was pretending to be a zombie.

Not-zombie Jill hesitated for only a moment, but in that instant the zombie horde was upon her. Candy groaned and waved her arms. Some zombies ran to the left, some to the right. In seconds, they surrounded Jill. Candy reached out and yanked off the zombie mask.

"Barb!" Skylar shouted.

"Don't say anything else!" Killin said. "You'll mess up the spell. We've delayed too long. Finish the story."

I dashed toward Barb, but the zombies were all around her, turning her in a circle, groaning as they went. Barb's mouth was set in a tight determined line as she grappled with the woman she'd murdered, but her eyes were wide with horror. How did she think she was going to get out of this? I looked at Detective Duke, who stood transfixed at the end of the driveway. He had his pistol out, aimed toward the zombies. His mouth was open. He was pale as a ghost.

Behind me, Skylar shouted the story in a shaky voice:

> He instructed her on her part in the spell, recounted the story of their doings since noon, and finished with a benediction: "The dominion of life is broad, crossed with storms that reach into unseen canyons and caverns, drowning rivers that rise and vanish as clouds ceaselessly rearrange the affairs of water. So it is upon land and sea with the lives of people who sojourn across the earth. Let them find safe harbor, a plot of land. Let them rest."

As the moonlight dome flickered, our zombies did not rest. They continued to press in on Barb. Her determined look was gone. She wore an expression of pure terror, and kept repeating, "No, no, no…" Her hand thrust up out of the pressing mass of zombies holding a long knife. She plunged it into Candy's chest.

"The spell isn't working!" I shouted.

"Just wait," Skylar said.

The Woad plant shot green filaments across the ground. They grew around us and extended out to the edge of the yard. As they covered the grass and the driveway in lacey traceries of spring-green tendrils, the air filled with the twittering of birds. The glowing shapes of birds darted across the dome in every color of the rainbow.

Again and again Barb stabbed at Candy, who didn't react to the cuts. The zombies snatched Barb's hand from the knife and held her arms straight out, still turning her around in a circle. With the long knife quivering in her chest, Candy fastened her hands around Barb's neck.

I looked away. Killin gripped my shoulder. He looked as horrified as I felt. He watched the zombies and gripped my shoulder tighter. Skylar was on one knee, facing the house, her head down.

The spell wasn't working. What were we going to do with a yard full of murderous zombies?

Chapter 25

Magic, like life and love, is frightfully uncertain. Your father laughs when you talk about becoming a veterinarian, and you end up running a plant nursery. Cast a spell to put one zombie to rest, and a pack of undead nightmares take the law into their own hands. Fall in love with a heartthrob sorcerer who *would* cheat on you to save his life, and you forgive him because he holds you while the zombies run riot in your yard.

These things happen.

They don't make sense, not in the way we think life should. At the moment, nothing made sense except having this man hold me. I clung to him desperately.

What was I doing? I struggled out of his grasp. When did I turn into a clinger? He released his grip reluctantly. Who was clinging to whom?

"We have to keep the zombies from getting away," I said in Killin's ear.

A little green around the gills, he was watching Candy finish off Barb in the whirling zombie rampage. "First you don't want them, and now you don't want them to leave. Candy seems to be in charge. Maybe you can talk her into calming them down."

"Is Barb, uh, done for?" I asked.

He nodded yes, still looking at the zombies. "I wonder if she'll turn into a zombie?"

I looked over at the zombies then. They lifted Barb's lifeless body into the air and carried it around the yard like a trophy. I turned away again and put my hand on Skylar's shoulder. She was still kneeling on the grass.

"Are you okay?" I asked her.

She wiped her mouth and raised her head to look at me. "Never better."

"Any idea how to corral the zombies?" I asked.

"Are they leaving?"

I glanced over at them. "They're carrying what's left of Barb around the yard, but I'm afraid they'll run off any minute now. They don't seem attracted to the magical barrier anymore."

"Maybe they'll run to the police station and turn themselves in," she ventured.

"Speaking of the police, Detective Duke is still standing at the end of the driveway with his pistol hanging out. From the look on his face, I'd say he's clear that these are genuine zombies."

"Does that mean he'll let Emma go?"

As I was about to point out that he couldn't know Barb was the perp, the screech of a hawk cut me off. The twittering of sparrows stopped. Then, the whole world changed around us.

The moonlight dome evaporated with a fizzing sound, and in its place was a late afternoon sky with clouds scudding across the blue expanse. Our house was gone. All the houses in the neighborhood were gone, and in their place was a forest that stretched north and south along a dusty road that ran where the street used to be. Almost out of sight to the south was a sign with barely legible letters that said White Raven Inn.

Killin, Skylar, and I were in a small clearing in the forest. Then the chunk of granite we'd used in the spell crackled and lurched into the shape of a small headstone. We jumped this way and that as other headstones erupted out of the ground beneath our feet, and the iron nail we'd put out clanged up into a gate in a rail fence. We stood amid the headstones, watching the zombies sway in place outside the iron gate.

"The spell is still playing out," Killin said.

"Will the zombies return to their graves?" I asked. "And where will Candy and Barb end up?"

"We'll soon find out," Killin said.

The zombies milled around for a minute and then shuffled toward the gate. A white-haired zombie in an ancient green gown and a rust-colored shawl opened the gate with a skeletal hand. She minced through the opening, turning slightly sideways with each small step. She stopped just inside the gate. The other zombies came up behind her and pushed her forward until they were jammed together in a small area like a bundle of drab undead jellybeans.

"They're not going to the graves," I complained.

"That woman in the shawl stopped where the objects were — the granite, the nail, and the Tannis Beltane."

"Which substitutes for the newt," Killin pointed out. "Where was the newt in the story?"

"The story didn't have a newt in it," I said.

"So where would the newt be if there was a newt?" Skylar asked.

"In the grave!" we all answered together.

Spells didn't generally make sense. Magic is a way for the universe to go sideways on itself, after all. But sometimes you see how the pieces go together when they go sideways. Now we had to hope we were seeing the puzzle correctly, because otherwise we were stuck with a big party of undead homies. Also: one bewildered detective. What were we going to do with him? But first the zombies.

"If we sprinkle the Tannis Beltane in the graves, the zombies will dive in?" Skylar ventured.

"One of us needs to get the Tannis Beltane from over there and see if the zombies follow," I suggested.

Skylar and I looked at Killin.

"You want me to shove into that mob? How did I get stuck with herding zombies in the first place?" he asked.

"You volunteered," I reminded him.

"Out of a deep sense of civic mindedness," Skylar added.

"Yeah," he said.

"At least Skylar deodorized them for you," I said.

"Mother calls that her Secret spell," Skylar said.

"The Tannis Beltane is in a cup," I told him.

"They look like they're trying to squeeze into a mosh pit the size of a cup," Killin said as he plodded toward the zombie jam.

He pulled one of the zombies out of the way, and another filled in the space. He put his arms between two of the zombies and worked his way between them only to have the entire group shift sideways, leaving him further from the Tannis Beltane than when he started.

After a few more tries he came back to where Skylar and I were standing. "I need you guys to run interference."

I started toward the zombies, but Skylar grabbed my arm, saying, "Hold on, I have an idea." She put her hands on the Woad tendrils that were running here and there across the ground and bent her head in concentration.

Of course! This was her magic, controlling plants. We could have been using this in our back yard.

As Skylar bent over the delicate Woad tendrils, they grew thicker and squirmed forward like pythons, crunching against the headstones, rising upward. In a few minutes, they wrapped the zombies nearest us in fat green loops and shoved them forward to open a path to the Tannis Beltane.

Killin dashed through the gap and found the cup of herbs pressed halfway into the dirt by the pressure of zombies trying to get into it. Would the zombies follow it when Killin carried it off? Yes, they would, and Skylar couldn't contain them with the plant. Killin ran around the yard with the pack of zombies in hot pursuit.

"We need to get this stuff to the cemetery," he shouted as he ran. "And before you even suggest it, I can't run that far."

"We could rent a truck and lure them into it," Skylar said.

"They need to go back through the Waterway," I said. "Then maybe the magic they took out will go back in."

"So, you need to take this cup through the Waterway and let them follow you," Killin said.

"But how can I?" I protested. "The rest of the world is gone." I waved my arms at the forest around us.

"If you run out there where the street used to be," Skylar said, "it will still be there. You just need to go through the perimeter I marked out with the lime."

"Can the zombies go through that?" I asked.

"Well, *there's* a good question," she answered, or failed to answer. "Killin, run up this road a ways and see if the zombies can go with you."

He ran out where the driveway used to be, past Detective Duke, who was still standing there staring wide-eyed with his gun out.

"Excuse us," Killin said on his way by. "Could you put that thing away?"

The detective hopped several feet to the side as the zombies trouped past, still carrying the body of one dead perp. They disappeared at the edge of the road as though they'd passed through a tent flap. A few minutes later Killin reappeared with his undead entourage and announced that Redondo Beach was right where we'd left it. As he ran past, he handed me the cup containing the Tannis Beltane.

"I'm supposed to run several miles up the beach with these zombies and hope nobody sees us?" I asked as I started running.

"That's right," Killin said, running alongside me. "Don't worry. I'll be your wingman."

"What does that mean?"

"Guy who takes care of everything."

What did that have to do with having wings? In any case, I was glad to have help. We ran through the perimeter around the yard, and I stumbled when we were suddenly plunged into darkness. I'd forgotten it was night in the real world.

"If you fall," he said, "hand me the Tannis Beltane so the zombies don't run over you. And let me know if you need a break."

"This distance is easy for me. Are you in good enough shape to run all the way to the pier?"

"Beg your pardon? I'm in better shape than you."

"No you're not."

"Yes I am, and anyway, these goons behind us are not exactly savage runners."

"Okay, but I don't think I can get you through the Waterway. Skylar needs to pick you up near the pier. Wait!" I jerked to a halt and started running again. "This won't work."

We were in the street running north. I made a big circle through an intersection and headed back home.

"Run a little faster," Killin said. "The zombies at the back of the pack are cutting across the intersection. And why are we doing this?"

Holding up the cup, I said, "If I take this into the water, the Tannis Beltane will splash all over the place."

"You're so smart," he said.

"Yeah, and I think we want each zombie to go to his or her own final resting place, however final that might be. We need to grind up these few leaves of Tannis Beltane and sprinkle a tiny bit in each open grave."

"I'd be okay letting them buddy-up in one hole, but I suppose that's not a thoughtful way to do it. And we have way too many to fit in your average grave. Speaking of way too many, how are we going to find all the right places for a couple dozen zombies? That cemetery is a big place."

We ran through the boundary around the yard where the driveway used to be. It was afternoon in this bubble, blindingly bright. Detective Duke had put his gun away, but he was still standing there with his brow furrowed. Did he not realize he could walk out? Skylar was headed toward where the house should be. I called her back.

"I need a baggie for the Tannis Beltane. Could you get one, please? And we need to grind up the leaves so we can divide them across a bunch of graves."

Skylar's smart too. She understood immediately. In a few minutes she came back with a mortar and pestle. I ground up the Tannis Beltane on the run and dumped the shredded leaves in the plastic bag she handed me. "When you meet me at the pool, could you bring some dry clothes, please?"

She held up a cloth bag. "Got 'em. And a towel."

I gave her a thumbs up and pointed at Detective Duke, "Bring him, too."

"Are you kidding?" she said.

"We're going to need all the help we can get up there, and it might be good if he sees where the bodies are buried."

"You're so smart," Killin said.

"Can you stand it?" I asked as we sprinted up the street with the zombies in tow.

He didn't answer, but he kept running alongside me. I took that as a yes.

On the way to the beach, we passed a few dog walkers who stood and stared as the zombies clumped past. Did people think we were some sort of historical reenactment group? A tattered Renaissance Faire running society? Or a branch of the ministry of funny walks? To be fair, the zombies were making good time for corpses.

We arrived at the pier without drawing a police escort and found Skylar waiting for us. I let Killin lead the zombies around the beach for a few minutes so I could rest before taking the plunge to the Waterway.

Skylar told me that Detective Duke wasn't taking the situation well. He was too dazed to drive his own car, and sitting next to Skylar on the way to the pier, he kept saying, "I can't arrest dead people. I just can't."

"Poor man," I said.

"Yeah, I just hope he doesn't go cracker-dog on the way to the cemetery."

"Don't worry, Killin can be your wingman."

"What's a wingman?" she asked.

"Guy who takes care of annoying detectives."

"What's that got to do with wings?"

"No idea. Ask Killin. I'd better go, much as I don't want to."

"Have a nice swim," Skylar said.

I caught up with Killin, grabbed the bag of Tannis Beltane, and plunged into the frigid surf with the undead throng.

# # #

A couple of hours later, I was delighted to see Killin and Skylar waiting for me when I rose to the surface of the Waterway pool in the Angelus-Rosedale Cemetery. Killin extended his arm to pull me up, and I handed him the bag of Tannis Beltane.

"Why is it light here?" I asked.

"Killin cast a spell on the cemetery to light it up," Skylar said. She handed me a towel and peered into the pool. "Where are the zombies?"

"I hitched a ride on a shark," I said. "The zombies are swimming at a good clip, but it might take them another hour to get here."

"Good," Killin said. "We did some scouting around, and most of the open graves are in a swath on the western side of the cemetery. In another hour, we might find the rest of the graves, and we'll be ready for the zombies when they come out."

"While I was going through the water, I started thinking that a couple dozen zombies seems like a lot, but it's not when you think about all the graves in this cemetery. What if we don't have most of the zombies?"

"Yeah," Killin said, "I worried the same thing. I'm hoping Baldock figured out how to turn off his zombie maker, and that's why we only got a couple dozen."

"I don't suppose you've seen Baldock?" I asked.

"No," Killin said. "He'd better not show his face."

I looked around. "Where's Detective Duke?"

"He's off that way," Skylar said, gesturing to the east. "We asked him to find open graves over there, but I'm worried he might throw himself into one of them. He's still bewildered by the whole thing."

On the pretense that the detective might come back, I hid behind a big headstone to strip off my wet clothes and put on the dry things Skylar had brought. Really, I was shy of undressing in front of Killin. Maybe I wasn't ready to be his gf after all. I still had a lot to think about when I had a little spare time.

Killin took half of the Tannis Beltane to sprinkle in the graves he and Skylar had already found. He'd taken photos of them on his phone and swore he could find his way back to every single one.

Skylar and I headed in the direction Detective Duke had gone. We found him sitting on a granite slab across from a carved marble crypt that was the size of a small cottage. The crypt's massive metal door was mottled black and green and must have been an inch thick. It was hanging open on bent hinges.

The detective's elbows were on his knees and his head in his hands. He was staring at the stained white crypt and barely glanced at us when we walked up.

"Detective Duke," I said. "How's it going?"

He gestured at the crypt. "Look at the door on that mausoleum. It's made of iron or maybe bronze. Three men couldn't lift it, yet some force has pushed it open *from the inside*." He put his head back in his hands.

I looked at Skylar and twisted my mouth into an expression admitting that bringing Detective Duke hadn't been a good idea. I didn't want him thinking we could explain what was going on or — worse — that we were behind it all. Time to play dumb.

Shoving the metal door with both hands, I budged it barely enough to get slight creaks from the rusty hinges. "That makes no sense."

Skylar gave the door a playful kick. "Somebody forced it with a pry bar. Let's go see what else we can find." She tugged the detective's hands from under his chin and pulled him to his feet. As they walked away, she lingered behind and gestured at the baggie in my hand and then at the inside of the crypt.

I had to go in there and leave some Tannis Beltane. I leaned inside the marble doorframe. The interior was some kind of dark stone. It was black as midnight in there. I turned around, but Skylar was gone, and she had my phone. I could run after her and get my phone, so long as I was sure I could find my way back. Or I could toss a pinch of Tannis Beltane into the crypt and call it close enough. The zombies could sort out the details. Did I even care if they got it exactly right? I leaned into the crypt. It was so dark in there.

As I pulled away again, my hair snagged in the doorframe. That's when I noticed the wisps of spider web that filled the corner of the doorway where I'd been poking my head. I tore at my hair for a couple of minutes, running my fingers through, peering at my hands after each rip through my hair, watching the ground to see if anything fell out. Nothing did. Eventually, I noticed a big spider biding his time on the edge of the web. How many of his buddies were lurking inside?

Skylar and Detective Duke couldn't have got far. I walked away from the crypt, looking over my shoulder every three or four steps, memorizing my path. After about 20 yards, I stopped and put my fingertips to my temples. How dim was I? Stalking back to the crypt, I gingerly reached inside the doorway — on the side away from the spider — touched the stone, and asked it to light up.

Lit by the orange glow that suffused the chamber, Baldock Gunter bowed and extended his arms in a gesture of welcome. "Hayley West," he said.

I took a step back, but before I could get out the door, he had a firm grip on my arm.

Chapter 26

"Please abide with me for a brief moment," Baldock said. He waved his free hand over his shoulder and flung something toward the crypt's doorway. The metal door slammed shut with a dull clang behind me. He released his grip on my arm. "Have a seat."

He gestured toward a corroded metal coffin that had been ripped out of an alcove in the side of the crypt. Its mildewed lid was lying askew across it. No way was I sitting on that disgusting piece of furniture.

"What do you want?" I asked, rubbing my arm.

Baldock sat on the edge of another metal casket. "If I recall correctly, you've asked me that multiple times, and I keep giving you the same answer. I need help with the magic pool so I can straighten out a situation with Fel Dinaden. You've told me you would think about it, but I hear nothing until I find you and these other people traipsing around the cemetery doing heaven knows what with the whole place lit up like a Christmas tree lot. What are you doing?"

"We cast a spell to put your zombies back where they came from," I told him. "You don't need them anymore, do you? They're making a mess out there." I gestured toward the world at large.

"I don't need them, and I don't care about them. In fact, they became highly annoying in my little cemetery neighborhood, bumping into the stonework and groaning. I can't tell you how many times they woke me from a sound sleep."

"You don't live in this crypt, do you?" I looked around at the moldy black stone that loomed above us.

"This dump? No, no. I have a much nicer mausoleum that's white marble all the way through. I only came in here and cast a darkening spell to get away from you lot. Who's the dimwit in the cowboy hat? Your new lover?"

"He's a police detective named Harris Duke. He's been investigating the murder here in the cemetery, and he just saw the victim kill her own murderer. The victim was able to do that because your spell turned her into a zombie."

"Splendid!" Baldock said, clapping his hands. "What a lovely symmetry to the whole affair. I'm glad to hear my zombie spell was so helpful, and I see why your Detective Duke is going around with that gob-smacked look on his face."

"Yeah, well, he's also a dimwit. We're hoping he understands that the woman he saw killed today was the murderer so he'll release Skylar's girlfriend. The detective arrested her for the murder."

"What makes you so sure she didn't do it?"

"I saw Gucci loafers in the trunk of this other woman's car with a pile of raggedy clothes. Remember you told me you saw those loafers on the pretend zombie the night of the murder?"

He laughed. "Oh yes, I remember. Bear in mind I just made that up."

I stared at him. "Are you serious? You made up the Gucci loafers?"

"It made you so happy. A clue! You had a clue!"

I put my hands on my head and sagged against the stone wall. So Candy had strangled Barb in a random fit of zombie rage? Possibly motivated by the spell we cast? But why was Barb wearing a zombie mask? Why was she in our yard? Carrying a knife?

"Mind the spider," he said, pointing over my left shoulder.

"Gah!" I shouted. This place was crawling with spiders. I brushed off my shoulder, shook my head, and ran my fingers through my hair. I strained to see my left shoulder and tilted toward Baldock. "Is it on me?"

He didn't say anything. I shot him a glance. He was bent over, hands on his knees, shaking with laughter.

"Was there really a spider?" I demanded.

He shook his head no.

"Baldock!" I swatted him on the shoulder, hard. "What makes you think I'm going to help you with the magical pool when you jerk me around like that? When you lie about the Gucci loafers? Or were you lying about lying about the Gucci loafers?"

He nodded yes.

"What? Yes, what? You were lying or lying about lying?"

He sat up. "You are precious." He wiped his eyes. "That woman in the zombie mask might have been wearing Gucci loafers. How would I know? It was dark and foggy, and all I cared about was that *she* not see *me*. But she had on some kind of shoe with something reflective on it. I think she was shining a flashlight on the ground. I saw a little flash of gold light. So I didn't invent a Gucci loafer out of the whole cloth. Just think of this as a typically unreliable eyewitness report, okay? Now, will you help me with the pool?"

"Honestly," I said, slapping the sides of my legs. "You need help with your social skills. That's what you need. How about you work on —"

A dull banging on the metal door of the crypt interrupted me, followed by a faint voice. "Hayley? Are you in there?" It was Skylar.

Baldock put his finger to his lips. I made a what-are-you-thinking face back at him and shouted, "Be out in a second."

To Baldock I whispered, "I'll get back to you about the pool, I promise. We need to finish up with the zombies. Excuse me." I pushed him aside so I could sprinkle Tannis Beltane in the coffin he was using as a sofa. I put some in the other coffin and pointed at the door. "Open sesame."

He stood and caught my arm. "Hayley, I know what kind of person I am. I know what you think of me. But you should also know this: My task concerns your family. Now, dowse the lights."

He placed my hand on a relatively clean part of the stone wall. I asked the stone to shut off its glow. Was Baldock going to tell me another of his upsetting facts about my mother? Some comment she made about how glad she was to leave me?

When the stone's glow faded and we stood in complete darkness, Baldock asked, "Do you know your sisters?"

I heard a slight rustle as he moved his arm, and with a creaking groan, the crypt door swung outward. He pushed me away. I stumbled out of the crypt into the arms of Skylar.

"What were you doing in there?" She asked. "Why was the door closed?"

Killin was making his way toward us around the headstones and monuments. If he found out Baldock was here, we'd have a big fight.

"Tell you later," I whispered to Skylar. Louder, I said, "I went in with the Tannis Beltane, and, ah, took a minute to do another little bit of business."

"Did I just see this door swing open?" Killin asked as he came up.

"Apparently," Skylar said, "Hayley mistook this crypt for a public toilet."

Killin leaned into the doorway. "Spooky. I'd rather squat out here than go in there. Looks like Spiderboro."

"Where's Detective Duke?" I asked, tugging Killin away from the crypt.

"He's staring into another crypt down the way," Skylar said. "He finds them fascinating."

"It is amazing that the zombies can force these doors open," Killin said. He put his shoulder against the door and pushed. The hinges squeaked in complaint as the door swung an inch. "How on earth did you move this thing?"

"Got the rocks to help," I lied. "How much more of the cemetery do we need to survey?"

"Beyond this area around the pool we haven't found any more open graves," Skylar said. "All we need now is zombies."

We walked toward the pool, but since none of us knew how to get to the pool from that direction, we found ourselves on the other side of it after a few minutes of wandering. We had to go a ways toward the cemetery entrance. From there, we followed a route that led through the magical barrier and to the pool, where nothing was happening.

"Maybe I should go in the water and check on them," I said.

Killin looked at his phone. "It hasn't been an hour since you came out. Let's give them a little longer."

We sat on the edge of the stone platform around the pool, and a few minutes later the first zombie reached out of the water and clutched at the air.

"Nice effect!" Killin said. He took several photos from different angles with his phone as the zombie climbed out of the pool. "This is classic zombie stuff. I can probably sell these on one of the online photo sites."

"When somebody recognizes their grandpa in your photos, you might have to answer some sticky questions," Skylar said.

"Hmm," Killin said. He put his phone away.

We stood back and watched the first few zombies flail around in the water and struggle up onto the stone platform. They stood there dripping, swaying, looking around as if they were sniffing the air. The first one staggered off with Killin following him. Skylar followed a zombie woman in a tattered green dress but came back after half a minute and said she couldn't watch the woman get back in her grave. We waited by the pool.

In a few minutes, Killin returned and told us the zombie guy he'd followed had thrown himself into the casket at the bottom of an open grave, swung the lid closed, and somehow pulled the dirt back into the grave. The same thing happened at a nearby grave. The zombies were reburying themselves.

Killin went off with new zombies while Skylar and I waited by the pool. And waited. Would Candy make it to the pool? Finally, the last of the zombies came out of the water — Candy and two others carrying what remained of Barb Vanderberry. Where would Candy go? She had no grave to return to.

The two zombies carrying Barb shuffled off toward the marble crypt where I'd talked to Baldock. Candy followed them, and so did I. Skylar went to get Detective Duke from where she'd last seen him, but he was already sitting outside the marble crypt when I got there.

The zombies carrying Barb stopped a few feet from the crypt doorway and dropped the body on the ground with a thump. Detective Duke stood up as the zombies took Barb's arms and dragged her toward the opening. He'd worn a stunned look since he first saw the zombies in our yard. Now, his face contorted as if he'd been stabbed, and he clutched the front of his shirt. The zombies dragged Barb into the crypt, and as her feet bumped over the cracked marble threshold, the Gucci loafers came off and fell to the ground.

Candy bent to look at the shoes and backed away. The hollow where she was bashed in the back of the head was clearly visible, washed clean by two passages through the Waterway. The knife was still embedded in her chest. As she stood swaying a few feet from the threshold, one of the zombies came out, picked up the loafers, and threw them into the crypt. Then, he took Candy's arm. He tugged her toward the doorway.

A metal scraping sound came from inside the crypt.

"What's that noise?" Skylar asked from behind me.

I jumped. "Don't sneak up on me like that. It's probably the zombie closing his coffin lid."

"Ugh, great."

"That is what we want them to do," I reminded her.

"Yeah," she whispered. She patted my shoulder and cleared her throat. "Detective Duke is really having a hard time. Me too. I can't watch Candy go in there. What if she doesn't realize she's dead?"

Skylar's footsteps faded into the distance behind me.

Would Candy go in? What if she didn't? What if the undo spell didn't work on her? After all, she was killed while Baldock's zombification spell was still going. Maybe Candy never really died in the first place, so we couldn't undo her from undead to really dead.

I put my hands on my head. This was crazy. All I could do was hope that Candy would now find peace and a final resting place. Well, I didn't even care if this place was final, but —

The scraping stopped, and a louder grinding noise of metal sliding over stone erupted through the doorway. With Baldock and his darkening spell gone, dim light penetrated the gloom. I didn't want to see in there, really, but I couldn't resist stepping forward and peering in. The coffin was slowly grinding its way into the alcove in the wall of the crypt.

The three massive hinges on the door let out a slow rasping squeak as they turned the slightest bit. The door swung an inch and then another inch. Candy moved her head around dreamily and put her hands on the door. The zombie holding her arm pulled harder, and Candy tottered forward a couple of steps. The squeaking of the hinges continued, louder. The door swung faster. The zombie let go of Candy's arm and backed into the crypt, beckoning. Candy stepped languidly onto the threshold.

"Don't do it!" Detective Duke shouted. He rushed forward and gripped the back of Candy's shirt. "Don't go in there! It's a grave."

She turned toward him with a look of infinite sadness, and her hand gestured over the back of her head where she'd been wounded. She patted his cheek.

As the crypt door pushed against her leg, she raised her hand, palm outward toward him, stepped into the crypt, and crumpled onto the stone floor. Detective Duke stepped back. The door swung shut with a clanging thud.

He placed his palms flat against the door. The sound of metal scraping on metal resonated inside the crypt, followed by metal on stone. Then, the crypt fell silent as a tomb.

He leaned his forehead against the metal door. After a moment, he turned to face me. "She's dead now, isn't she?"

I nodded yes. "I think so."

"What just happened here?" he asked. "It doesn't make sense."

"No, it doesn't make sense."

"Will they come out again, the dead ones?" he asked.

I gave a tiny shrug. "No idea. I hope we've seen the last of them. I hope they rest in peace."

# # #

"Where on earth have you been?" Detective Nakamura shouted.

I held the phone away from my ear.

"Sorry we didn't call," I said. "We'll be home in half an hour. We've been tied up at the cemetery."

"The cemetery?"

"Angelus-Rosedale," I specified.

"Yes, I know your favorite cemetery, but why were you there instead of here so we can go into Barb's house? Yoshiko and I have been waiting at your place with a newt and a frog for two hours."

"Right, well, sorry about that. We don't need to go into Barb's house. You guys go on home, and we'll tell you about it in the morning."

Detective Nakamura spluttered on for a while about the unforgivable delay while his daughter Emma sat in a jail cell. And how could we go off and mess around in the cemetery? I finally got him to agree to go home and wait until morning.

I pressed the red disconnect button and put my phone down. "I'm putting off telling him what happened because I don't know how this will turn out. What will Detective Duke do now?"

Skylar was driving us south on the 110 freeway toward Redondo Beach. We'd just dropped off the detective at his police station, which was only a couple of blocks from the cemetery. Killin stayed in the cemetery to make sure all the zombies were accounted for.

"At least Detective Duke knows that Candy is dead," Skylar said. "He knows where her body is, so he can open that crypt if he wants to and let the forensics people work on her."

"Then they'll confirm that the bash on the head killed her," I said, "but she also has a knife in her chest, multiple stab wounds, and several bullet holes. They'll know she was shot by Georgina. They have her gun. They'll match it for sure. How they'll explain all that is a mystery. It would be entertaining to see them try."

"Will they still think Emma is the one who bashed Candy on the head?" Skylar asked. "That's the mystery that matters to me."

"Now that Detective Duke has seen Candy kill Barb Vanderberry, maybe he'll go find evidence that she was the perp."

"Evidence a little better than the Gucci loafers," added Skylar.

"Oh, yeah, the Gucci loafers," I said. "It turns out Baldock kind of made up the Gucci loafers."

"No way. When did you talk to Baldock? Oh wait, that's why you were in that white crypt with the door closed."

"He was hiding in there, and he grabbed me when I went in. He thought it was funny that I latched onto the loafers as a clue. He did see something shiny and gold on the perp's shoes, but it could have been anything."

"Candy obviously thought Barb was the perp."

"Or did she attack Barb because of something in our spell?"

"That doesn't make sense," she said.

"Well, there you go," I said.

We swung into the curving exit ramp to the west 105 freeway. When Skylar had merged into traffic, I said, "Here's something else that doesn't make sense. Baldock pestered me about helping him with the Waterway and said whatever he's up to involves my family."

"He's just trying to give you a reason to help him."

"Sure, but the last thing he said was 'Do you know your sisters?'"

"You've always said you're an only child," Skylar objected.

"That's what I thought. That's what I was told. But what if it's not true? What if I have sisters somewhere? What if my mother took my sisters away when she left? I've been thinking about it, and I have little memories of another girl. I see her on a pony next to me with a dragonfly on her hat. I see her looking across a table at me through the stems of champagne glasses. I see her in a white dress with pink ribbons, standing in sunlight next to white roses."

"You were five years old when your mother left. You can't rely on those memories. They could be of any little girl. And only one? Didn't Baldock say 'sisters' plural?"

"Right."

"He could even have been talking about the women in your life, your female friends."

"He said it right after mentioning my family," I said.

"And it was most likely the first thing he thought of that might hook you in. It came from the same place as the Gucci loafers."

"Maybe."

My phone rang. It was Detective Nakamura. He said Emma had been released from jail. The authorities had dropped all charges against her.

Chapter 27

The swells were big for mid-summer, but only one surfer was riding this evening at the south side of the Redondo Beach Pier. On the ocean side of this horseshoe-shaped pier, several fishermen sat on folding chairs, talking about beer and tackle. One of the regulars noticed me and nodded. I looked in his bucket.

"Nothing," I said.

"Yeah, couple a good 'uns got away," he said. "You're not running very fast today."

"Meeting a friend." I looked around. Detective Nakamura was coming around the far corner of the restaurants. "There he is now."

The fisherman stroked his gray beard. "Well now, sweetheart, if I'd a known a pretty girl like you was into older men, I'd a cast some of my classic pickup lures."

"Try me."

"Let's see, there's the one where I say you look like an angelfish, and do you want to hook up?"

"Not biting that one," I said.

"How about I ask if you're farm raised or wild caught?"

"Are they all that good?"

"Yep, 'fraid so. You can see why my bucket's empty."

I squeezed his shoulder and walked over to Detective Nakamura.

"How many boyfriends do you have?" the detective asked.

"That's a good question," I said. "Maybe half of one, depending on what day it is and whether I'm remembering that he cheated on me."

"I thought you forgave Killin for that."

"Yeah, I think so too some days." I walked toward the restaurants. "Thanks for coming."

"You ran here from home?" he asked, gesturing toward my running shorts. "I'm mostly a walker, myself."

"Walking is fine, so long as we stay out of the wind. I'll warm back up when I run home. How is Emma?"

"More than three weeks, and she still walks with a limp," he said. "The orthopedic guy says she'll be more or less back to normal in another three weeks. I owe you such a debt of gratitude for the effort you put into clearing Emma's name. I don't understand how you searched Landon Longstaff's house when you were hurt so badly."

I shrugged. "I had to." We reached the row of restaurants and went around the corner, out of the wind. "I heard on the news that Landon's been charged with a number of crimes."

"Along with that guy on the planning commission — bribery, blackmail, conspiracy to misconvey public property. They should get several years for all that. Who knows what the city will do with Barb Vanderberry's house. I suppose they could tear it down and put the park back the way it was. Or maybe they'll give you the house for saving Redondo Beach from the zombie apocalypse and getting Detective Duke on the right track."

"Assuming that Barb was actually the right track," I said.

"Right, meant to tell you first thing," he said. "The forensics report came in this morning. The trunk of her car had traces of dirt where you saw her shoes, and that dirt matched what's in the Angelus-Rosedale Cemetery. She was the perp for sure."

"That's a relief."

"What I don't understand is how Detective Harris Duke suddenly knew that three weeks ago. He hadn't done the investigations needed to identify Vanderberry. And where is she now? She's vanished into thin air. For that matter, where is Candy Longstaff's body?"

I leaned against a wall and looked at Detective Nakamura. He knew the zombies were real. He hadn't seen Candy as a zombie, but he had good evidence that she became one. I'd told him we "dealt with" the zombies, and he knew that the open graves in the cemetery had mysteriously filled themselves in. If the police wanted to find Candy's body, they had an obvious place to look, and Detective Duke knew exactly what crypt to open first.

"The guy who should be finding Barb and Candy is Detective Duke," I said, "It's his case. Where is he?"

"People in the Pico Union station tell me he's been very quiet lately. He seems to have lost his cowboy hat and the swagger that went with it. They even say he's talking about giving up police work and taking a job at his uncle's winery in the Napa Valley. I don't know what happened, but he sounds like a totally changed man. Did you do something to him?"

Did I do something to Harris Duke? Not really. And how much would Detective Nakamura want to know if he could choose? How could I decide that for him? But that's what I had to do. If I told him what happened, he'd want to open that crypt for sure.

"No," I said. "I didn't do anything to Detective Duke. Maybe he realized he didn't have good evidence against Emma, and he was upset by the idea that he'd almost nailed an innocent person."

Detective Nakamura snorted. "More likely someone took him down a notch."

People were trickling into the restaurants around us for the early-bird specials. I started walking again, staying away from the areas where the people were passing. "Detective Nakamura, I was wondering if you could do me a favor."

"Sure. You know we owe you so much. What do you need?"

"I've always thought I was an only child, but I learned recently that I might have sisters. Did you know my mother left my father and me when I was five? Yeah, and my father is off in his own remote world of finance. I have an aunt in a nursing home whose memory is gone. So if my mother took my sisters with her when she left, that would be a big deal for me. I might have sisters out there I could be close to — real family."

"Sounds great," he said. "Are you in touch with your mother?"

"No, that's the problem. I haven't communicated with her since she left 26 years ago. I don't know where she is or even if she's still alive."

We walked beyond the restaurants, and the wind hit me. We kept going, walking along the pier railing. I hugged my arms around my body.

"Why don't we go inside?" he asked. "Have a snack, maybe a drink?"

I shook my head and kept walking. "I was wondering if you have a way to find people, like you can look in a police database to see whether my mother had other children, you know, and where they might be, if they even exist. Or something."

His face darkened. "That's illegal. You asked to meet out here so you could ask me to break the law as a favor to you." He stopped walking and glared at me. "Well, I'm not doing that."

"What happened to owing me so much, being grateful and everything? Why can't you do this one thing? Just tell me if I have sisters out there."

"Look on the Internet," he said. "You can find anybody on the Internet. Or hire a private investigator. Or how about the method you used to find Angelina Martinelli? You found that little girl. Why not use it to find your own sisters?"

I put my hands on the wooden railing and gripped tight. "Can't do it. Won't work. I already hired a PI. He's barely found any evidence that my mother existed, never mind my sisters."

"Has it occurred to you that they don't want to be found? People have a right to disappear, to start over, to not be found by you. I won't violate their privacy."

I let go of the railing and got in his face. "What happened to owing me a debt of gratitude? What happened to being so thankful for what I did for you? You can't even capture Baldock Gunter. That's how much you're doing for me."

His face flushed red. "Gunter's on the FBI's most-wanted list. They're coordinating the search. There's nothing more we can do."

The lone surfer next to the pier had given up for the evening. The empty waves rolled to the beach. The sun was gone behind a fog bank out to sea. More people were coming to the restaurants around the corner. Their voices carried over the sighing wind and the crashing waves. I would not cry in front of this man.

I ran. Fleeing past the restaurants, I dodged the people going this way and that without thinking about where they were going. I ran off the pier and past the shops on the plaza. I ran south toward home, wishing I had more than half a boyfriend, wishing I had a family to call my own. My running shoes felt like lead on my feet. They slapped at the hard surface of the path.

My friend Skylar was at home. She'd have a good vegan supper ready for us.

We'd solved the murder case, freed Emma, drawn the magic back into the Waterway, and put the zombies to rest. Our neighbor Georgina was home from the psych ward, ready to annoy us at every future opportunity. The world had returned to normal.

Killin told me fate had brought me to Redondo Beach. He said it was part of a plan put in place centuries ago, and greater than that, I was the walker of the Stoneway, the only witch who could repair the patterns that kept the world working. But what about me? What about what I might want out of my life? Or was that a selfish question?

It was wrong to ask Detective Nakamura for police info about my sisters. Was everything I wanted self-centered and out of line?

I ran faster. I willed my feet to carry me along like a wild animal, like a gust of wind, like a storm-driven wave. Life was waiting out there, possibly a family. I would go find it.

The mystery and magic continue

According to legend, an ancient Chinese dragon called the Shuilong could stop gunpowder from working: Guns no longer bang, bombs no longer boom.

If the dragon emerges from fire into the modern world, what then? Evil people might take advantage.

Not if vegan witches Hayley and Skylar have anything to say about it…

Newt Kid in Town
(The Vegan Witches of Redondo Beach #5)

Get a free short story about the vegan witches

Everything is going great for the vegan witches until their happy magical lives are thrown sideways by a hex, a barking dog, and a bad haircut.

How can they stop the hex?

Will that dog ever shut up?

Most importantly, where do they find a magic spell powerful enough to undo a bad haircut?

Get this free short story when you sign up for the latest newts!

Go to: bit.ly/veganwitch

A Note from Emily McVie

Thanks for reading The Vegan Witches of Redondo Beach. If you enjoyed the adventures of Hayley and Skylar, please let me know by leaving a review on Amazon.com. I read all the reviews and appreciate your thoughtful comments.

www.ingramcontent.com/pod-product-compliance
Lightning Source LLC
Chambersburg PA
CBHW050726180626
46814CB00002B/618